CARIBBEAN HEAT

By

Ophelia M. Turner

For ordering contact:

Tmissot@verizon.net

Dedication

Dedicated to the loving
memories of my three
daughters:

Eleasha Irene (Cookie) Ray,
Remethia (Remy) Garrett and Rose
Taylor.

Cookie was my special gift
from God, who always believed that
I could do anything except fail.
Cookie's love and belief gave me
two more beautiful daughters, Remy
and Rose. Cookie believed that
blood does not make a family, but
love does. I can testify to the
truth of that, because when she
introduced these two young ladies
to me as her sisters, it was with a
lot of love and sisterly
interaction. Because of Cookie's
love, I shared the immeasurable
love of these two wonderful young
women as daughters. God bless the
ties that bind. I am happy to know
that love never dies. I will always
love and miss you Cookie, Remy and
Rose.

ACKNOWLEDGMENTS

Sometimes thank you isn't enough, but that's all I have right now so Thank you! Thank you! Thank you! To begin with the beginning, thanks unto God and my parents, Roselia and Joshua Knight, for their love, guidance and protection. To my editors, Amy Byle, Sheila Baggett and Janielle Edmonds, what would I have done without you? To my children, George, Alan, Arthur (Sly), Sidney (Sonny), Helena (Nina) and the memory of Eleasha (Cookie) Ray, your encouragement and your faith in me will always means so much to me. To my daughters-in-laws, Clarinda Fitzpatrick Ray and Valerie Ray, their shoulders are often wet with my tears due to life and its problems. Thank you for being there. To my sister Mary Williams and family, Virginia Knight and family, my brother Maylon Knight and family. To my two love-sent daughters, Carol Dennis and Sabrina Johnson and their families, they have always let me know that I am not alone because they were always there. To my grandchildren and great-grandchildren and countless number of friends special thanks to some of the **dearest of the dear friends**, Dr. Lucile Ijoy, Georgia Davis, Mike Lemon, of Mike Lemon Casting and Virginia Moore. They always gave me those much needed words of encouragement and extra shoves that kept me going. Last but far, far from the least are my manuscript readers without whom I would have been lost, especially my niece **Denise (Niecy) Gomez.** Niecy you were there from the beginning and never grew weary or tired of my endless mistakes or pleas for help, I love and thank you baby. There is also Virginia Knight, my sister and my niece Robin (Missy) Hudson, my readers, thank you, and other reader and love daughter, Charlene Bailey, thank all of you.

A special thank you to Mark at Colorfile in Newton, Pa for my cover and Cindy Smith at Whitehall Press, her patience matches that of Job's.

CHAPTER ONE

St. Croix, Virgin Islands

In a state of pure euphoria, Sandra Lee Hayward Dubois left her office at Robbins and Robbins' International Construction Company, located on the south shore of St. Croix, U.S. Virgin Islands, where she has been employed for over three years. Two things fostered Sandra's happiness. The first was she knew that today was the day that Mark Landers, her ultimate lover, was officially moving in with her and their plans to marry were definitely underway. The other thing was the big grin that she saw on her boss Trent Robbins's face when he said, " Damn girl, you pulled that crew together in record time. I don't know how you did that but I'm damn glad you did. For a hot minute I was sweating there! We'd have lost a hell of a contract if you hadn't come through."

On short notice early that Thursday morning, Hess Oil had called for one hundred twenty five men for an emergency 'turnaround,' an equipment overhaul that was scheduled to begin in three working days.

To organize such a crew at this time was not an

easy task. The availability of reliable manpower with the right experience was at an all time low and required a lot of searching, re-assigning and re-organization to fill Hess Oil's request, especially with Martin Marietta going full blast and WAPA was also hiring for an overhaul.

Robbins and Robbins had contracted to provide these men, as needed, to periodically break down sections of Hess Oil's plant for overhauls of their equipment. They were required to replace needed parts and do other types of maintenance to insure the safe operation and efficient production at the plant. 'Turnarounds' are fast moving and demanding work. Hess stipulated that only seasoned, experienced workers be assigned to these crews, especially in key positions and each worker was subject to Hess' approval before entering the plant.

In accordance with Hess' request Sandra Lee Hayward Dubois, the Personnel Manager for Robbins and Robbins Construction Company, managed to pull together a crew of: six supervisors, twelve foremen, twenty first-class pipe fitters and a number of millwrights, carpenters, welders and their helpers, as well as general laborers.

Somehow Sandra accomplished what others may have perceived as being near impossible and she felt mighty damn good about it. She had satisfied everyone, herself, Robbins and Robbins, and especially Hess Oil.

Sandra visualized Blake Feinmann, president of the Feinmann, Heights and Davison Construction Company, the next largest construction company on the island and a hostile opponent of Robbins and Robbins,

eagerly standing by waiting for her to fail. That would
have allowed his company to step in and grab Hess Oil's
contract. Sandra had only been a clerk for eighteen
months when Trent promoted her to Personnel
Manager. Feinmann never viewed her promotion with
much respect and he laughed at Trent's judgment for
promoting her so soon after Jason Baldwin had
resigned.

Upon hearing about Sandra's promotion,
Feinmann refused to believe that she was ready
for the position and had openly expressed his
opinion to Trent during one of their love-hate
conversations. Besides, he never felt any woman
was capable or possessed the fortitude that was
required for going one on one with hundreds of
rough and tough male construction workers.

As Sandra envisioned the look of
disappointment on Feinmann's face when he
heard that she has succeeded, she relished it and
smiled.

Getting the promotion to Personnel Manager
hadn't come easy for the novice, five foot three, one
hundred twenty two pound, stateside born, almond
complexioned, ambitious, independence seeking young
woman.

Trent imported at least five state side applicants
to fill the empty position after his Personnel Manager,
Jason left the island to return to Boston. Since Trent
never really educated himself regarding the personnel
office procedures it was left to Sandra to show each new
potential applicant the required routine. This position
included hiring, retaining a skilled workforce,
organizing and scheduling crews, acquiring supplies,

maintaining insurance programs, as well as handling immigration paperwork, workers compensation and submitting bids after Trent's approval, also numerous other responsibilities.

Sandra instructed Trent's prospective Personnel Managers in the performance of each task; still, none of them could handle the workload.

A few days later, at nine thirty on a Monday morning after attempted to train a fifth applicant, while Trent Robbins was sitting at his desk concentrating on some paperwork, a nervous and irate but spirited Sandra marched into his office and said,

"Trent Robbins that's it! I'm not going to train another person for a job I can handle myself. You hired me to work here as an office clerk yet you've had me doing a Personnel Manager's duties every since Jason quit. Now you are telling me to train men that you expect to place in a position that you know is rightfully mine."

With a look of surprise and complete bewilderment Trent immediately raised his head from the work that he was deeply involved in and he slowly sat erect in his high-backed brown leather chair and folded his arms across his brawny chest. Trent was caught completely off guard when Sandra looked directly into his eyes and said, "If I can train these men for the position I can do the job. Why don't you promote me and stop this nonsense of having outside people coming in here wasting my time, not to mention the cost of air fare, hotel, meals, training and God knows what else, just to have me continue doing the job.

"Now Trent, with all due respect, if you won't
promote me to that position please do one of two things,
fire me if you must or leave me out of it and train them
yourself. If you should choose the latter while I'm still
here I'll only perform as an office clerk -- no more and
no less. Do you understand me?"

After a few minutes of mulling Sandra's
unexpected, heated words around in his startled mind,
frowning, with a raised eyebrow and one eye squinting,
he stared at Sandra, totally taken aback by her fiery
and somewhat impertinent remarks.

The six foot three, solidly built, deeply
suntanned, sandy haired, good-looking Texan was still
frowning as his baby blue eyes tried to read Sandra's
solemn face. After the gravity of her words finally sunk
in, he asked in his Texan drawl, "What goddamn bee
got under your damn bonnet so early this morning?"

Sandra instantly replied, "Bees don't have
anything to do with it Trent. I'm just tired of always
being used and taken for granted, especially by you."

"Ain't you being paid for what you do around
heah? What in hell else you want?" asked Trent in a
partially jovial, but slightly irritated voice.

"If it was money I wouldn't be standing here.
It's the principle of the matter. By giving me a hefty
raise in salary you are admitting that you know I can do
the job, but by not promoting me is your way of saying
you don't want a woman doing what you consider to be
a man's job. Well, since that is the case, do it yourself.
Unless you promote me... I won't do it anymore no
matter what you pay me.

"Here is my promotion application; I have
filled it out. My raise in salary as Personnel Manager is

retroactive from the day Jason left. Now you can sign it or fire me and train them yourself. This nonsense doesn't matter to me anymore."

"Girl! What in hell you trying to do blackmail me or something?" yelled Trent.

"No Trent, I am just asking you to be fair and give me what is rightfully mine. As I said before, I'm the only one here including you that is capable of doing this job and you know it. So you decide. What will it be? I'll be waiting for your answer."

Tossing her completed promotion application at him, she watched it gently drift down landing on his desk directly in front of him, just before she defiantly turned and swiftly walked through his office door, leaving it open.

As weeks passed Sandra confined herself to doing her job as an office clerk filing information, typing request documents, keeping the coffee pot filled and performing other minimal tasks. Her office was bombarded with requests for services, which she passed on to Trent.

Trent had been unapprised of many of these requests because Sandra had been addressing them. This constant demand for his attention was wearing his nerves thin and he became even more desperate to find a new Personnel Manager.

One morning Sandra arrived for work, entering the office that she once shared with the former Personnel Manager, to find Trent sitting across from another prospective new face. He was trying to instruct the potential manager in hiring procedures, which included immigration paperwork verifying citizenship, work permits and immigration status required for bonding.

Sandra went to her desk and began her duties. She intentionally gave no notice to Trent and his blundering, inept performance. Realizing that he was stuck on some issues concerning the correct procedure for filing a certain immigration paper, he turned to Sandra asking, "Sandra, in a case like this, what do we do next?"

Without ever looking up from her desk Sandra replied, "Don't ask me I've never been a Personnel Manager, remember? I'm just the office clerk." Then she causally continued with her work.

Thoroughly vexed after Sandra completely ignored him, Trent sat steaming for a short while before he stomped out of the office leaving his confused trainee sitting there gawking at Sandra.

Several days later one of the first things to happen on a memorable Friday morning, was the issue of a foreman being missing from his assigned work site at Hess Oil. Trent rushed into her office saying, "Sandra, handle that mess at Hess."

She replied, as she continued her typing, "I can't. I'm only your office clerk remember? This is a Personnel Manager's job, you do it."

As always Trent was livid, he got on the two-way radio that broadcasted throughout Hess to his supervisors and began blaming them, other foremen, or whoever was in earshot of the radio for the emergency.

For several weeks Sandra had ran the office smoothly before Trent became bent on an all out effort to secure a stateside, preferably a Texan for the position of Personnel Manager. She followed to the letter every instruction that Jason had given her and every procedure he had taught her, especially for those nine months after he confided in her about his intention to return to the states. From Sandra's first day on the job at Robbins and Robbins, when Jason was required to teach Sandra the responsibility of an office clerk, he admired her willingness to work hard, endless enthusiasm in combination with her ability to learn quickly. They became close comrades and enjoyed a sincere working relationship and he began teaching her all other phase of the business.

In order for Sandra to gain hands on experience Jason allowed her to assist him with carrying out many of the Personnel Manager's office procedures under his supervision. In addition she also assumed some of those responsibilities.

Sandra's job at Robbins and Robbins elevated her attitude about herself to a higher level. She gained knowledge, confidence and learned to speak for herself. At first some of the men coming into the office frightened her and they knew it. Jason encouraged her to be more assertive and outspoken in order to prove that she was strong enough to handle the job. Often he refused to intervene when she had issues with the men. Instead, he forced her to stand up and take control of the situation. That didn't come over night. But Sandra kept pushing becoming stronger and more secure in her job and her abilities.

When Jason told her that he was vacating his

position and expressed his intentions to train her in even greater detail for his job. Sandra's self-esteem skyrocketed. He chose not to mention his intention to leave the island to Trent before it was time to give his mandatory two weeks notice, for fear of creating a stressful working environment that would remain until he left.

With his decision to leave firmly in place Jason made sure that Sandra was well prepared for the position with the hope that she would secure it upon his departure. He even encouraged her to take some business courses at the local college, especially those related to office management, which she did immediately and was still continuing to do.

Trent couldn't deny the extent of Sandra's knowledge and her ability to run the office but still he continued to refuse her the position. This stand off persisted over the following two months until a request for an emergency 'turnaround' crew had be scheduled, just like the one she had just manned.

Feeling the pressure of Hess' demands and the fact that he had not found a capable replacement as Personnel Manager, Trent was forced to promote Sandra in order to get the necessary hiring done. Trent stormed into her office and slammed the signed promotion form on her desk saying, "Here is your damn promotion. This job is yours as long as you can keep it. The first time one of these crazy-ass men run you the hell out of this damn office just keep on running. You got that!!"

Sandra triumphantly smiled sweetly and said, "Yes, Trent, I got it." Sandra immediately began the hiring process. She had earned enough respect from the current workers and the West Indian community to send out an urgent call for the rehiring of all former employees and qualified new arrivals. Their quick response allowed her to fill the quota needed in record time. The professional way she handled the assignment and all other facets of the job earned Sandra, Trent's reluctant recognition, gratitude and a permanent position.

Not only did Sandra prove to be an excellent Personnel Manager, but she also upgraded hiring procedures and implemented new procedures for issuing equipment to all employees, saving the company thousands of dollars.

One of her lauded procedures was the creation of an equipment list for each worker. This form listed every piece of equipment that was issued to each man upon hiring according to his skill.

Each piece of equipment that was issued to the employee required an initial beside it. When the list was complete it was signed by the employee and then witnessed and dated by Sandra or Trent. Each piece of equipment that was not returned upon dismissal was deducted from the employee's severance check, from a hardhat to work gloves and everything in between. After Sandra's list there was minimal need to repurchase equipment. Prior to this new system at the beginning of each turnaround there was always a rush to repurchase needed equipment.

It is now two years later, on a Friday, about five thirty in the afternoon and Sandra had had manned the

turnaround crew that Robbins and Robbins, needed for
Hess Oil on the following Monday morning and
satisfaction filled her.

Unconscious of her footsteps echoing sharply
throughout the beautifully manicured grassy landscape
bordered by the white concert sidewalk, Sandra raced
toward the entrance to her third floor unit in the
Harbor View Apartments Complex in Christiansted.
The vast picturesque courtyard encompassed all of the
surrounding three story yellow limestone buildings.

On her climb up to her floor Sandra looked out
over the courtyard below. She is mindful that it was
almost empty except for a few small children running
about at play. The tennis court was host to a pair of
young male players. None of what she saw was unusual,
since this was a working community and most people
were just beginning to return home.

Reaching the opening in the second floor
staircase landing before mounting the remaining
staircase leading to her third floor apartment, Sandra
felt compelled to stop a moment to take a more
appreciative glance at the breathtaking landscape.
There were clusters of flowerbeds filled with an
abundance of various tropical flowers in bloom. At the
end of each row of buildings in every direction were
sprawling flamboyant trees and wide areas of evenly cut
grass framing the entire setting.

The palm trees along the shoreline of the beach
just across the road swayed in the light tropical breeze,
making a flapping sound as their branches struck
against each other in the busy breeze, as they seemed to
be bowing in her direction sending her a hardy
greeting. She could hear the rattling and rumbling of

slow moving cars thumping over rows of speed bumps
lining the back road and the constant clanging and
grinding of the machinery at the water and power plant
located about a half mile away. From time to time she
heard a sea gull's cry in the distance against the
backdrop of the roaring sea racing to the rocky shore
and crashing with rumbling thuds. Sandra never
wearied of the way they all came together to perform
their daily orchestration. The eternal flow of their
rhythmic sounds always added enjoyable harmonizing
tones to the atmosphere surrounding her.

After lingering briefly on the second floor
landing to admire nature's handiwork embellished by
man's creativity, Sandra smiled... heaved a sigh of
contentment. Carrying her light blue briefcase in her
left hand she continued her rapid climb to the top of the
stairs. Sandra's right hand fumbled around inside of
her shoulder bag in search of her key ring. Finding the
ring she held it between her long, lean, well manicured
fingers and began a clattery gyration of the ring of keys
in an attempt to single out the key to her front door.

Just as she rounded the last flight of steps that
ended on a platform just outside her doorway she found
her front door key. Then Sandra stopped abruptly.
Lying coiled on the welcome mat in front of her door,
blocking the entrance to her apartment was a nearly
new, long, green garden hose. The hose appeared to be
about a hundred and fifty feet in length. Surprised, her
jaw dropped in bewildered. Filled with disgust she
drew in a deep, sharp, breath and paused a moment to
regain her composure before muttering in a low voice,

"What the hell?"

Without making a sound, her next door neighbor, Lillie, suddenly appeared in the adjoining doorway. Her dark brown, moon-shaped faceglowed in the reflections of the retreating evening sun. Upon seeing Sandra, her dark eyes beamed and her broad, thick lips flashed an impulsive grin.

Speaking with a very distinctive West Indian accent, she said, "Hi Sandra, I hear' footsteps. I kno' someone was comin' up to dis' floor. I thought it might be yuz' but yu' can't be to sur' bout anythin' dez' days."

Without returning her greeting Sandra blinked her widened, big brown eyes several times before looking sharply at the woman. With keys in hand, Sandra motioned toward the hose asking in a very curt voice, "Is this yours?"

The baffled woman gave Sandra a surprised blank stare. Still grinning she instantly replied, "No! No! No! I never see it befor' til I reach home dis evenin'. Twas lain' dar'. I thought it twas yors."

"Mine? Mine? No way in hell," Sandra angrily declared. "I just wish I knew who in the hell piled this damn thing up in front of my door. I can't get into my apartment."

"Well," Lillie shrugged her shoulders and in a very meek tone said, "I don' nuh what to tell yu' 'cept it ain't none of mine."

For a brief moment the two women stood staring at the hose. Then, Sandra said, "If I expect to get into my apartment I'll just have to move this damn thing."

"Throw it, sister! Throw it!" Lillie suddenly

pleaded.

"Throw it where?"

"Over de sid', sister. Over de sid'," urged Lillie.

Completely bewildered by Lillie's advice, Sandra asked, "Why? Why should I throw it over the side when I don't know why it's here or who left it?" Then as an after thought, Sandra said, "I will just lay it inside my doorway until I get some answers."

Lillie cried out in panic saying, "No! No! No, sister! 'Tis too dangerous."

"Dangerous?" echoed Sandra. "What in the hell are you talking about Lillie? Dangerous?" She snapped.

"It could be Black Hand, sister. Yu' neve' know!" Lillie informed her with much sincerity. "If 'tis' Black Hand sister, yu don' wan' no involved."

Lillie always appeared to be a person of very little conversation and she completely surprised Sandra with such a sudden rash of strange words, annoyed Sandra inquired, "What in the hell is Black Hand? What are you talking about?"

"'Tis bad sister. Yu don' want to nuh'. Don' take de chance. If 'tis obeah,'tis really bad sister, throw it!" pleads Lillie. "Thro' it now!"

Lillie was a hardworking woman filled with kindness, generosity and possessed a very gentle nature. Seeing her so upset and completely irrational mystified Sandra.

Sandra said, "Lillie, that talk is just plain stupid if ever I heard it. How can you believe in such nonsense? Why are you talking crazy? I swear I thought that you were much smarter than that," scolded Sandra.

"'Tis' true sister!" said Lillie. "'Tis true, sister! In dis world der' is people dat'll use Black Hand or as yu' say in de states, black magic or roots to hurt yu'. Yu' can't be too careful I tell yo'."

Angered by the entire situation and Lillie's conversation, Sandra said, "All right Lillie believe whatever you want to but you Jumbie and I'll Jesus and we'll see what's true. There is no way I'll ever believe that damn crap."

Lillie's ashen face reflected the pain of Sandra's hostile rejection. Bowing her head and lowered her eyes Lillie quietly made a slow retreat back into her apartment and softly closed the door.

As if unaware that the woman is no longer standing there Sandra took another long, hard look at the cumbersome hose and complained loudly, "This is so disgusting! Absolutely and totally disgusting finding this mess here!"

Then in a low, almost inaudible voice she mumbled, "Mark must have been here and left it."

As if speaking to some unseen person, Sandra asked loudly, "But why?"

She began to reason aloud, "Yet that just doesn't seem likely."

While still searching for some logical answers concerning the hose, Sandra reached over the hose holding the door key between the fingers of her extended hand she made a clumsy attempt to unlock the door. Frantically struggling to keep her balance she made several stabbing attempts at the keyhole. After repeated instances of lurching back and forth she finally succeeded in unlocking the door.

Stepping back to regain her balance, she lifted up the narrow skirt of her tailored floral-patterned cotton suit above her knees and stretched her long shapely legs as far as she could. With first one leg, then the other, she stepped over the high piled hose stubbing her toe in the process causing her to stumble forward.

Slightly limping, reflecting her pain Sandra slowly hopped down the short hallway covered with the same thick, white-carpeting that covered all of her floors. Entering into her living room she angrily threw her briefcase and shoulder bag onto the red velvet sofa, rushed over to the nearby matching chair and grabbed the telephone sitting on the table beside the chair and dialed the number to Mark's office. She dropped heavily into the chair as she waited for the call to go through. Her rapidly beating pulse sent blood rushing to her head causing it to pound.

As she waited for telephone number to ring a strange humming filled the telephone line. The humming is followed by a series of sporadic clicking signals. Then the telephone went dead. She shouted, "Hurrah for Vitelco." In complete disgust with the local telephone company Sandra slammed down the telephone picked it up again and immediately redialed the number, only to get a busy signal.

After several unsuccessful attempts to reach Mark, visibly annoyed, Sandra realized that the telephone only added to her frustration and increased her anger. She slammed the telephone receiver into its cradle, leapt up and heatedly stalked back to the still open apartment door.

She gathered up portions of the large clumsy, hose, only to have it repeatedly roll out of her arms. Cursing under her breath, Sandra said, "Who in the hell needs this shit on a hot ass day like this?"

Attempting to get the hose inside the apartment, impatiently she grabbed on to as much of the sliding hose as she could. After much dragging, tugging, and stumbling, she managed to get it piled up on the floor against the wall of the hallway that led to her living room.

Totally exhausted Sandra stood for a few seconds staring at the hose. Her entire mood of joyful exultation was now shot to hell. She thought instead of holding Mark I'm forced to fill my arms with a damn hose.

Sandra slammed the door shut, spun around and walked swiftly through the living room into her bedroom. She switched on the stereo to a local Cruzan station featuring her favorite D.J., Chaz "Hollywood" Nibbs. His sexy voice was soothing, chatty and very informative. He had the ability to play the right music at the right time. The soft island music flowing from the stereo's speakers, replaced the depressing silence throughout the apartment, soothing her weary mind.

The late evening sun tinted her bedroom with a rosy red. Sandra stripped off her clothing. The perspiration soaked garments were difficult to remove. The sweltering Caribbean heat in her small office seemed to have fused them to her body. After much struggling and wiggling she finally ridded herself of everything except her panties and bra.

Breathing deeply and almost nude Sandra stood

staring at her ruined fingernails the result of her
encounter with the hose. Soaked with perspiration and
physically drained from the effort of undressing she
turned her attention to the full-length wall mirror. She
observed the reflection of her smooth skin glistening
with small beads of moisture that kept oozing out of
her. The only redeeming act she could imagine was to
step inside the shower and get lost in a steady spray of
cool, refreshing water.

A sudden gust of cool air rushed through the
open louvers of the bedroom's window washed over her.
It lightly fondled her exposed soaked flesh with such a
cooling affect it caused her to briefly postpone her
immediate intention to shower. With raised arms she
twisted about allowing the breeze to thoroughly
encircled her, sighing she relished the pleasure of living
in the moment.

The rhythmic vibrations of the soft island music
consoled her weary mind and body. She exhaled deeply
in response to the absolutely relaxing atmosphere.

Later, inside the shower, covering her body with
mango scented shower gel lather she became
determined not to allow any more negativity to further
invade her space. While allowing her hands to linger in
all her most sensitive areas she leisurely stroked her
body and envisioned Mark's nude body standing before
her, close and hard.

After fifteen minutes the beneath the pulsating
stream of refreshing water and entertaining adoring
thoughts of Mark permitted her to emerge from the
shower feeling fresh, rejuvenated and calm. The fruity

aroma of her shower gel made her smell like a delicious appetizer.

She slipped into a pair of silk panties to provide a soft touch to the throbbing area between her thighs. Feeling very appeased she wrapped snuggly in a bath towel and returned to the living room. Sandra stretched out on her red velvet couch. Closing her eyes she breathed in the intoxicating perfume from the tropical flower garden below that hitched a ride on the rampant breeze. Their aroma added a healing touch to the breeze that caressed her.

The tranquilizing affect sent her thoughts racing back to Mark and her earlier stated expectation. Relishing the refreshing fragrance of her shower gel and her desire for Mark, she said, "Since I smell like an appetizer why not become a full course meal?"

Arising she leisurely strolled to the telephone on the other side of the living room. With slow, deliberate' feline movements, she sunk into the chair beside the telephone table. Swinging her leg over the plush chair's arm she picked up the telephone. Once again she dialed Mark's number, the line clicked several times, indicating that the call was going through.

The constant breeze and the flowing music generated an aura of comfort as she waited for Mark to come onto the line. Silence filled the air on the line before the telephone began to ring. A sudden click indicated that the telephone was being answered. Sandra waited with restrained breath for Mark to speak. The smooth, amorous, masculine sound of Mark's sensuous 'Hello' enticingly fondled her ear and tightly encircled her body like a warm embrace. Sandra thought how good it is to feel his voice. Then she whispered into the phone, "Hello yourself." Her escalating, titillating emotions forced her to take a moment to compose herself before she said; "When I got home I expected to find you here. What a hell of a disappointment that was. I tried to reach you but your line was busy. What happened?"

Mark quickly replied, "Yeah, I know. I should have been there. I'm very sorry but things got a little fouled up around here and I had to sort them out."

She slid her free hand between her widespread legs, pushing aside her silk panties she began to entwine her fingers in the moistened hairs covering her throbbing need. Mark's face floated vividly before her eyes, as she said, "I was very upset. My body was so ready and sure that you would be waiting. It prepared itself for the moment that it would receive you. You'll never know the suffering I've endured not finding you here."

Pushing her fingers inside herself dispensed very little comfort. Inhaling longingly between her clinched teeth she only prompted the fire within her to build even higher than it was earlier, with each step that she took toward home.

Mark's voice managed to filter through her imagination saying, "I'm sorry, baby. Can I do anything to make it up to you?"

She replied, "Yes! You can bring my missing stuff over here and put it into operation as fast as possible, like right now."

"All right, baby, I'll do just that as soon as I finish here, I promise. It won't be too long. As you speak, this bad boy of mine is turning to cement and he hurts like hell."

Sandra's legs trembled and her fingers became covered with the evidence of her passion. With her long fingers she firmly pushed against her moistened haven of vibrating longing as she attempted to pacify her ravenous craving for Mark. Closing her eyes Sandra inhaled deeply and moaned, "This waiting is just too damn hard. I need you so badly. I'll be glad when we don't have to do this shit anymore. All I want is to simply roll over and have you whenever I want to instead of playing stink fingers while I wait for you, like I'm doing now."

"I know, baby. I feel the same way. The more I have you the more I need you. We are almost there. Think of that and please take it easy for a little while longer," he pleaded.

Tension in Sandra increased by the moment. The more she fingered herself the greater her desire for Mark became. She tried to force a climax but couldn't. Without Mark her longing for him only grew.

Still stroking her pulsating space she was on the verge of tears with longing. Her faltering voice wavered, as she complained, "I might have been able to do that if things hadn't gotten so fucked up when I came home. I guess I became a little too sure that you would be waiting when I got here. You promised, you know! This was supposed to be our big day."

Squirming around in the chair in disgust she turned and saw the ugly hose curled up inside of her doorway only added to her anger. The sight of it instantly sent her mind hurrying back to her earlier disappointment causing even more anxiety to etch its way into her voice.

Looking at the hose she snapped, "I only wish I knew what kind of business is going on around here. Even if it's some monkey business."

The stress in her voice evoked deep concern in Mark, prompting him to ask, "What else has happened to you today Sandra? Why are you so upset?

Still gazed angrily at the hose, she said, "I wish that I knew what's happening with all of this crazy business going on around here."

"What are you talking about? What business?" Mark asked.

Really emotionally strung out, almost reduced to tears, Sandra replied, "All of this dumb shit that went on when I arrived home."

"What in the devil are you talking about Sandra? Make some sense. What's the matter baby? Is it something that I've done beside being late that's bugging you?"

Sarcastically, she stated, "Well since you are asking, yes there is! Did you leave that damn appalling hose in front of my door? If you did it really pissed me off, Mark."

Relieved to learn that a hose was behind her apparent anger, with a chuck in his voice Mark tried to suppress his laughter.

Sandra shouted, "It's far from being funny Mark."

Still slightly laughing Mark tried to appease her by agreeing, "I know it isn't, but I didn't do it. Why would I?"

"I don't know! That's why I am upset. I could barely get into my apartment. I even hurt myself. Then you not being here made everything worse."

Still trying to control his laughter, Mark snickered as he said, "Well baby please believe me, it wasn't me." Then attempting to become serious he asked, "What kind of hose is it anyway?"

"What do you mean what kind of hose is it? It's a damn garden hose. What other kind of hose is there?" she shouted. "It's light green with darker irregular green spots. It's ugly as hell and really very long. It was rolled up on the mat in front the door outside of my apartment. It's well over a hundred and fifty feet long."

"Wow! That is large. Where is it now?"

"It's rolled up beside the wall in the hallway just inside my apartment's door."

"Why?"

"Because I thought it was yours that's why"

Mark reassured her again saying, "Well no it's not mine. I didn't leave it there. Maybe Scottie put it there. Maybe he came by and you weren't home and he just left it there for you."

Pausing for a moment to consider Marks words, Sandra thoughtfully said, "That is quite possible you know, knowing him, he probably did."

Scottie was a shy, gawky and mentally challenged young man that assisted with the grounds keeping around the complex. He is overly fond of Sandra because she was friendly to him. A kind word and attention was all Scottie wanted and having been there herself, she gave him these freely. She always found time for him and shared in his dreams by listening to him. Therefore, he was always bringing her presents such as lamps salvaged from the trash bins, chipped statues and vases that he viewed as valuable, things he found, things people gave to him as well as things he bought just for her.

Sandra never offended him by refusing his gifts or making them seem useless even though most of them were.

Accepting the possibility of Mark's suggestion Sandra immediately agreed with him, with her attitude mellowed out said, "Yes...that does seem like something that Scottie would do. But what in the hell do I need a hose for in a third floor apartment?"

Without fear being scolded Mark chuckled, "I don't know. But you know Scottie he doesn't think about a thing like that. If I didn't have a hose I would take that one. Mira just bought a hose for the shop a few weeks ago and she has a large one that her grandmother gave her about a year or so ago. From the description you gave it's just like that one or close to it."

"Yeah! No kidding. Just imagine that. Tough shit, huh?" quipped Sandra. Completely aware of the reason for her sarcasm Mark intentionally ignored it, saying, "Yeah! Some tough shit. It seems like you've got yourself a hose."

"Yeah, so it seems until whenever Scottie shows up. This is one time I am making him take that damn thing out of here. This hose is one more thing I can definitely do without. But for now let's just forget it," she insisted.

After a short, silent pause to reflect on her

intimate needs, once again Sandra allowed her thoughts to wrap around Mark. Drifting into a more serene state of mind her voice trails off into a teasing sexy whine as she suggested, "Let's talk about something much more pleasant."

The brief conversation with Mark had adjusted her attitude properly allowing her to recapture her former state of mind. Sandra became aware that her hand was no longer engaged in intimate foreplay instead it lay idle against her thigh. Once again, she opened her legs and began touching the dry, stiff hairs that bore witness to the heated desire that she experienced just minutes ago. Her nimble fingers proceeded to explore the damp walls of her tingling organ. She commenced to fondle it into a slush pool of longing.

Her voice softened and trailed off. It became low, teasing and filled with sexy whines, "Let's go some place genuinely pleasant."

Mockingly Mark asked, "Like where?"

"Like right here at the end of my wet finger tips. Can't you feel yourself surrounded by soft, warm, pulsating flesh, while tight, massaging walls oozing with moisture filled with famished little nymphs greedily gnawing at you? Can't you feel those nymphs twisting and turning all hot and cozy, as they suck you in deeper, getting you wetter, seeking to provide satisfaction in a world that belongs only to you? Can't you feel them baby?"

Mark took in a long, deep breath, held it, and then slowly released it, letting her know that he was there.

She went on taunting him, "I've had a ferocious

craving for you all day. I guess that is why I am so damn testy now. I started to come to the store today on my lunch hour. I wanted to serve your noonday brunch of succulent goodies up on the counter while they were sizzling hot. Then I thought that your partner Mira might have been there. I know she's due back from Haiti late tonight or early tomorrow. Since you told me how she feels about our relationship I don't want anymore problems, especially right now while this steaming, hot host of my busy fingers' is demanding an encore of last night performance."

"Sandra you are hurting me with your mouth. You damn well know that? Don't make me come through this damn telephone and fuck your ass off. You are deliberately inflicting pain on me. I can't handle this baby. So please cool out just a few more minutes please," pleaded Mark.

"Well, next time I'll just stick an ice cube in there instead of my fingers to remind me of what you are not," teased Sandra. "I wish I had stopped by anyway. Whatever happened would've been worth a good healthy workout, especially since I'm still burning."

"Listen baby," said Mark. "You're right not to have stopped by. Mira got back early this morning rather than tomorrow. To avoid any further confrontation with her about our relationship I left her in the store and went over to a client's office to work on some sketches for new furniture we have in mind for his office. When I got back she had closed up the shop and left. I put my drafting tools and some other equipment away.   Then I returned a few telephone calls, that's what threw schedule my off."

"Mark please tell me that Mira's return won't change anything," pleaded Sandra. "I'm on hell's fire here. I'm burning up from the inside. I need you to do me right now to keep me from losing my mind. So, no matter what she says, don't let her influence you. Don't keep me waiting a minute longer."

Mark quickly replied, "Slow it down baby, one thing at a time. No! I did not change my mind. I'm hotter than you can ever be I need to do you. What in the hell do you think has been happening to me with what you've been saying on this damn telephone? There is nothing or no one that's going to keep me away from you tonight or any other night. So, until I get there, please keep it hot, I'll bring your coolant."

"I say prove it," she whined, as she challenged him.

"I damn right will, I hope you can stand what you have talked up."

"In that case I say bring it on and find out. I'm waiting," said Sandra

"Damn right I will within the hour," he solemnly promised. "When I get there I don't want anything between us, not even air."

As an after thought, Sandra asked, "Hey Mark, does Mira know that we will live together until we get married? Then she added, "After all you know that we did consolidate most of our plans while she was away,"

"If she doesn't know, she'll know before I'm out of here. I'm sure that she'll do everything possible to try to change that. She really hates you that much. But

I meant it when I told her, no matter how she feels about it, I love you."

"I thought she had accepted all of that by now," asserted Sandra. "I thought that's why she took off to Haiti the way she did. Sometimes I wish I understood her."

"Sandra, I gave up trying to understand Mira and what she thinks, what she says and what she does. Soon she'll be out of our lives for good. I'll be there just as soon as I can so get ready."

"Ready? You told me to strip. Have you changed your mind? Are we going someplace?" asked Sandra.

"Damn right we are! Out of our fucking minds, right in the center of your big old bed, where you'll be working like hell under me for the rest of the night."

"Oh...so you want to be chief administrator, well on top of this situation, huh?" giggled Sandra. "Well far be it for me to keep you from letting me assume my rightful position. I'll get off of this telephone so that I can stop keeping me from doing my job. I can barely wait to get you started. Your work is waiting and the heat is definitely on baby, inside and out, so step it up. Make it happen much sooner than later. I love you!"

The telephone clicked softly and Sandra was gone. Mark was still holding on to his telephone receiver when she eased her into its cradle.

Sandra lay back in the chair and her head practically swam with exciting expectations and near disbelief. Everything had finally come full circle and was falling beautifully into place. Her mind rambled over the many events that had led her to this day--- the day that she views as the happiest day of her life. She thoughtfully whispers, "How did Mark and I ever survive those moments of pure unadulterated hell? Have those awful times really been wrapped in forgetfulness and cast into the sea of time never to rise again? I wonder. Oh Lord, how I wonder."

CHAPTER TWO

Looking Back At Yesteryears

Over three years ago, at age twenty-nine, Sandra Lee Hayward Dubois fled her home in Hillsboro, a small community just on the outskirts of Durham, North Carolina, and came to live in St. Croix, Virgin Islands. Until then as the youngest of seven children born to Hattie Lee and Philbert Hayward, her entire life was extremely empty, sheltered and controlled by everyone except her.

Sandra's mother, Hattie, was an only child. Hattie's mother died during her birth and she was reared at her father's side as the son he had been denied. Beside her daddy Hattie lived her life like a man. She worked like a man, thought like a man and acted like a man. She was healthy, strapping and spunky. Hattie became her father's strong right hand. She learned to ride, rope, brand and plow. She more than carried her weight and expected everyone around her to do the same. At age sixteen it was easy for those around Hattie and her father to see that she was the boss.

What started out as a large sized farm, located just outside Hillsboro near the main highway with access to through traffic, grew and developed into a thriving small community over the years. In addition to their large farm Sandra's grandparents owned now had developed into a general store, a garage, a very large boarding house to accommodate travelers going to and from Hillsboro, as well as a few local people. There were other business established on land that her family leased to other family members and residents. The immediate residents consisted mostly of family and a few outsiders who began their lives among them as hired help.

Sandra never knew her father. When she was very young he was killed in a hunting accident. She recalled how from the age of ten to about fourteen she derived almost all of her family's information from the older female family members and outsider women often during quilting parties. Those women took great pleasure in gossiping about her family, especially her mother. There they could speak freely about Hattie, because she never came to any quilting parties. She had no use for such 'carrying on' as she called it.

Whenever Sandra knew there would be a quilting party she made it a point to hide in the attic of Aunt Lucy's house, where they always met. Those gossiping older women delighted in speaking of her family, especially of her father. It was as if all of them had wanted to lay with him. Since they couldn't bed

him they gladly shared every secret they had about him
and the rest of her family.

Over the years Sandra obtained a lot of little
well hidden facts as they were revealed according to
each of the women gathered around the quilting poles.

"Why God Almighty?" said Aunt Sally. "He
sure was one handsome body, that Philbert Hayward,
Lord he was somethin' but he was too mild mannered
for that tomboy Hattie. Why he was pure putty in her
hands. I 'member when Philbert Hayward was the
foreman on her parent's farm 'fore marrying her,
Hattie was barely sixteen years when she 'come his
virgin bride, so she done said."

Then Aunt Lucy snarled, "That gal got
married in plain old Levi's overalls and a blue cotton
shirt to a man eighteen years her senior. Almost
immediately after that marriage Hattie blew up as big
as a tick with the first of them seven children. Before
they married she was always helping him in the hay loft
and believe me they wasn't pitching any hay."

"Well," declared Aunt Mary, who was not really
anyone's aunt anymore than Aunt Sally. The name
aunt was a handle of respect that the younger people
attached to them. "That there was a shotgun weddin if
you ask me. That' man ain't had no choice."

Then, looking sly and almost whispering, Aunt
Lucy said, "If you asking me, dag blame it, just as sure
as I'm born she raped that old fool so fast that he
couldn't help himself. You can bet your boots that she
rode that old fool like she rode them horses, hard, long,
fast, bare back and often." Then like a church mouse

she snickered squeaky and soft.

Hoping that no one would find her there sitting silently on the attic floor peeping through the cracks above the gossiping circle of women, Sandra absorbed every word.

Aunt Sally went on saying, "Motherhood was Hattie's only female virtue but I believ'e dat even back then Hattie had her own plan. That why when her belly bulged with child she went on daily working 'side her husband and her father."

Anna Bell, a New Yorker imported by marriage by a tenant farmer, who was there on the farm from the beginning and prized herself on knowing everything, she said, "Well…. She has always been more man than woman has anyhow. Huh, if you ask me, taking on those manly looks and ways of hers. She appeared to me to be one of those "morph dikes" that city folks talk about. Why anybody with two good eyes could see that she only needed a man to do the one thing that she couldn't do for herself and that was to breed. From the minute that man got took on by her daddy to work, just like a coon dog, she took site on him…or should I say took site on his crotch, is more like it. From the minute she got her hands on him she led him around by it and made him do her bidding, especially providing her daily studding service. She lapped her legs around old fool so fast and tight that it made your head swim. The Good Lord in heaven sure knows she kept his old hind parts busy day and night. She had him plowing field's days and her at night.

"Then on top of that she always worked from the day that she got bigged, right up until time to delivery of each one of those babies, which came almost every year. Them babies came one right after the other.

"Until the day of her husband's death and then her father's, she never left their sides. She works hard and underwent more than most and under the worst conditions. There was nothing womanly about none of that. That's why everybody calls her 'Momma Too Tight.' She is a pistol alright."

"More like dat double-barrel shot gun if you askin' me," Aunt Sally laughingly declared.

Aunt Lettie reared back to make sure that she was heard. She held her needle in her right hand and used it to weave an inference into each word as she went on to say, "Yeah, after de loss of he' men, Hattie becom' sompin' else. She was a force to recko' wid. Der's no tenderness in dat woman a'tall and she tolerated none in anybody else, 'specially dat der gal of her'. From birth, dat gal Sandra twas discounted fer being a female. Hattie done always steeled he'self to 'cept de unavoidable facts of life. She ain't never give' to female 'motions. She always clenched he' teeth, or bit he' lip, and proceede' forward in all matters such as death, personal or business tragedies. I know what I's talking abou', 'cause I been dar wid he' all de time. Now de birth of dat gal, dat was sompin' else, I was right dere when dat gal poppe' out he'. I kin tell yu' for a fact, 'cause like I said, I was dere. When dat gal Sandra twa' born, dat twa' probably de only time in Hattie's adult life dat she cried. He' heart and mind twas set on de seventh son."

Aunt Lillie May chimed in, "Why the way that woman carried on you'd think that somebody died instead of somebody getting born."

Aunt Sally licked her old dry lips as she fumbled on the floor for a tin cup of water that she had been sipping on earlier that evening when they were mounting the quilting frames. Finding the tin cup, she took a long swig of water before continuing her story. Then she put the cup back on the floor and joined in saying, " Well you sure do got dat right." Nodding her head in approval she went on, "Almost from birth, Hattie trained dem other children of he's in de work dat needed to be done in order to maintain dey environment, from feeding dem chicken' to running dem stores and knowing de bookkeeping of family-owned businesses. Them der six boys twas willing, fast, and excellent learners, but, dat gal Sandra couldn't be taught nothin'. It weren't dat she was stupid or nothing of de kind she was too down right always too scared to death at de sight of anything dat crept, crawled, or wiggled. At first she even feared the chickens, hogs, and other farm animals. Such things would set her off screaming as if she twas in mortal danger. Dis was de reason Hattie was always on he', most time it resulted in Hattie severely scolding he' or giving he' a sound beating. Lawdy Lord, I use to feel sorry for de way Hattie flailed dat gal's hind part at times."

"Lord knows you are exactly right," interrupted Bertha, who had married into the family through some cousin, boasting that she was mostly Indian. She had been all ears up until then, but now, bound to put her two cents in. Bertha said, "Why the good Lord in heaven knows that I'll never forget that day I had come for hog killing. That little child was about eight years old or so. It was one Saturday, towards noon, as I recollect, and Sandra was on the way home from the general store, which was about a mile away from their house. She had been there helping out behind the counter, you know. She carried a little bag of household supplies, such as sugar; store bought bread, and few other things that Hattie had told her to bring home. Within yards from the house she heard a loud squealing. Then oh My God, that poor child looked around to see this hog running right at her with a stream of blood gushing from a cut in the throat. Her young brothers and some other men were chasing the hog. One of whose men's loud voice shouted, 'Catch him, you stupid ass'.

" Someone else among the men with a very loud voice shouted, 'Catch that damn hog. How in the hell did you let him get away?'

"That huge old hog just kept on running towards poor little Sandra, from the minute that she looked around and saw that large hog, that poor girl damn near died. The bleeding hog was running and squealing in a high, shrilling, blood curdling sound that kept on coming.

"With the men in hot pursuit, the hog was heading directly for her. Sandra tossed the bag into the air, its contents raining down and scattered on the ground where they may, as she screamed and ran for the house. Later on she told me that her heart was pounding wildly, her knees were weak, and her head was twisting and turning with fear. Once inside the house everything disappeared in an envelope of blackness. That child absolutely fainted clean away.

"Sandra told me, as quiet as it was kept, that when she came to she was alone in the room lying across her bed. She recalled the bleeding hog and fear began smothering her. She cried and screamed, but no one came to comfort her. She said that Hattie had gone on about her business. My heart ached for that poor child. But my hands were tired. As you all know, my dears, if I had got mixed up in it, Hattie would have had my head on a platter."

"You sure is right 'bout that," said Aunt Doddie, "'Cause I was the one that told Sandra later that one of her brothers was doing his first hog kill. He missed severing the jugular vain, and the animal got away. Later he ended up shooting the run away hog through de head and Hattie blasted his hind parts loud and long. Yu' know, I believe that terror still haunts that gal to this day."

"All I know is this," said Lucy. "After so many tries by her mother and brothers to force her to stop being so squeamish and do her part of work, they give up on her, and see'd her as hopeless and useless. They cast her aside and she was near forgotten."

"In a way," said Aunt Sally, "yu can't really blame Hattie and dem. Dat gal didn't even try to live up to he' mother's standard."

"Sally, you ain't right in what you saying," interrupted Aunt Lucy. "That gal can't be expected to be something that she ain't. Why can't nobody let people be they self?"

Some of these things that Sandra heard made her very depressed, yet she felt compelled to listen. She learned of her mother's selfishness, her disappointment when she was born and her cruelty to other that refused to agree with her. Later when everyone lay sleeping Sandra relived their words as if freshly spoken ...and often cried.

By the time Sandra came along the older boys had formed a tight bond with each other and drew the younger boys in. Hattie's attitude toward Sandra became their directive and like their mother, they had no time for her.

Sandra was sentenced to what she deemed maid service for her mother and brothers, who took their lead from Hattie. She polished their boots, waited on them hand and foot when they came to the house, and cleaned up whatever mess they left behind when they went.

There were occasional moments of pleasure that came when she was allowed to work in the general store, but those were short lived. Hattie accused her of being too friendly with the men customers, too talkative with the women and not working hard enough. As a result, sometimes despite her fears, Hattie or other family members, ordered her out of bed early on any given mornings of their choosing to work outside until late into the night. There she assisted in work that any boy her age would be expected to do, such as thinning brush, grass cutting, or crop dusting by hand. Sandra spent those days crying, trembling, and jumping with fear at every sudden or unfamiliar touch of a leaf or insect. Then at the end of each day she was tired, sore, and a nervous wreck. When her mother and brothers gathered on the front porch and engaged in conversation concerning the events of their day she was told to get up and find something to do some place else.

Approaching her early teens Sandra still was unable to adapt to the lifestyle her mother demanded her to live. Knowing that she could never live up to her mother's expectations, Sandra learned to accept whatever happened to her as destiny and dealt with it as best she could. She did as she was told, and didn't expect anymore from her mother than what she had always gave her, food, clothes, and a place to sleep.

Alone and lonely in her formative years Sandra's consolation came in believing in fairy tales and playing make believe. She pretended that Hattie was not her mother but some wicked old stepmother that stole her after her father died. She imagined that one day a '*Knight in Shining Armor*' would rescue her, such as she read about in Sleeping Beauty and Cinderella. She chose to be Sleeping Beauty because she had the worst stepmother of all. Her games of pretend would take her to a far away, shining castle that had flowers, birds and no bugs or worms. The birds and flowers would talk to her and be her friends. Then one day a 'Knight in Shining Armor' would come, kiss her and they would live happily evermore. Then in bright daylight she realized that she was only daydreaming in the middle of the night and her drab little room would condemn her to another long, lonely day.

The older Sandra became the more her life became subject to dictation by everyone older than herself. She was given more responsibility with the expectation that she would perform them without question. Soon the entire burden of keeping the house was left on her. Everything that she did was taken for granted especially by her mother. Until the age of fifteen, Sandra's days consisted of endless drudgery without any other expectations.

The first Sunday in August meant the beginning of church revival that lasted for an entire week. It also meant homecoming, old friends and visiting churches' congregation.

During the church service fifteen year and a half year old Sandra sat in her family's pew and watched the people as they filed in and took their seats, each displaying their personal attitude of being humble, pious or acting just plain sanctimonious. To watch them was a form of entertainment for Sandra, especially since she had no particular role in the service other than just being there. Then suddenly in the midst of those strangers a young man walked through the door. To Sandra, his appearance was like an emerging light in a world of darkness. He looked so handsome and so wonderfully different that Sandra's eyes only focused on him. Her stare was a magnet that drew his eyes to her. He gave Sandra a meaningful glance and her face burned with embarrassment, but she didn't have the strength to look away. She became so excited that she was sure he heard her heart beating. She slowly lowered her eyes and folded her hands across her breast to quiet the sound of her heart. Then she didn't have the courage to look at him again. All she could do was hope. Sandra closed her eyes and dreamt her favorite dream of a "Knight in Shining Armor."

CHAPTER THREE

Entertaining A Stranger

Raymond Dubois Jr., appearance at Mt. Sinai
Baptist Church was not an accident. His father,
Raymond Dubois Sr. was the guest speaker for the
church's weeklong revival and his church family
accompanied him to Hillsboro. As the church's guest,
during their stay the minister and his congregation
lodged at Sandra's family's boarding house.

If the hours of preaching were left out and
concentration on the good food and new people were
emphasized, Sandra would view church revivals as fun.
Church gatherings were one of the few places that she
was allowed contact with people outside of her blood
relatives. Sometimes even in church there was no
escaping her family's watchful eyes. Somehow, through
some miracle on this first Sunday during the lunch
break, Sandra and Raymond met without complications
or interruptions from her family.

After lunch break Sandra wandered to the far
end to the last of several long rows tables lined up in a
designated area of the yard. They were shaded by a
cluster of tall pine trees and laden with home cooked

food of every variety. She stood there allowing her eyes
to drift from one huge dishes of food to another. They
were filled with country fried chicken, baked ham,
string beans, smothered cabbage, candied sweet
potatoes, roast wild turkey and many other dishes of
food. Sandra was completely unaware of the arrival of
the handsome man that she had dared to admire when
he walked into the morning service just as everyone else
was comfortably seated. When he walked into the
church and Sandra looked upon his face, she instantly
became excited and fidgety. His appearance caused her
seat to become as a bed of burning embers.

Sandra carefully marked the aisle that he slid
into in hopes of seeing him again after service.
However, at the church's dismissal the crowded
building became a beehive of activity, as people met new
people and greeted old friends. Not knowing where the
young man had vanished she slipped out of the door
looking for him in all directions.

Finally Sandra stood alone resigned to the fact
that unnoticed he had left when suddenly she sensed the
presence of someone close behind her. Turning, she saw
him standing there smiling down at her. Surprised,
Sandra jumped, saying, "Oh, you startled me. I
thought I was alone."

"I'm sorry, I didn't mean to frighten you," he
said. "That is the last thing I wanted to do, especially
since I've been looking for you. My name is Raymond
Dubois Jr.. My father was the speaker for this
morning's service. I noticed you when I came into
church and I made up my mind to know you."

Gazing deep into her eyes he stretched out his hand offering it in a handshake.

Sandra looked up at him. When their eyes met a slow burn crept over Sandra's being. She didn't dare admit that upon seeing him her fondest wish had been granted.

At age twenty-six, five foot nine Raymond were about two hundred pounds, with short cropped, thick, black hair and a deep brown complexion, intelligent looking, appealing and seemingly very proud young man. He appeared gentle, polite and considerate, so unlike the men that she saw daily, whom most of the time was rude, crude and uncaring. She reached out her slender hand, and managed to say, "My name is Sandra Lee Hayward. I am a member of this church."

Shaking her hand firmly, Raymond replied, "I'm glad to meet you, Sandra Lee Hayward."

Suddenly the air around Sandra sent chills rushing through her, only to be followed by heat equal to the burning rays of the summer's sun. She shook inwardly as her voice failed her.

Lost in the presence of each other for a few brief seconds they stood speechless. Then looking at the table that surrounded them spread with a variety of delicious-looking, good-smelling, hot food, Raymond timidly asked, "Can I get you something?"

Sandra nervously replied by the shaking of her head to indicate no, before she able to voice, "No! No, I'm not hungry."

"Well," said Raymond, "I'm famished."

Moving towards the table filled with barbeque, steaming hot corn, mashed turnips, and countless other foods, he smiled and asked, "Would you mind keeping me company while I eat?"

Sandra returned his smile and said, "No, I wouldn't mind. Help yourself."

Raymond filled a paper plate with small portions of a variety of foods, while stealing glances at the beautiful young creature standing beside him. Sandra was a picture of sheer loveliness; her long auburn hair fell loosely over her shoulders. Her wide, brown, innocent eyes would have shamed a saint. All of her five feet three, weighing no more than a hundred ten pounds if soaking wet and curved in all of the right places, could have easily caused him to sin in his thoughts.

Together they walked over to the picnic area and there they sat on a bench beneath a huge pine tree that sheltered them from the sun, while Raymond leisurely consumed his meal. There, under the trees protection they talked, laughed, relaxed and enjoyed in each other's company.

Sandra learned that he was an only child and like his father, was a minister. But, he still attended Seminary College.

While they were together she received all of his attention. He made flattering gestures such as dusting the bench before she sat and later bringing her refreshing water from the fountain. His words of 'Thank you' and 'Please' fascinated her. Raymond showed Sandra kindness in even little things. This was a new experience for her. He made her feel special.

The naïve, starry-eyed girl had never had anyone treat her like anything other than a servant or a nuisance. Raymond's attention was overwhelming. During their short time together Sandra surmised that despite being so big, especially his large, thick hands, there was only tenderness in him.

Having talked with Sandra during their entire lunch break Raymond Dubois became completely attracted to Sandra because of her sweet childish ways.

When Sunday service was over Raymond and his group headed for the boarding house a mile or so away, Sandra dreaded seeing him leave, but she delighted in the possibility of seeing him the next day.

After being alone with Sandra several times during the weeklong revival, not including the hours of service, Raymond's great attraction for her made his growing interest in Sandra known to Hattie. Surprisingly, despite her age, her mother gave consent for him to call on Sandra in the future. In the months that followed under strict watchful eyes there were many visits by Raymond and their relationship became extremely binding. Believing they were in love, Raymond readily admitted to Sandra's family that he wanted to make a very serious commitment to her.

Hattie Lee Hayward made it clear that it didn't matter how he felt when she said, "Sandra is still a young gal, and I'll still be watching everything that you do, so you better watch your P's and Q's."

Having no desire to wrangle with Hattie, Raymond readily agreed with her. When they were together, other than a greeting embrace or departing kiss on Sandra's cheek there was no other physical contact between them. Raymond handled her gently, with great respect, while all of his conversations were

centered on what "Thus said the Lord." Even his
passion for Godly conversation was refreshing to
Sandra, in view of the harsh words and stern attitude
she had always been subjected to.

After a six months of courtship consisting of
many visits, doting behavior, gifts and much mail
correspondence, with the approval of her mother,
during her sixteenth year, Sandra and Raymond
announced their plan to marry in early June.

Hattie had no objection to the marriage,
especially since she assumed that Sandra and Raymond
would settle down in or around Hillsboro. She viewed
their marriage as the prefect opportunity to exchange
Sandra for a hardy male addition to her family.

Sandra knew little of marriage or the
requirement of such a relationship, even though she had
six married brothers. Despite the fact that all of her
sisters-in-law were young and in their childbearing
stages, Sandra lived in a cocoon as far as sex was
concerned. Sandra was not allowed to ask any question
about sex and was never given any answers. Hattie
believed that Sandra had no reason to be privy to or be
concerned with married life matters or become involved
in grown people conversations before her time. Hattie's
reasons for never permitting Sandra to have any form
of sexual conversation with her or anyone else was
Hattie's belief that children already knew "too damn
much."

Beside the idea of Sandra having a man never
crossed Hattie's mind. She still saw Sandra as a child
and a necessary burden. Hattie believed that Sandra

had no need to "waste her time with grown up business before she needed to." Therefore, she never allowed Sandra many visits with her sister-in-laws; beside she always had too much work to socialize.

Even after Raymond suddenly came into Sandra's life, Hattie still didn't see her as a woman. Instantly Sandra became a commodity that she could readily exchange to further her plans for boasting of her family's male power by having seven sons.

The wedding couldn't happen fast enough for Sandra. Although she lacked sexual experience, she had her dreams and infantile imagination. Within months Sandra and Raymond were married. For Sandra her wedding meant that for the first time in her life she was someone very special.

After the wedding Raymond carried Sandra to their house. It was located five miles south of her family's Hillsboro home.

Upon their arrival Sandra was led into the neatest, most tastefully decorated six-room house that she had ever seen. From the foyer to the upstairs bedrooms with their wide windows and high ceilings, each room was decorated with Early American furniture, and floral print wallpaper with colors consisted mainly of soft dusty rose, light green and white.

In the dining room a light dinner was set out on a beautifully decorated table, which she bashfully but happily shared with her new husband. During dinner Raymond told her, " My family prepared everything for us including this food. They have also stocked the house with groceries, I hope that you don't mind."

Unable to overcome her shyness, Sandra only

smiled.

After dinner Raymond showed Sandra to her bedroom. It was located at the front of the upstairs hallway. It was unique. The furniture in it was more elegant than the rest of the house, with one exception the huge four post bed stood apart from the rest of the furnishings. It was so high that a footstool three steps high was required to get into it.

Looking into the room was like peeping into a dream. The brightness of the white canopy, soft white linen sheeting and the bedspread dazzled her eyes. Sandra was greatly surprised when Raymond stood just outside her door as she entered and explored the room. She wanted him at her side. When she was finished he called her to him and gave her a kiss on the cheek and said, "Goodnight."

Sandra thought he would come back later after she dressed for bed.

Although no one prepared Sandra for this night she dressed in her finest feminine nightwear and laid there waiting for her 'Knight in Shinning Armor,' that was now her husband not knowing exactly what to do or expect from the man she had seldom seen except under the presence of watchful eyes.

She was alone and frightened, yet excitement filled her heart as she joyful anticipated clarification of life's secrets. She lay trembling, wondering and waiting for her husband. All the while, the hours crept by minute-by-minute, she went on waiting for her adorable Raymond to appear, but he never came. Late into the night, from the depths of her loneliness, Sandra tossed and cried because she never dreamt that her loving husband would not come to her. On the first night of their marriage she and Raymond didn't share a bed.

With her eyes puffy from weeping, the next morning Sandra arose, dressed and went down to prepare her husband's breakfast. She was confused, hurt, and fearful of facing him.

Raymond arrived in the kitchen fully dressed, behaving like the same man that stood beside her at the altar on the day before. His dark brown eyes were warm and sparkling with the joy of seeing her. His manners were cordial, polite, caring and he smiled at her with the same tenderness she always saw. There wasn't any change in him.

In the midst of inquiring about how she slept and commenting favorably on the enticing smell of breakfast, as the tantalizing aroma from the well-prepared morning meal filled the room, Raymond took his seat at the head of the table. She began to fill their plates with fried country ham, scrambled eggs, home-fried potatoes, and hot baked biscuits. When she finished, Sandra took her seat facing Raymond, who sat at the opposite end of the table.

After bowing his head and blessing the table, Raymond straightened up in his chair, gazed into his wife's face, and said, "Sandra, I guess I should've explained to you before we were married that due to my religious beliefs our marriage is on a much higher plateau than most. Therefore, we are much more seriously committed to 'Thus Say The Lord ' than other couples. Most marriages are steeped in sin with loose morals that dictate practices that lead to a life of sin, fornication and divorce."

Surprised by the solemn, hard tone of Raymond's voice, as well as the strange course of conversation, Sandra sat silently, wide-eyed and mystified, staring at her husband and intensely listening to each of his unexpected words and understanding very little.

Raymond went on saying, "I don't know what you have been taught, but there's much you must learn about marriage according to God' s Will. But, I'll teach you the laws of marriage sanctioned by the Bible. My wife, marriage vows are very sacred. They come with a set of golden rules meant for us to abide by. These rules are very hallowed to me. According to God, lustful intercourse is a sin before him. God created nature in man for the sole purpose of propagation. In every phase of life, sinful mating is devastation to those that uses it. Illicit intercourse breed's heartaches, harm, and danger to all involved. Lustful men build worlds of chaos upon fornication and other illicit behavior. Weak, foolish women's lives are destroyed by fornication, and they are enslaved by their own weaknesses'.

Suddenly, Raymond was sounding like every Sunday school teacher she ever had, only his Sunday school book was absent. In deep sincerity, Raymond began to instruct her, "Mating between all of God's creations is not meant to be used in a lustful way, especially by man. Mating is meant for the sole purpose of propagation. In other words it's an act that allows a male to seed his mate. In the act of fertilization God does not require any unnecessary futile sensual exhibitions or beguiling passionate act of arousal to accomplish His will."

Sandra was so intent on grasping the meaning of what he was saying that she couldn't touch her food. She sat rigid with her eyes, mouth, and ears wide open, because many of Raymond's words were baffling to her. She had never heard most of them before.

"Therefore," Raymond explains, "We'll not indulge in lurid behavior of any kind, because it's despicable, dispensable and forbidden. I didn't come into you last night because it was not yet time to seed you, my wife. I know that you are innocent and ignorant to the ways of men, but still I must see the proof of your purity by your issue of blood. Then ten days afterward, I'll come to you, only if we are ready for children. Right now I've much that I must first do to prepare myself and there's much for you to learn before you are ready for seeding."

Still staring wide-eyed with bewilderment and stunned by Raymond's words, she was immobilized, disappointed and not fully knowing what he meant. Being completely at a loss, when Sandra did become able to speak she asked, "Raymond what are you talking about? I don't understand what you mean by 'futile exhibition, seeding, lurid behavior and mating.' Mating! It's only animals that mate. We're not animals and fields alone get seeded. We are human beings as well as husband and wife. We are people in love, so what're you talking about?"

Raymond looked tenderly at her and said, "My dear, we're more animals than any creature God ever created. We're dumb, sinful and rebellious animals that disregard God's laws, but this will not be so in my house. We will obey. Just as I believed, you're truly very innocent. I cherish your innocence. It's precious in God's sight and mine. I'll instruct you daily in God's Will."

"Innocence! Innocence of what?" Gasping, Sandra cried out, "What're you talking about, Raymond?"

Raymond replied, "Just as I surmised when I first laid eyes on you, you are completely innocent to the wicked ways of men and their lust. There is not one sinful thought in your mind. You'll be a good wife, Sandra."

She attempted to absorb her husband's words, but all she could do was sit there feeling confused.

Raymond proceeded to explain to Sandra, as gently and simply as possible, the meaning of what he had said, word for word, precept upon precept, he versed her on the meaning of lustful sex. He did little to display the pleasures some found in it because he viewed them as sinful. Raymond read her passages of scripture from the Old Testament concerning the Garden of Eden, Adam, Eve, and the serpent. He explained their disobedience in detail. When he finished talking she knew enough to know that all the wonderful romantic fantasies that her imagination had conjured up from bits of conversation she had overheard through the years, Raymond was denouncing.

Sandra was completely disappointed. She wanted him to at least introduce her to the womanhood in her that her mother spoke of when she turned thirteen and had her first period.

Without any tactful, adoring words, her mother told her, "You have womanhood in you now, so keep your dress down, your legs closed and your belly won't get big with some young scoundrel's baby before you are married to a decent man. Men only marry virgins."

Even though, after being told that, she still had little concept of virginity. Once Sandra's mother caught her using her fingers, trying to touch her virginity and feel her womanhood and she was beaten severely for being fresh. After that she always sat with her legs crossed and her dress tucked beneath her legs to make sure she had both womanhood and virginity when she married. She knew enough to know that sex played an important part in it.

There was no honeymoon and no sex for the young couple. Instead they traveled to his family's home, seventy miles away and stayed there for two weeks. During that time, Raymond's mother assisted him with instructing Sandra in everything concerning the duties of a good Christian wife except the descriptive facts of mating.

Since beyond childish thoughts and innocent curiosity, sex hadn't ever been a part of Sandra's life, with no sexual experiences there were no yardsticks for guidelines, nor any sensual pleasures for comparison or to evoke any remembrance of sexual pleasures. Therefore she had no feverish longing for an experience of what she never knew.

Yet, there was much she longed to know. She wanted the answer to why her breasts tingled when she got close to Raymond, looked into his eyes, or smelled his aroma. She needed the answer to why her knees weakened when their flesh touch. Often a look from him sent warm waves washing over her and caused twitching in the secret part of her body. Far too long there had been much she wanted to know with no one to tell her. Now Raymond was calling everything that she once desired and often imagined experiencing lustful and sinful.

Other than her limited imagination and youthful inquisitiveness, her obscure knowledge of sex allowed Sandra to accept Raymond's strict propagation rule and settle down and become a desirable, satisfying and contented wife.

Sandra, now seventeen and married, with her only form of sex education, being seeing the rooster jump the hen. While digging his spurs into her back and striking the back of her head repeatedly with his sharp beak, causing her feathers to fly. He beat the hen with his widespread wings as he mated with her and wallowed her in the dirt. All the while the hen squawked pitifully. Sometimes the rooster was so rough with the hen that Sandra chased him off.

Once, young Sandra saw mating dogs become stuck together. They yelped and whined while locked together, and the slobbering male dog's dripping tongue was wagging, as the female desperately struggled for freedom. On quivering hind legs they were pulling each other back and forth while bound together by a length of round, wet, red flesh. She watched in horror as the small bitch yelped and whined pitifully in ongoing intervals, as she was dragged behind the large male dog that was tightly wedged into her. It all seemed to be so horrible and painful that Sandra cried and cried. Later, when she shared the frightening experience with her mother, again Sandra was beaten severely for her boldness.

After that, Sandra was afraid to speak about anything of such a forbidden nature. With no one to talk to, everything concerning sex was left to her virginal imagination. Therefore Sandra found it impossible to imagine what she did not really know anything about.

When Sandra was thirteen she over heard two of her young sister-in-laws talking about "doing it." They spoke of how it felt when their husband's peckers went inside of them. Because of her curiosity about sexual intercourse and the feeling of a male part going into her, Sandra decided to find out how it felt by trying to push a hot dog into her. Hattie caught her attempting to masturbate and once again she was beaten so severely that she could barely sit for weeks. Sandra was warned to never touch herself like that again because it was being nasty and sinful.

After that act of inquisitiveness she never attempted to have any form of sexual or any other intimate experiences. Her fear of her mother was too great and she had no desire to lose her virginity. Besides, before Raymond, no men were allowed near her except her brothers. Therefore, Sandra's asexual mind was the fertile ground for her husband's strict religious cultivation and left her wondering would she ever truly understand any of this womanhood.

Sandra listened intensely daily to Raymond's

teaching, and they became deeply ingrained in her mind. She remembered the long list of begets in the Biblical passages as Raymond had pointed them out about the issue of blood women shed for proof of innocence and maintaining their uncleanness.

After learning all of Raymond had to say was based upon Bible's teaching, as well as recalling the way Hattie had treated her desire to know about nature, Sandra wondered if her romantic dreams were just some extension of childhood fairy tales. Like Hattie, Raymond was calling everything that she had imagined wicked and offensive.

Sandra thought of Hattie's teaching and how her sister-in-laws kept having babies year after year. She recalled the hen and the dog's experiences, Sandra readily justified Raymond teaching by telling herself, "I've not seen nor heard of any pleasure in those animals during mating at all, so why should man be any different? Besides God's Word doesn't lie."

She declared aloud, "They must be right. Mating is only meant for reproduction of life."

When Raymond's teachings were complete all of the laws of the Biblical laws were established with all of the inhibition boundaries firmly rooted in Sandra's mind. This knowledge caused her to accept everything else that Raymond had to say or do.

The lack of any sexual involvement didn't prevent Raymond from being a good husband, nor Sandra a good wife.

Raymond made sure that Sandra's life was completely independent of her family's finances, opinions and other resources. As minister, teacher and lecturer he was able to provide her with a good home and every material thing that she needed. He also forbade her from having any discussion of their private lives with anyone, especially concerning the law of propagation. Raymond said, "Lustful people would never understand the meaning of God's Word."

Raymond was a strong-minded man. He had no intention of following the imaginary role that Hattie had envisioned for him. His main goal was to advance himself in the ministry and spent most of his free time studying.

It was harvest time and Hattie needed all of the help that she could get. Sandra and Raymond had been married for three months or more, when early one Monday morning Hattie showed up on Raymond's doorsteps saying, "You have had plenty time to settle down into this family. Since you have not come forward freely to help out I am here to see that you do just that."

Raymond stared at Hattie standing there dressed in blue overalls and wearing boots and a straw hats that had long out lived itself, tapping her thigh with a riding crop as she spoke.

For a moment he was speechless. Then he said, "If you one time think that I have any obligation to work in your fields or anyplace else you are sadly mistaken. I am my own man with my own plans and none of them include you in my life other than as my wife's mother."

"Well if that your way of thinking, let me set you straight. When you married my gal she didn't become a DuBois, you became a Hayward. As a Hayward you owes this family. So you may as well get off you high horse and join the rest of us and start doing your part," shouted Hattie.

Hearing the commotion Sandra came to the front door, asking, "What's going on?"

Hattie shout, "This lazy ass husband of yours thinks that he is too damn good to join hard working everyday people."

Before Sandra could say anything Raymond said, "Get back into the house Sandra, I am the head of this household and nobody tells me what to do, and besides, you have nothing to say I speak for the both of us."

Sandra turned immediately and went back into the house. Turning to Hattie, Raymond said, "Stay away from my door. Stay out of my business and keep away from my wife. Until now everybody else may have jumped when you ordered, but I'm not everybody else. Come here again without being invited and I will have you arrested."

Then Raymond slammed the door in Hattie's face.

Raymond designed their lifestyle according to his religious beliefs. When compared to life before Raymond, Sandra viewed her life with him as being happy. She became a member of his church and later she was assigned to assist on different committees. As she gained in experience her social life expanded. Raymond's family and friends embraced Sandra. She relished their warmth; it filled the void created in her life by so many years lacking in love and attention. She and Raymond were the best of friends and were a good team that worked well together, but at home they had separate bedrooms and bathrooms.

With the assistance of Raymond's mother, Sandra became a better housekeeper and an excellent hostess. Raymond established a routine that required unconditional protocol and tolerated no unscheduled interruptions in their lives. He was short on patience when it came to Sandra's family, especially her mother.

Even after her and Raymond's earlier encounter, Hattie still insisted on displaying little or no social protocol. Often Raymond and Hattie clashed head on, especially when she willfully interfered in their private affairs. She had no respect for Raymond's position in Sandra's life and placed his authority over Sandra second to hers. She was brash and outspoken, whether she was right or wrong.

Sandra still retained childhood fear of her mother and would have become submissive upon her mother's demand had it not been for Raymond, because of this, Hattie began to despise Raymond.

CHAPTER FOUR

In The beginning

Sandra and Raymond had been married for a year, and she was happy with her life and felt very secure in their relationship. She enjoyed a childlike existence, as she went about her daily activities caring for her already immaculate house, her husband and carrying out her church duties. Sandra and Raymond established themselves in the church community and among the local residents as being an ideal, happily married couple that most young couple eagerly emulated.

It was on a Thursday evening in June, just a few days after their first wedding anniversary, when Sandra returned home early from a church fundraiser; she was exceedingly happy. The president of the Ladies' Auxiliary had informed her that she was the best chairperson they'd had in a number of years and that single handedly she was responsible for raising the highest financial contribution in the history of the

Ladies Auxiliary Committee.

Sandra flitted about the kitchen, happily preparing dinner for Raymond. He was at a late church meeting and she knew that upon arrival home he would be famished. Just when everything was prepared and the table was properly set, Raymond walked through the door.

Seeing Sandra looking so radiant, he smiled. During dinner, bursting with excitement, she eagerly shared her thrilling news with him, "Raymond you would have been so impressed with me, maybe even proud if you had been at the Ladies' Auxiliary meeting today."

She smiled proudly as she looked at her husband seated across from her.

With curiosity, Raymond laid his dinner napkin in his lap as softly he asked, "Why? What happened to make you say that?"

"Well," rather coyly said Sandra, "Today I was told by the president of the Ladies' Auxiliary that I'm one of the best chairperson that they have ever had. Beside that, I raised more money for our treasury single-handedly than anyone ever has."

The smile on his face exhibited his satisfaction for his wife's accomplishment. He said, "It was all of those bake sales, tea parties and May Day activities that you wrapped yourself up in that generated so much revenue. I am truly very happy for you."

Then he leaned across the table and with his finger tips, he gave several very lightly taps to the table top near the hand of his still virgin bride and said, "I've news of my own tonight, Sandra."

Still smiling broadly, Sandra excitedly asked,

"What is it Raymond, dear?"

"I've decided that it is time."

Bewilderment reflected on Sandra's face. She asked "Time, time for what, dear?"

"It's time to begin our family."

At his words Sandra's eyes lit up; as her excitement increased, her lips moved slowly, she was so happy that she could barely speak. Then in a timid voice she asked, "Do you mean that I can really have a baby?"

"Yes you can in a matter of time, if it's God's Will," explained Raymond. "If we are successful when we have our first union, it'll be within the year."

Extremely delighted Sandra eagerly asked, "When Raymond, when? When will we start? When will we do it? Will it be soon?"

Her heart raced knowing that now at last she would experience the 'Will of God.' She was on the verge of having answers to every secret question that she had buried beneath prayers and fasting, Raymond was about to unfold secrets from the book of life to her. She said, "Oh Raymond, at last you're going to make me all grown up. You'll show me the womanhood that's in me."

She looked at Raymond. His face was no longer smiling, a very solemn, pious look shrouded it as he said, "Sandra, remember your teaching. It's our duty, my dear not our pleasure. It is not our intention to become lustful. This is a holy venture."

He reminded her, saying, "You must keep your mind stayed on God and His Word and not on what we are about to do."

Just as a small child who was chastised by her father Sandra's face stung from his verbal slap as she said, "I'll remember, Raymond. I'll remember."

His eyes were fixed on her face seeking any evidence of undue insincerity. Sandra lowered her eyes and shyly asked, "When, my husband?"

Without any emotional display, in a low inexpressive voice Raymond said, "Tomorrow night. Until then we'll pray for spiritual guidance and cleansing."

They finished their meal in an atmosphere of heavy silence. In his presence Sandra didn't even dare to allow her thoughts to embrace the idea of becoming intimate with her husband. Later that evening, after Sandra had finished cleaning the kitchen, they sat at the table and Raymond read to his wife from the book of Ecclesiastes. The poetic passage about a good wife gave her much comfort.

When he was done reading night had come into its fullness. He gave Sandra her usual adoring goodnight kiss on the cheek and each retired to their bedrooms.

Alone, still filled with the excitement that she dared not show in Raymond's presence, happiness stirred in her, she allowed it to fill her heart. The desire to know her husband was one that she had secretly entertained so many nights. Now that the reality of it was so near, she still had to rejoice secretly. Try as she may, the law of God failed to control her overwhelming desire to know marriage's most intimate secrets. She created her own innocent scenario concerning the events in the lives of loving couples trying to imagine what it was like by building upon the fairy tales of her childhood. In her mind generated Garden of Eden, she became the sleeping beauty that's awakened with a kiss in the strong arms of her adoring prince Raymond.

In the past, when Sandra received no real gratification from her vague visualizations, she had followed her husband's instruction and prayed past them. But tonight despite all of Raymond's instructions, Sandra was so excited it was impossible to pray into calmness and settle down enough to sleep. It was impossible to concentrate on any of Raymond's instruction; so she could only returned to entertaining her fantasies. Trying to imagine having a real kiss, to boost her imagination, she slid her hand through her long, satiny soft auburn hair that she inherited from her Comanche great-grand mother, and pulled it over her face. Caressing its softness she pressed it to her mouth to practice tender touched of kisses that she had envied of other couples and now eagerly expected from Raymond.

Sandra huddled against the pillows lined headboard of her oversized bed, drew up her knees and embraced them, whispering aloud, "We're about to have our first moment of an acceptable union. I'll not be like Eve in the Garden of Eden succumbing to a cunning, deceitful snake. Instead, my husband will lead me in the way that God would have me to go. Raymond said that Eve was beguiled into sin by the serpent, making sex sinful, but Raymond and I will be doing God's Will."

Even if it was an act of holy participation for

Sandra, the mere thought of experiencing a touch of intimacy added an air of excitement that made her tingle all over.

Sandra recalled her lonely wedding night of endless waiting for Raymond to come to her and unfold the mystery of marriage. In defiance of Hattie's warning and Raymond's preaching, with trembling fingers she dared to touch her genitals. With timid fingers, using slow, gentle movements, Sandra circled the tiny mound above the slit leading to her virginity. It was warm, soft and foreign to her. Her innocent mentality had not begun to fathom the depths of pleasure that was a real possibility. The more she massaged her clitoris the greater the sensation became. Her legs shook, as she became alive beneath her fingertips. The amazing affect filled her with thoughts of great pleasure as well as pangs of guilt. Still she didn't dare to push her finger inside of the fleshy mound for fear of rupturing the seal that Raymond informed her that God had placed inside of her. She knew that according to the bible, rupturing that seal was a privilege that belonged to Raymond alone. Hattie had warned her that men only marry virgins. Because of this seal she was a virgin, and she knew if she broke it Raymond would despise her. But when he breaks it they would be physically as well as spiritually united. Now they were on the verge of becoming one in body, mind and soul. She whispered, "Now I'm only hours away from having him really belong to me."

Sandra closed her eyes and tried to picture what it would be like to have her husband completely possess her and break open her heavenly seal. Would she be afraid? Would she laugh, cry or shout for joy? Then

she shivered knowing that she was already afraid, but
she was even more inpatient. If her fingers felt this
good how much better must he feel? But how could she
ever know what he felt like unless tomorrow came?

Mind chatter kept Sandra awake until the wee
hours of morning. At long last, she closed her eyes and
collapsed into a dream filled sleep, allowing tomorrow
to advance forward.

The next day, the rising sun sent its breaking
rays through the kitchen window, located above the
sink, flooding the neat, moderately sized room where
Sandra prepared her husband's breakfast. Her heart
was as light as the morning's air and her thoughts were
bright as the sunlight.

It was Friday morning; Saturday was one of
Raymond's days of rest with Sunday being the next.
They leisurely enjoyed a delicious breakfast of fruits,
omelets, and baked muffins that she lovingly prepared
and placed on a plate before him. She filled his cup
with coffee. After Raymond had been well served she
sat down opposite him. She looked at him without any
outward display of the churning sea of excitement that
flooded her body. After breakfast she happily cleaned
up the table putting everything back into its place.
Raymond retired to his room for meditation and Bible
study. It appeared that for him this day was like any
other. But not so for Sandra, even though she went
about her housework and her daily church
responsibility, taking care not to get exhausted, the day
was too long and it dragged by far too slowly.

Tonight she anxiously anticipated receiving her

husband, an experience that she wanted to be prepared for emotionally and physically. She was elated when at last the dinner hour passed and the last dish had been washed and put away.

During dinner when she looked at Raymond's adorable face, a flicker of emotion arose in her, but she withheld any expression of eager anticipation because she didn't know how to express her happiness without offending her husband's beliefs.

After dinner Raymond looked at her and a placid voice said, "It's time, Sandra dear. Cleanliness is next to Godliness. Go and bathe."

Nothing ever he said had sounded so sweet to her. Her heart skipped a beat, and her blood ran so hot that she shivered with sheer excitement at hearing him saying, 'It's time, Sandra dear.'

Enthusiastically, Sandra hastened to obey her husband. In the bathroom, she filled the tub with water covered with foaming white perfumed bubbles. Her adjacent bedroom smelled of rose petals that matched the flowers that filled a vase sitting beside her bed on her dressing table—she relished the scent of roses, all freshly cut from her spring garden. She had designed her own wonderland.

During her bath Sandra's mind rummaged through her cache of memories drawing on all Raymond had taught her about this moment. As the minutes for "propagation," as Raymond called it, grew near, her stomach churned and her hand grew cold with a combination of excitement and fear. Their holy matrimony ritual was about to begin. Sandra thought, "Oh God, what'll it be like?"

CHAPTER FIVE

A Time of Reckoning

At age ten Sandra realized it was not the stork that bought babies, and she had seriously doubted the story about the Doctor's black bag containing them, and they certainly were not in stumps like Aunt Sally had told her. She had seen the big bellies in women and was told that they had swallowed a watermelon seed and it grew inside of them. But when dogs had those same big bellies she saw puppies coming out of them, but the truth about the mystery of it all still eluded her. Knowing how babies ever get in and out of their belly still was not entirely clear to her?

She was now eighteen; and she would soon know it all. Raymond had promised her that he would perform the monthly ritual of prorogation regularly, according to his plan and "The Will of God," until she had a baby of her own, but thoughts of thoroughly knowing still engaged her mind. Questions such as how would it feel? How would he give it to her?

Now Raymond was about to bring an end to her wondering exactly what was the real truth about babies and how they were made, how it felt when they were made, how did you know when you had made one, where did they really come from, and how did they really get to be here in the first place was about to be made known to her. She took comfort in Raymond's promise that only when she was with child would he stop.

After bathing, Sandra went into the bedroom and nervously began to prepare to receive her husband. Smiling, she put on her silkiest gown and best perfume and then spun around before the mirror to view her shapely reflection. Her protruding breasts were like large, firm, sun baked, satin smooth balls. Her raised, budlike nipples pressing outwardly from beneath the soft silkiness of her white gown had begun to tingle from her excitement. Her entire body was filled with a new and strange sensation. It was a degree of excitement such as she never experienced.

Her moment of self-adoration was suddenly interrupted when she heard Raymond's approaching footsteps.

Raymond came and stood outside her bedroom door and knocked lightly, as he called to her through the closed door, "Sandra, have you bathed?"

Rapidly she repeated smoothed her gown over hips with the palms of her sweaty hands and stood in nervous anticipation of greeting her husband. Expecting him to come in she quickly braced herself mentally for his appearance and made ready to receive him. She softly replied, "Yes, Raymond dear, I have."

Raymond immediately said in a very solemn

voice, "Then get fully dressed and meet me downstairs in the living room right away."

Sandra was shocked by such a request. Completely bewildered she thought why doesn't he just come in? Curiosity took a firm grip on her mind, but obediently, she hurriedly dressed and rushed downstairs to find her husband standing waiting for her in the living room.

Raymond's face was clean-shaven; his hair was well groomed and his eyes were clear and steady. He looked so handsome, but frightfully serious. Draped over his arms he carried a long white cotton gown much like baptismal clothing.

In direct response to the apparent look of surprise exhibited in Sandra's face at seeing the outfit, he said, "This is the traditional propagation outfit that once belonged to my mother and her mother before her. Mother is now past her childbearing years; now as my wife, it's yours."

With the snow-white garments draped covering his forearms and hands, his arms stretched toward Sandra as he handed them to her. Then in a tutorial voice he issued her instructions saying, "Take these and put them on."

Too stunned to speak, Sandra stood staring at Raymond, as she wondered what was it that he was really telling her to do.

Smelling the fragrance of perfume exuding from her body, Raymond said, "And go and wash yourself again. Then, without any scent except the one God gave you, put on these clothing. Now take them and get dressed. When you are ready, I'll come to you."

This unanticipated occurrence left Sandra completely astonished. Stunned by Raymond's words she stood looking at him bewildered and motionless. There was a brief silence between them before he slipped the outfit over her outstretched arms. Sandra looked at the white cotton garment, then she looked back at Raymond, not sure what to make of what was happening. She nodded timidly and accepted the outfit and folded it to her breast.

Raymond gave her further definite instructions, saying, "Once you are bathed and dressed in this outfit go into your bedroom and lay flat on your back at the very foot of the bed, place your feet upon the footstool, and wait for me."

Dazed, confused, and feeling overwhelmed by Raymond's behavior, Sandra returned to her bedroom and spread the garments out on the bed to further examine them. She had never seen anything like them. There was a pair of almost new, long, white, drawers designed to completely cover her lower body and legs, with a slit in the seat from front to back. This went with the almost new long white gown. The head wrap was long and meant for a number of laps around her head. Trembling and sorely confused, feeling like a wounded child, unquestioningly, Sandra re-bathed and dressed as she had been instructed to do.

After a short while, re-bathed and wearing the outfit, she went over to the bed and walked around to its foot and stood staring at the footstool as if she was seeing it for the first time. Suddenly, Sandra lost all of the childlike remembrance of the dream that she had on her wedding night about her having a princess-like bed, and the thoughts that she entertained when dreamingly she first sat on the side of her bed a year ago.

Raymond's solemn attitude suddenly made her doubt if there were any fairytale reasons for the high, firm bed and the three-step footstool that never completely went with the rest of the bedroom's furniture. Suddenly everything was giving the impression of having another purpose, the robe, the bath and now the bed and footstool, but what was their real purpose?

Feeling abandoned, Sandra slowly ascended the footstool. Fearfully she climbed onto the bed. She thought this footstool was always intended for me to use in this manner, but why? So many questions swamped her mind, as she lay flat on the bed on her back with no pillow beneath her head; her arms were stretched down at her sides. Nervous and tense she laid there barely breathing, waiting, as her feet rested firmly upon the footstool.

CHAPTER SIX

Keeping His Commandment

Almost an half an later, very politely Raymond knocked on Sandra's bedroom door. After hearing her telling him to come in, he entered dressed in a white cotton pajama suit. Its long top had long sleeves and a wide panel concealed the frontal slit in the pants. He carried a white towel on his left arm that concealed a pair of white gloves that he also carried in his hand.

Raymond approached the bed slowly, appearing slightly frightening, as he loomed over where Sandra laid spread before him like the feast on those tables in the churchyard on the first day that they met. In total perplexity she lay wondering when would he uncover her and how much of her was he going to take?

Again she heard Raymond in a very distant, detached voice, issue to her another firm order, "Close your eyes, now, Sandra and keep them closed until I say differently."

Even more confused, disillusioned and subdued, her will was now withered. She immediately closed her eyes without questioning him.

With his head raised and his fluttering eyes cast upward, sanctimoniously Raymond entered into the portal of her open legs. He uttered a boisterous fervent short prayer, "Oh God all power is in your hands. You know all and see all, so it's with a pure heart and a clean mind that I ask you to bless our union with fertilization. Thanks and praises be unto you. Amen"

When his prayer was finished his voice became low and almost consoling as once again he reaffirmed his instructions to her, "Keep your eyes closed no matter whatever takes place here Sandra. This is a very sacred moment, so treat it as such."

With closed eyes, Sandra felt the warmth of his nearness. She visualized his handsome face and athletic body hovering over her. Once again her expectation rose; she anxiously waited for the wonderful surprise that her husband obviously had in store for her. The slight hint of tenderness in his voice allowed her imagination to once more take over. Her lips trembled in anticipation of his sacred kiss. The hardened nipples of her heaving breasts tingled as they waited to be crushed beneath his ardent, tender touch. Wonderful, handsome Raymond was really going to touch; taste, caress and lovingly take her body in a wonderfully exciting and divine way. She lay in anticipation of being swallowed up in his strong arms.

For a few moments Raymond was very silent. Those moments were like having all sound sucked out of the universe. Her body grew taut as anxiously she waited and longed for some gesture of adoration, a caress, a word of enthusiasm, or a mere touch to

indicate the beginning of their marvelous journey.
Then she realized the magnitude of her flawed thinking
when Raymond harshly commanded her, saying, "Your
eyes better remain closed Sandra no matter what,
because it's sinful for you to look upon my bare flesh or
me upon yours."

The sudden change in his voice was shocking.
Now, more-than-ever, Sandra was completely mystified.
She thought why can't I see what is going on? What is
so secret that even now, married, I can't know?
However, she would not be entirely discouraged, as she
still awaited the one gift that her husband had yet to
bestow upon her, womanhood. She was all set to receive
and experience all of it whatever that might be.

Raymond's eyes remained uplifted towards
heaven and did not look down on Sandra's beautiful
face, nor did his hand pull up the long, white robe to
reveal the smooth, flawless skin of her outstretched
body. He ignored the rapid rising and falling of her
bountiful breasts that made the cotton robe covering
them alive with movement. Raymond didn't dare move
his face near her full, trembling lips that called his
name so sweetly and had spoken to him so tenderly for
over a year. He welcomed the white head wrap
covering her mass of soft auburn hair that served as a
lovely frame for her smiling face. Raymond knew that
he couldn't even dare to think of her in such a manner.
To Raymond her physical beauty was only temptation
that Satan had intentionally set before him to provoke
him into committing a multitude of unforgivable sins.

For Raymond, at this moment of prorogation
Sandra had to become to him as Lot's wife, when she
turned to a pillar of salt. In all of her loveliness, he

could not afford to look at her. He had to keep his thoughts pure, his mind focused and his hands clean, according to God's pre-ordained instructions.

Sandra shut eyes didn't allow her to witness Raymond' s manhood enter into a state of transformation, rising up, solidifying and stretching out to its greatest potential, preparing to administer to her as the designated instrument of 'God's Will.'

Once thoroughly physically prepared, Raymond meticulously slipped on the thin white cotton gloves. Then, with a gloved right hand, he reached down into his pajama pants and released his primed holy tool from behind the cotton wall and quickly concealed its stoutness inside the white towel.

With half closed, fluttering eyelids, he stood erect between Sandra's well-covered, open legs. While positioning himself to move even closer to his wife's outstretched body, his feet struck the footstool where her small feet rested. In doing so, he caused the stool to slide closer to the bed, suddenly shifting Sandra's trembling legs backward, raising them even higher.

With her eyes still shut, Sandra's heart fluttered as the sudden jolt sent her mind groping for some idea of what was taking place around her. At that moment, she felt Raymond's hand as it skillfully moved between her thighs until it identified the slit in her drawers and at the very same time located the slit in her. His pressed his stout finger beyond the slit in her drawers and dipped it onto her. There was a roughness associated with his touch that was unfamiliar to her. Not having seen him with the gloves on, she couldn't visualize the reason for his coarse touch and she shrunk away.

Like some unfamiliar invading prowler, the forefinger of Raymond's glove covered left hand moved gradually over Sandra as he began to summarize the perimeter of her narrow channel nesting beneath a layer of soft curly hair. Prudently touching every inch of her opening, he was apparently exercising a form of fundamental measurement upon her.

Beneath his slow moving, probing touches Sandra suddenly began to experience an exciting twitching as a series of warm sporadic waves stirred in her. It was so similar to the sensation that she felt the night that she dared to touch herself. Then she recalled that according to Raymond's instructions she should lay motionless and subdued before him and remember that she was strictly forbidden to receive any pleasure from whatever occurred between them. However, with each touch of his hand the excitement in her increased.

Raymond's gloved right hand took a firm gripped on his erection and by touch alone he guided it between the soft perimeters of his wife's tiny opening and targeted her center. While the thick fingers of his left hand pried her open, spreading her just enough for him to become fixed into her narrowness. With a slight shove he nuzzled his God's chosen instrument into the rim of her and rotated it in place several times, exerting enough pressure to keep him in position. Having certified the preciseness of his location with great objectivity, he bore down in forcefully readiness to fully engage her.

Upon the launching of his portly mass into Sandra, she experienced for the first time the great dimension of her husband and knew the hugeness of his instrument. She instantly reacted to the unexpected hardness his prodding instrument and the pain it caused. She cringed beneath the tremendous pressure of his fleshy wedge. Twitching and turning she tried to shut him out by closing her legs. When Raymond felt her resistance and resenting it he pressed down into her even harder, generating more pain than Sandra expected or was prepared to endure. Raymond's intense effort to breach Sandra hurt her severely. Finding no pleasure in it, crying she pushed hard against him and opened her mouth to beg him to please stop. But, before she could speak to make Raymond know that mating was something that she didn't want after all, without a word or further warning, a sudden heave of Raymond's heavy hips sent him hammering into her. With one devastating thrust he fully engaged her instantly shattering her virginity, obliterating her innocence and rupturing her heavenly sealed orifice. Upon impact her body seemed to explode. She felt the rasping, gouging and burning abrasion of her flesh. Gripping pain slashed through Sandra in jarring waves and she was agonizingly aware of being ripped apart.

Until that moment Sandra had no idea of the enormity of her husband's manhood. She wasn't prepared for the severity of Raymond's devastating assault upon the small niche that barely accommodated her finger. When his hunk of steel-like muscle tore her apart, she immediately knew his strength and lashing power. Her body vibrated from the sudden shock. In reaction to her pain, Sandra's mouth flew open and she rapidly tossed her head from side to side, as salvia flowed freely from the corners of her lips. Her wide, terrified eyes that instantly flew open were gushing with tears.

She had not dared to attempt to see what was happening before, because she feared the wrath of God and adhered to Raymond's warning. Now she willingly accepted the price of disobedience, as she looked to see if this was her handsome husband, her adoring friend, and her constant protector who was doing this to her.

As she gazed through tearing eyes into Raymond's stony face, she screamed out in excruciating agony and from somewhere in the far distance she heard a series of blood chilling screams that kept on coming. Only when Raymond's hands released their steel grip to her quivering thighs and flew up to grab the sides of her head and shoved it down into the bed pinning it there, as he bored further down while executing into her blistering organ a series of hard, grinding thrusts. It was only then did she realize that it was she who was doing the screaming.

Like the slobbering dog, Raymond was stuck inside of her. He was wedged into her so tightly that her legs couldn't even tremble. He was buried so deep in her that their pelvic hairs were inseparable. Her body was thoroughly riddled with debilitating pain and she kept on screaming, screaming and screaming.

Then, for the first time, she witnessed harshness in Raymond that she had never imagined existed. His face grimaced, and his eyes had hardened like those of a Bible-thumping preacher observing the most extraordinary performance of a sinful act.

With his face pushed close to hers, squeezing her head hard between his hands, his voice boomed harshly

Ophelia M. Turner

over her screams as he shouted, "Shut your mouth and shut your eyes woman of perdition and bear your burden in silence. It's the price of sin that you are paying. You are only carrying out your wifely duty by doing God's Will."

Raymond's face held no expressions of sympathy. The lines of his jaws were set with hardness. Raymond grinded his teeth as his piercing eyes searched Sandra's tearful face for any signs of rebellion as he set out to execute "God's Will," upon her.

Fearful of Raymond and God, Sandra shut her eyes and her mouth and bites her lips until blood filled her mouth, while pain like shoes of iron with cleats of steel, raced through every fiber of her body.

Raymond raised his body up over hers to the point of almost total withdrawal. His protruding instrument rested above its searing host, with his hard plow like instrument momentarily pauses in a downward position, on the very edge of her furrow of pain as Raymond stopped for another prayer in which he said, "Help me Lord. Please help me to deliver your seed to this rebellious woman and forgive her in her ignorance."

Breathing deeply Raymond spread out Sandra's legs as wide as he could and held her fast, as if waiting on God for his next holy command.

Before Sandra could begin to relish any thought of possible release, with a loud "Amen," and a forceful lunge, Raymond's powerful hips sent his inflexible muscle slamming into her, again. Sandra knew she was trapped like the hen beneath the rooster, and there was no one to save her.

After each devastating thrust Raymond repeatedly paused and momentarily hovered over her before delivering another calculated blow, continuously compelling Sandra to accept his full dimension. The fear of sinning kept her lips sealed as she screamed inwardly.

Without any form of loving preparation from her husband, or advice or words of knowledge from her mother, armed only with the lies of her aunts and her childish imagination, and limited amateurish mind, she had no substantial knowledge of how to protect her traumatized body from the torment of Raymond's onslaught. Bloody and torn, Sandra lay pinned beneath her husband. She was helplessly and hopelessly unprotected from Raymond's and God's Will. Sandra could only bear the pain that Raymond inflicted, as he, with only his mission in mind, went about the task of fertilizing her in a no frills, sin-free way.

Sandra laid suffering while God with his eyes wide-open watched Raymond viciously tear into her. God's voice remained silent as Raymond's hand dug into the flesh of her thighs like steel vices, as he pressed her legs apart until they ached. With each awesome shove he intensified the strength of his powerful hips. Her legs were as dead logs; her body was a mass of excruciating pain and her mind was spent from the continual hammering from Raymond on his Godly mission.

Sandra's eyes became tearless. She had no voice. All she could think was someone should have warned me. She cried silent tears asking within, Momma, Momma, why didn't you tell me? Why did

you allow me to walk blindly into this living hell filled
with so much pain and disappointment? If this is the
womanhood in me why didn't you give me some
protection against it or prepare me for it? Why did you
lead me to believe that I should protect something that
would only bring me so much pain?

In one stifled inward scream Sandra saw her
foolish envision of "Fairy Tale's Princess' and Knights
in Shining Armor" vanish behind a veil of complete
disappointment, agony and sorrow.

Now, all she possessed was the stunning pain
radiating through her battered and torn body and
dreams of it ending. Unrelenting in the performance of
his holy quest, pausing, counting and slamming
Raymond administered with great precision each
penetrating blow into her.

On the last impact Raymond positioned himself
deep inside of Sandra and the only feeling she had
beside agony was the constant vibrating thumping of his
convulsing instrument as he released himself into
completion. Becoming satisfied that his task was well
done, with the utterance of a short parting prayer, he
said, "Thanks be to God for this holy union. I'm asking
for your forgiveness for any sins I may've committed or
any pleasure of the flesh that I might've given or
received at any instant while seeding my wife. Oh Lord
bless my seeds that they may fall on fertile ground. For
I have humbly sought to redeem her body and my soul
by the full deliverance of thirty-nine blows into her,
such as those that you endured for our sin. Oh Lord,
my God, please forgive me if I've sinned in my attempt

to do your will and pay our pennants. Please forgive my wife for rebelling against Your Will and her duty. Amen."

With his brief "Amen," Raymond quickly withdrew his wilting erection with his glove covered hand and wrapped it in the waiting towel, as he rushed out of the room, leaving Sandra to deal with her pain. Bloody, aching, and alone, only then did she dare to weep outwardly.

Ophelia M. Turner

CHAPTER SEVEN

Aftermath

The next morning Sandra's awakening was like the completion of a tormenting nightmare. In the midst of broad daylight, shattered, shaken and ashamed, she remained traumatized by the horrible experience of their union. Her body felt foreign, dismembered and throbbed with pain.

She managed to pull herself together enough to drag through dressing and performing her duties of making breakfast and being available to Raymond when he arose.

Raymond demeanor was pious and stern when he entered the kitchen. He offered her no sympathy for what he referred to as, "Doing her duty." He casually suggested to her to care for her battered body with warm soaks and natural herb compresses that his mother in anticipation of her needs had sent over for her along with the propagation outfit.

Sandra had no words. She silently served her husband breakfast. As she carefully sat down at the table to face him the searing pain left her no room for comfort. Sandra felt Raymond's staring eyes resting on her face. They held no compassion. After a long silence Raymond spoke firmly as he readily cautioned her in no uncertainty, "Sandra now you must always be on guard against any wicked urges or sudden desires of your flesh for spontaneous sex that may occur now that you've tasted the 'Root' of sin. You must keep spiritually prepared to work through any such feelings by following the Word."

Sandra's sore body, mind, and spirit were so devastated and abused that she could barely remain seated before him. It was almost impossible for her to look into his face much less desire him. As he spoke, deep in her mind she was wondering, how could anyone in their right sense ever deliberately want anything like that again? She wanted to scream out as loud as she could, never, never, never again is far too soon.

Daily Sandra diligently prayed for fertilization. But, then at the end of the month with the appearance of her menses, she realized that God hadn't heard her prayers or any other words that she had said.

Once again she saw the white robe hanging outside of her door tears filled her eyes and her heart stumbled and skipped a beat. Sandra's breath grew shallow while her body quaked at the prospect of what lay ahead.

When the time arrived, filled with fear and dread, Sandra prepared for the unavoidable. Her previous experience magnified her fear and caused her to offered up her own prayer for a quick deliverance. Without hesitation, showing no tenderness or loving concern, Raymond once again mercilessly plundered

Ophelia M. Turner

her. As he thrust into her Raymond appeared angry at having failed to breed her on his first try. From the first moment of contact he was more forceful and intense than before. His engorged instrument became a mandatory statement of his determination to fertilize her this time.

Unlike her first experience Sandra now knew what to expect, but knowledge alone offered no protection against being brutalized. The occurring pain appeared to exceed all previous memories. Physically cringing beneath her husband she attempted to shield herself emotionally by recalling his teaching and painfully accepting her fate. Instead of screaming, her closed, tearing eyes provided her with a psychological secret closet that she immediately slipped into. There she prayed for strength and stamina. Then she laid her spirit at the foot of the cross and submitted her body unto Raymond to do his and God's Will.

As Raymond repetitively prodded her toward his fulfillment of "God's Will." Sandra clenched her teeth and tried to rationalize her purpose, as well accept her reason for being. Those unrelenting waves of pain now came with some understanding those thirty-nine splitting strokes were her payment toward the price of her forgiveness. Her husband was God's instrument of choice through which he sent forth some of his blessed seeds for multiplication and she was the gateway through which they would flourish. Anyway, that is what Raymond said when he explained her duty to him and God.

However, there were times when Sandra often

questioned God, wanting to know if propagation was His Will, why did it take so long for fertilization, and why did he require so much pain?

By the third month, Sandra had learned to mentally remove herself from the unavoidable. To mate without fertilization was a grievous sin that Raymond had no intentions of bearing. At the sight of the robe, like the utensil she had become, Sandra shut down her feelings to dull the harshness of the impending experience. Mentally she grouped the blows into an uninterrupted chain allowing them to become as one event, knowing that the repetitive links in this chain of pain couldn't extend beyond the thirty-ninth. Silently, submissively, emotionally and physically detached, she committed herself to wait for the moment of Raymond's fervent closing prayer and dying withdrawal.

At the end of the third month Sandra had no menses. She knew then that for nine wonderful months she was free from the Will of her husband and God.

Sandra soon learned that the price of freedom from monthly union came at a very high price Raymond believed that God did not need man's help to do His will. Those nine months she had no obstetrician and her pregnancy was not easy. They were fraught with morning sickness, backaches, swollen feet, an encumbering enlarged body, and long lonely hours as Raymond never varied from his schedule and would not accept any changes in their household routines.

When time came for delivery, a midwife and some female members of Raymond's family assisted Sandra., Raymond's mother had previously told her as much as possible about the ordeal of childbirth, yet Sandra had no real concept of childbirth. When the first contraction set in Sandra realized there were no words to describe the awesome pain. Nothing that had been said by anyone came close to recounting the agony of childbirth, and neither did any experience that she ever had, not even when Raymond first ripped her body asunder. There was nothing in heaven, hell, or in between that could be compared to it.

According to scriptures and her husband's beliefs she was compelled to endure natural childbirth. For seven hours she was propped up on a birthing table with five tubs filled with boiling hot water sitting on the floor beneath it. In a steam filled room with her bound legs spread wide and knees bent upward, Sandra lingered helplessly in a world filled with steam and wrenching with pain. All she could do was endure and scream. Raymond's mother stood faithfully by, from time to time she placed linen towels over Sandra's mouth to muffle her loud cries, which never ceased until the healthy bellowing of eight pound Raymond Dubois, III, split the air.

Breastfeeding became Sandra's greatest pleasure. Her baby was two years old when Raymond ordered her to completely wean him. Sandra's objections went unheard. She needed her baby's mouth pressed against her breast. She needed to be stroked gently with his soft, warm, tongue and patted by his smooth, tiny hands. It became the only source of pleasure that she could draw on. It was the only demonstration of affection she had ever known and she needed it to make her life worth living. Nurturing her baby had made her life of motherhood so wonderful that she almost forgot and forgave the brutal demands of their unions that had brought him into her life. Now she was being forced to relinquish the only real meaningful part of her existence.

When their son was almost three years old Raymond informed her that it was time for him to enter into a man's world. She could only watch as her son was practically ripped out of her arms and turned over to the elders of the church for the beginning of his religious education. They kept her son from early mornings until Raymond's arrival at home, even if it meant keeping him over night. Raymond and the elders controlled her son's life.

Hugging, kissing, and motherly fondling was strictly forbidden. According to Raymond's religion, it was believed that mothering, smothering, pampering and overrated affection weakened males. Raymond made her know that at the age of twelve their son must acquire the full obligations of manhood, becoming responsible for his own sins, and assume his place in life as a man. Until then, he and the elders alone were responsible for his training as well as his welfare. Once again Sandra became a voiceless, disposable, invisible figure.

Then, a few weeks later, after being deprived of her son without any prior indication, Raymond said to her, "Its' time to add another child to our household."

The dreadful memories of those violent moments caused trembling to seize Sandra. Her body and mind was instantly traumatized at the memory previous monthly unions, the horror of natural childbirth, the forced surrendering of her son and all of those heavenly duties that were pure hell.

On the day she entered her bedroom and saw the white robe hanging beside her door, at its sight her entire body recoiled. Then she knew why Raymond had sent their son to spend the weekend at his parent's home. He did not want their son in the house during her fertilization.

Dressing for the occasion Sandra assumed her position on the foot of the bed. Sandra closed her eyes and waited for her destiny.

She listened to his prayer, dreading the debilitating thrust that would come at the moment it end and she whispered a prayer of her own.

For a year, once a month this religious stranger invaded her body and she was compelled to accept him in the name of God. Fearing that she had become barren during childbirth she wondered how long Raymond would keep up their mating before he decided it had become futile, and lustful, and stopped.

After twelve months of unions Sandra accepted her fate as an endless exercise in pain to be measured out eternally by thirty-nine strokes at a time. When all appeared hopeless, God stepped in and sent their second son, Saul, and she knew that he too would soon be taken from her.

After their second successful mating Raymond informed her that there would be no more unions because two children were enough responsibility until their lives were more financially stable.

Inwardly Sandra shouted with joy. God has been listening, she thought. She had to literally bite into her lip to keep from screaming out her happiness. Sandra thrived on knowing that her education in fertilization was over. No longer having God's Will interrupting their lives she tried to recapture the life that they once had. Their friendly relationship had become constrained. Previously, Sandra had hoped to become happily absorbed in her role as a mother and minister's wife, while Raymond went on with his career as well as being a husband and father. Now with no children to mother, and no need for further fertilization, she again found herself virtually unnecessary.

Raymond remained the primary figure in all of their lives retaining much of the inflexibility that he exhibited as the rigid executor of God's Will. Only now he was the controlling father, and she was only allowed to be mother in name only. The elders had more authority over her children than she could ever hope for. All Sandra could do was stand helplessly by as Raymond became the architect of their lives and emotions. Her children became strangers without any regard or apparent love for her. To Raymond, she was a vessel depleted that stood idly at his side, ready to do his bidding. Void of emotions, empty of dreams, Sandra methodically moved around in the world that Raymond had created, performing her duties in the church, hosting his guests, cleaning up his messes, preparing his meals and carrying out his instructions.

Four years later, after ten years of Holy Matrimony with much hard work and adhering to

Ophelia M. Turner

God's Will, Raymond was finally called to pastor a church on the west coast. His individual happiness was overwhelming. However his call would lead to disaster for him and Sandra, especially since he always remained inflexible in attitude towards her family's desire to keep close to her and share in the lives of the children, which he had always firmly denied. His desire to go west became his primary concern and was decided without any consultation with Sandra or her family.

Then one morning Raymond decided to revealed to Sandra his plans for what he viewed as improvement for their lives and he joyfully announced, "We are moving to the West Coast. There we'll have a very large parish with a spacious house. You'll have even more help for the children. At a much earlier age they will go to live in the church's boarding school. This will allow us to have at least three or four children in a much shorter period of time. Everything will be wonderful."

Raymond's overwhelming joy instantly became Sandra's trauma, with her feeling having been completely excluded from day to day, Sandra mulled over her fate, until for once in her self imposed contentment she had squeeze out of it a smidgen of happiness at just knowing that she did not have to do anymore mating. Now Raymond was telling her that security was being ripped asunder. With Raymond speaking of his expectation for even more children her hope of freedom from pain had been shattered like a frozen glass in a three hundred degree oven.

For over twenty four years. Hattie had ran the

family and its businesses with an ironclad fist, and no one ever darted to neither challenge her authority nor defy her decisions until Raymond Dubois came along.

Upon hearing that Raymond was very close to solidifying his plan to move Sandra and their two boys to the West Coast, Hattie's temper exploded.

This infuriated Hattie and she yelled, "This shit's all brought about by that goddamn no good Raymond Dubois. He has done everything that he can to split up my family. Now if he expects to take my two grandsons, my own flesh and blood as well as my gal, completely out of my life and take them to some damn West Coast, well it'll be done over my dead body."

She vowed to prevent him from carrying out his plan at any cost, declaring, "I'll not listen to any of that damn shit. I'll not hear a damn word that he is saying. There is no way in hell I will ever allow any of that to happen."

Like a penned up animal, Hattie paced back and forth across the front porch almost frothing at the mouth as she vented her rage before her family. "Why, we Hayward's built this damn community," snorted the two hundred and thirty pound, five foot six, Hattie. "We own every goddamn stick and stone around here, from the lumber yard to the tooth picks in the restaurant, from the farmland and dairies to every damn thing else in between. This is my town and my family. Nobody is taking my family, my land, or nothing else away from here, and certainly not my grandchildren.

"That damn outsider Raymond Dubois sashayed his fancy ass in here full of pretense and snatched up my gal with his pretty words, smooth acting ways and his high and mighty attitude. Claiming to be so damn religious, promising he would keep living here knowing damn well that he was lying, just to get his hands on my gal. Now he's talking about going west to be some big time pastor and church overseer taking my grandsons with him.

"Him with his pious ass has always acted like he is too damn good to put his shoulder to the wheel along side of this family. Now he is a big time preacher man, so he says. Well damn him, his plans and his pious ass. He will not rob me of my grandsons nor my gal. Hell will be completely refrigerated before I'll ever let that happen."

All of Sandra's life, she feared her mother when she bordered on the edge of insanity, like now, and so did everyone else. Whenever Hattie became locked into a violent mode and made her opinion known no one dared to go against her. That was a lesson that all of her children learned at a very early age and often at the end of a whip.

Hattie was a vicious woman, especially when she was defied, and many men could testify to that. Hattie made it a point to let Sandra know how she felt, making Sandra fear for herself and for Raymond.

The day before their scheduled departure, knowing that he was unwelcome there, Raymond allowed Sandra to go to Hattie's house that morning alone to say her goodbyes. But after six hours Sandra had not returned. Becoming very concerned he went after Sandra. When Raymond arrived at Hattie's house in search of Sandra, he was not allowed to enter into the front yard.

By her appearance when Hattie stepped onto the porch with Sandra trailing behind her, Raymond knew that Hattie was extremely angry. With her hands placed firmly on her hips, her face was scowling and her squinting eyes were furious.

Although Raymond knew that Hattie was angry, he had no idea of the extent of her rage. From the moment that Hattie stepped out onto the front porch and laid eyes on Raymond she began berating him and accusing him of destroying her family. That afternoon Hattie's confrontation with Raymond was bitter. Hattie threatened to shoot him over the way that he was trying to control her family. As unpredictable as Hattie was he still stood his ground.

Raymond knew that Sandra was terrified of her mother and as for him there was no friend in their midst, not even totally Sandra.

Hattie began demanding Sandra to remember her family's loyalty.

Raymond retaliated by ordering Sandra to stand firm against her mother as he said, "Don't let her threaten you or tell you what to do. She has no authority over you. God gave you to me. You are my wife and you only belong to me and God so remembers your commitment woman, to Him and me."

Sandra had left the porch and stood in the yard just feet away from Hattie, placing hers between Hattie and Raymond. She was torn between her husband's demands and her mother's anger. With divided loyalties between Raymond, her mother and fear of

God, she turned into a nervous wreck as she teetered on the edge of an emotional melt down.

At the height of their confrontation Raymond called out to Sandra giving her an ultimatum, "Sandra-Woman, you need to make your choice right now."

Fearful of both of them Sandra was drowning in by indecisiveness. Her mother's angry demands and Raymond's orders raced around in her head. Out of desperation, she placed her hands on her head, making a pleading gesture. Confused and doubled minded hesitatingly Sandra stood speechlessly gazing at Raymond with wide tearful eyes, then at her mother. This irritated him beyond description. Raymond despised Sandra's inability to give him the immediate commitment that he felt that he rightfully deserved. He refused to be kept waiting for a reply that apparently she was not ready to give.

Infuriated, Raymond angrily demanded, "Woman, you will decide right this minute. According to God you are only subject to me. Who are you going to obey, your mother or God?"

The man that was the faithful administrator of God's Will and the father of her children was calling out to her, yet, Sandra could not make any reply. Her flooded eyes sent large tears rolling over her quivering cheeks.

Without any compassion in his voice, Raymond said, "Woman decide now or I am leaving tomorrow morning without you and taking the children with me!"

Hattie stood by in the background with her hands on her hips, looking on, hearing Raymond's words, shouted at Sandra, "Let him go. Goddamn him, he'll be back. No man has left a Hayward woman yet," she boasted.

Raymond turned and headed towards their car. Hattie was livid and Sandra was devastated. Still crying, without answering either of them, Sandra stared at Raymond as he drove off, disappearing in the distance.

The evening was fading into night and with no transportation Sandra remained at Hattie's home that night. It was the first time since her marriage that she had not slept under the same roof with her husband.

Hattie used every minute she could to make sure that Sandra fully understood how she felt about Raymond.

Hattie said, "That damn man! is damn near more woman than you are, with his manicured nails and baby butt smooth face. Never wanting to get his hands dirty with honest work. He is always prancing up and down pass here dressed like he is somebody special. I should have known that he would never be the man this family needs. Now he has you walking around here like some mindless creature. You ain't good for nothing no more. You can't even come here to give me a hand once in a while. He got you living, eating, and breathing every word that he stuff down your damn throat in the name of God. It's bad enough that he has taken your children from you and delivered them to that damned church, now he is taking all of you to only God knows where. I wish that the son of a bitch would just drop dead as hell."

All through the night Hattie never stopped berating Raymond. Having spent the night being forced to listen to Hattie curse Raymond, Sandra became desperate to be near her husband.

After tossing, crying, and getting no sleep, Sandra arose just before dawn, while Hattie still slept, dressed and slipped unnoticed out of her mother's house and hastily headed home. Her heart was heavy and ached with loneliness. She had almost forgotten what life with Hattie had been like. She had almost forgotten her mother's bitterness toward her, now Raymond suffered the same fate.

During the five mile journey home, sometimes walking, sometimes running, she reconsidered her years with Raymond. Until the mating and the children he had been a good husband. He treated her with kindness. They shared pleasant hours together at home and away. He made her feel appreciated and loved in his own way. She thought how could I blame Raymond for fulfilling God's commandments? It was his duty. As his wife, it was my duty to submit. I am subject to my husband and to do his and God's Will.

She knew that Raymond was the only life that she had, regardless of what it was, and she could not let him leave without her.

In all of those years of their marriage Sandra had never gone to Raymond's room while he occupied it. It was an unwritten law that forbids it, and he always insisted that she obeyed it. She could only clean it in his absence when he told her to, and she had to be very careful about it, leaving everything as he had placed it. But today she felt compelled and justified to make an exception to Raymond rules. She had to see him as soon as possible, to let him know that she would follow him anywhere, no matter what. She was his wife, and he was her husband, and it had to remain that way according to God.

Dawn was just breaking on the horizon when Sandra arrived home. The wind was still and the air was thick with the smell of damp earth, and laden with morning dew. The sun had just begun to emerge over the gray horizon of the approaching dawn. Its warmth could barely be felt. Sandra's body gave a slight shudder from the chill in the air and a reflection of her nervousness, as she rushed on.

Upon arrival, the silent house appeared strange and deserted. She entered as quietly as possible. The house's stillness was stifling and only slightly disturbed by the minute creaking of the floor as she stepped over the threshold. As quietly as possible, easing the door shut behind her, she slowly walked very softly down the carpeted hallway. Raymond's room was at the opposite end of the hallway away from hers. The distance seemed farther than ever. Her heartbeat wildly and she trembled with a fear that increased with each step that bought her closer to Raymond's door. Her footsteps were leading her to a place she had only dared to enter in broad daylight, alone.

Her body quaked uncontrollably, as with much apprehension she approached Raymond's door. At times her thumping heart seemed to stand still. She recalled every word that her husband ever issued as a warning about coming to his room. However, she remained determined and kept moving forward.

Stealthily approaching his room, took a deep breath and paused before she raised her hand to lightly knock on the closed door. But at the mere touch of her shaking hand sent the door silently gliding open. Surprised by the door's sudden, unexpected movement Sandra sucked in her breath and held it as she stood fearful of being there, unannounced. Still, she dared to peep into the room swimming in the pale light of the breaking dawn. Blinking her eyes several times as her misty eyes became adjusted to the light and they immediately widened when to her shock they fell upon the bare flesh of Raymond's broad, bent back. He stood totally spotlighted in the rays of the emerging sun that generous washed over him, fully displaying him before her eyes. He stood wide legged, nude, hunched over and firmly pressed against the bent over bareback side of another person.

Only when the swinging door struck the wall with a light tap did both Raymond and his companion turn to look into her face which allowed her to look directly into their. Suddenly Sandra was staring into the face of a handsome, young elder that she had hosted on countless occasions at their dinner table.

The astonished, nude man was leaning down face forward over the foot of Raymond's high bed. He knelt on a step of a footstool that was built exactly like the one in her bedroom. Raymond's stooping body was molded tightly to his and Raymond's pelvis was jammed firmly against the young man's behind with his manhood fully engaged between the round fleshy mounds of the young elder's bottom. They were so surprised by her appearance that neither man could move. The two men's actions were momentarily suspended in time. Startled, they became too frozen with panic to make any attempt to become disengaged. It was apparent that Raymond was the male hound and the little elder was the bitch. They were locked together like those dogs only neither made a whimpering sound.

Sandra eyes were glued to the unbelievable scene. She stood with her mouth wide-open before she became able to cry out in anguish, "Oh my God! What are you doing? What is going on here?"

In dismay she tried to cover her eyes in an effort to erase their living images. Sandra attempted to shut out the horrific sight of her husband's nakedness and the young elder's nude body glistening with the sweat from their feverish mating.

The young man didn't lay with his feet on the footstool with his legs spread and his eyes were not closed. He knelt on the stool, leaning over the foot of the high bed of propagation, with his legs closed and his fleshy backside pushed up to Raymond.

For Sandra the terrible truth became totally unacceptable. It was one of the vile evils that Raymond had preached to her about, a man lying with a man. At that moment, Sandra willed herself to reject all that she saw, finding it easier to believed that she alone had committed the ultimate sin by entering her husband's room, against God's Will, and looking upon his nakedness she cried out in repentance.

Sandra turned and ran screaming down the hallway and out of the house. Pain, fear and disbelief clutched her heart and mind. Crushed beneath the sudden flood of conflicting emotions, waves of cold rigor threw her body off balance causing her to sometimes stumble during her flight, without looking back,

Ophelia M. Turner

wondering what could she do? Who could help her? Totally traumatized, Sandra ran away from the only shelter that she had ever called her own as fast as she could.

Blinded by tears, confused by her surroundings and overwhelmed with grief, Sandra didn't realize that only a few paces behind her, Raymond was in fast pursuit. With his long robe flapping in the morning breeze, revealing his naked swaggering manhood in its fullness, he took long, angry strides in his attempt to overtake his fleeing wife. The sudden gusts of chilling wind over his nude body seemed to spur him on. He caught up with Sandra at the edge of the woods beyond the house.

When he was within hand's reach of her Raymond gripped her arm and swung her around to face him. Trembling with fury, his eyes blared and his clenched teeth bit into his lower lip as he raised his open hand above his head and slapped her with such force that her body spun as she fell to the ground.

In a heated, loud, harsh voice he shouted "You Jezebel. You defiant wench! How dare you disobey me, woman? How dare you disobey me? How many times have I forbid you to ever come to my room? How many gosh darn blessed times?"

Sobbing into the ground where she landed, Sandra cried, "I'm sorry. I'm sorry, Raymond."

"You broke my rule and God's commandment. You looked on my naked flesh," he shouted. "What have you done, woman? What have you done?"

In that instance truth dared to rear up inside of

Sandra with the sharpness of a two-edge sword, cutting through the self-imposed shield of denial that she had drawn over her mind's eyes, she screamed out, "No more Raymond, no more! The lie ends here. It is not me that has sinned. Oh no, Raymond this day you will not force your guilt upon me. No, no, no, I didn't just see your bare flesh; I saw the bare flesh of you both in a sin fest. It's what have you done," she cried. It's what in God's name has you done Raymond?"

Raymond shouted, "Just like Eve, woman, you are lying in face of your disobedience, you are refusing to accept the fact that it is you who has sinned. Say what you will it is you that has become unforgivable. I'm leaving you Sandra and my sons are going with me. If you ever dare mention anything that you think that you may have seen today I will make sure that you never see them again"

Sandra leaped up and lunged at Raymond, yelling, "No! No! You will not have my sons. They are all that I have. They are mine." Blinded with desperation, swinging her fist wildly, Sandra flung herself at him.

Raymond blocked her attempt to strike him, then he slapped her several times fully across the face with all of his might cutting her lips, as the hard, raining blows impacted her face almost blinding her. Then he flung her to the ground, without looking back he turned, and rushed away, leaving her lying face down on the ground, crying out in agony to God, begging him to erase all that she saw and heard from her memory and to save her sons.

While Sandra lay in the woods crying in physical pain, filled with shock and completely emotionally destroyed that she didn't even feel the pain of Raymond's open hand blows. Their smacking sounds resounded in her ears along with the ringing of the Raymond's awful threatening words, "I'm taking my sons."

Raymond madly rushed home, gathered up his sons and their belongings and drove away.

By the time Sandra made her way back to the house Raymond had left taking their children with him.

Sandra never spoke of the morning when she last saw Raymond. She closed her eyes and mind to that day. She refused accept or acknowledge the truth of it again. She didn't bear to sever the last connection of her marriage and all she held sacred. It was her only lifeline. Love, as far as she ever knew, was always Raymond.

After that horrific morning, for one year with each passing day Sandra bled inside and bore her pain in silence. There was no one that she could turn to. How could she admit to anyone what she had seen? So she buried it deep inside and covered it over with self imposed guilt. Each day, her life became just a little more empty, lonely and more unbearable than it had been before her marriage.

Without Raymond everything became even more chaotic. She no longer had a bumper against her mother's overshadowing presence. At every opportunity, Hattie readily sought to beat her down and destroy all of her memories, especially those of

Raymond.

No longer able to maintain her home, Sandra was forced to move back into her mother's house. She had to abandon every routine that Raymond had taught her, and conceal any positive image of herself. The mere remembrance of being a wife, a mother, and a viable person is what she needed to cling to for the maintenance of her sanity

Just as before, no one respected her, not even her sons, when they were there; Raymond had seen to that. She was their birth channel, but Raymond's voice was the only one they ever heard, besides the elders.

Raymond managed to have her ostracized by the church, and his family shut her out. Her work at the church, being a wife and mother as whatever personal freedom she once had was gone. Now she had nothing and no one, not even her work at the family store.

Sandra felt like an insignificant talking doll with a crushed voice box. All of her life she was owned by someone, first her mother and then her husband. In their own way, neither allowed her the freedom of being, of feeling, of having an undirected thought, or to make her own pathway to anything that may have led to as much as a independent smile. But deep inside in of Sandra something began to stir. It was a growing unconscious aspiration for freedom and a radical desire to take control of her life. So she began to look inwardly, leaning toward her own reasoning and understanding, and seeking strength. A longing to pursue her personal need for total independence took root and slowly begun to sprout.

Raymond had been gone for over a year, when one morning, Sandra woke up in a cold sweat, choking

and gasping from a severe emotional attack that
triggered an upset stomach that sent her rushing into
the bathroom, where she tempted to heave out her
insides. She shook like a leaf in a windstorm and her
skin was damp and clammy. It seemed to be peeling off
in minute sections. Her vision was doubled, and her
head spun as darkness enfolded her and she passed out.

As the personal maid she had become, when she
didn't show up for her morning duties, Aaron, her
younger brother, came looking for her to prepare their
breakfast. He found her lying on the bathroom floor.
She had regained consciousness but was weak,
lethargic, unresponsive, and totally unaware of her
surroundings. Aaron rushed her to the hospital's
emergency room. Hospitalized, Sandra became
subjected to endless evaluations both physical and
psychological. It was with psychological assistance that
she learned, as she put it, "Suffering from an emotional
hemorrhage that was causing her very sanity to slip
away."

While she lay in her hospital bed drained and
lost, her deep longings revealed themselves. She
realized that for her entire life she had stood on the
sidelines and watched as her life slowly ebbed into
oblivion. Now, for the first, time she wanted to live her
life in her own way. She realized in order to do that she
had to sever all ties with her past, her family, their
unrelenting habit of taking over her life. Without
further consideration, determined to grab up what little
life she had left, along with the handful of dollars that
she salvaged from Raymond's support checks, Sandra

decided to run as fast and as far as she could away from Hillsboro, North Carolina and everyone connected with it.

Sandra knew she had given up and given in to her family for the last time. There was no more to give. Life with Raymond and everything that it entailed had been the only thing that was really hers, and even though he took large chunks of life out of her, what was left of it was still hers. Even though he still financially supported her, reconnecting with him was not an option. He had served her with divorce papers and a custody suit for the children within months after he left. The church and its money supported Raymond. Sandra realized that she would never win that battle.

At the root of her illness and all of her problems was her family. Her mother had always delivered damning blows to her marriage. Raymond Dubois and her family had stolen her will, her belief, her children, and her physical and mental health and strength. Sandra's only ark of safety rested in her ability and willingness to flee from all of them, immediately.

Early one Sunday morning the undeniable urge to flee beat unrelentingly in Sandra's mind, overshadowing every strangling hold of the past and every tie that bound her.

She heard about the Virgin Islands from a West Indian teacher that she had when she was in high school. This teacher had painted such a romantic and beautiful picture of the islands that in her loneliness she had longed to someday escape there, and that someday was now. For once, Sandra did as her mind dictated. Unannounced and without fanfare she suddenly fled her mother's home and ran all the way to St. Croix, leaving no word as to her whereabouts. In doing so, she was certain to rock her family's foundation with shocking disbelief.

All Sandra needed to leave Hillsboro far behind was an airline ticket. On a Sunday over three years ago, with her savings in hand and the barest of necessities into a suitcase and while the Hayward clan was still in a Hillsboro Baptist church day long service, Sandra headed for the dreamy little island of St. Croix.

From her seat on a Prenair small airplane, high in the air overlooking the Caribbean Sea, bound for St. Croix, she was amused and amazed at the incredible scene below. The nightmare of Hillsboro and all that it was didn't exist for her any more.

CHAPTER EIGHT

New Places. New Faces.

Sandra had never traveled over a hundred miles away from home and was panicky about what she would be facing and how well she would adapt to her new surroundings.

From the moment she viewed the beautiful island of St. Croix from the window of the struggling little airplane that she had boarded in Puerto Rico, theirs was a love affair. The island's rugged shore was an enchanting sight. She had never seen white caps leaping across a blue sea, yet there they were right below her, rising and falling in long irregular rows of white water. The waves sped out of control, rushing to the shore like speed racers, touching and crashing before reaching the finish line, reviving and then continuing on with the race. They touched the shore and washed upon its beach, then rolled right out to sea again.

As the airplane approached the island the blue, rolling sea gave way to mountains and valleys of deep green, flourishing plants, and trees decorated with an enchanting array of the most beautiful and colorful flowers on earth.

Countless sea gulls, like small white kites, dipped and dived as they sailed between the green earth and pale blue sky. The morning sun was bright, and the sky was clear over the land below that looked almost like Raymond's description of the Garden of Eden.

Sandra's flight brought her over the city of Fedriksted, on the west end of the island. It was scattered with large estates and sprawling hillside homes along with several large hotels and streets lined with waterfront businesses.

Upon arriving in Christainsted Sandra quickly saw that she was in a very different and new world. The west end of the island was so physically unlike the east end. Yet, each end of the island relished its differences, cherished its individuality and took great pride in its uniqueness.

Sandra found herself surrounded by people whom nationalities she had only heard about and seen in books. There were people from, India, China, Denmark, and England and other people from all parts of the world. They dressed in many different fashions and presented a very colorful scene. Some wore their native attire and others darned American high fashion, beachwear or local outfits. These people spoke many different languages and with various accents. Even though there were a lot of American tourist coming and going still her entire surrounding made her anxious, but Sandra had no choice except to make her own way.

After checking into The Windward Passage, a

Best Western hotel located on the oceanfront in downtown Christensted Sandra decided to explore her immediate surroundings. She found that the hotel housed Guthrie's restaurant that was open twenty hours a day, this made meals very manageable. The hotel was also accessible to many businesses that addressed her personal needs such as laundries, drugstores and banks, allowing Sandra time to begin focusing on her top priorities of finding a job and a place to live.

Eventually Sandra learned that the town was comprised of apartment houses, large hotels, a variety of stores and an influx of people from all over the world. Some were residents, while others were just passing through. Other people were imports, transports and implants. Some were famous, and others were not so famous, but all were welcome, and many were set to remain there for a lifetime.

With large groups of tourist invading the little island cities, especially Christainsted, the atmosphere of busy, big cities had crept in. Buying and selling merchants occupied every vacant spot. The entire Christainsted scene was unlike anything that Sandra had ever seen. Despite her uncertainties, Christainsted amazed her. She decided that end of the island was where she really wanted to be.

After lots of searching among real estate offices, newspapers ads, and following leads that even took her to private homeowners that rented out their properties, finding an apartment was appearing hopeless. Then by sheer luck, Sandra found an apartment with three rooms and a bath in the Harbor View Housing Complex.

Ophelia M. Turner

A friendly waiter working in Guthrie's restaurant who had become her only form of a social life told her about it. The tip was very welcome, because the hotel was making huge dents into her small savings, especially after at a very low price she bought an almost, new red and white convertible from someone leaving the island.

She was able to get the apartment because of superstition and fear. A woman died in it and no West Indian wanted to rent the place. Upon hearing the story, Sandra welcomed the information and had no problem acquiring or living in the apartment knowing that harm only comes from those that are living.

The building that Sandra moved into was only one of many modern cubical apartment complexes that had mushroomed up in recent years within and around Christiansted. These buildings were situated on a hillside overlooking the harbor that lay nestled along the shoreline of the blue Caribbean Sea, majestically stretching out in the glistening evening sun that drenched them and their sister building the Harbor View Hotel, that stood just across the road. There were many such structures of multi-level three-tiered buildings that consisted of twenty four apartments in each unit. Each unit had four entrances that allowed access to two apartments on each level of those three-tiered buildings.

During the sixties and the seventies, which was about the time of her arrival, independence was granted to many of the neighboring islands. A huge influx of immigrant and migrant working families poured into the Virgin Islands. These units and many more were erected to accommodate these people. All of these buildings were filled to capacity.

Christiansted, the largest city on St. Croix was heavily populated. The island housed two major industries: Hess Oil Company and Martin Marietta Cooperation. These companies offered numerous positions, lucrative salaries and often steady employment to skilled and unskilled workers. Therefore, the island became a magnet, allowing many islanders and stateside drop-ins to fulfill their various needs, from lifetime employment to subsidizing their vacations. For many, St. Croix was a gateway to the mainland as well as place to gain a financial head start.

Like many new arrivals on the island, after much searching, Sandra got a job working at the airport hotel answering telephones, assisting with reservations and checkouts. She was given the morning shift. The manager found Sandra very likeable as well as a willing worker, but because of a lack of experience it was difficult for Sandra to answer telephones, log in the reservations and keep up with the checkouts. Rather than letting Sandra go he switched her over to the night shift. The telephones quieted down at night. There were a lower volume of reservations and checkouts. The night shift was manageable for Sandra and she had an opportunity to learn more about the business at night and the island during the day.

After a few weeks, Sandra was very comfortable in her position. The manager noticed that Sandra had a lot of free time on her hands so he suggested that she help out at the bar when things were really slow. The switchboard was just a few feet away from the bar,

making helping out easy. However, the late night bar
had periods of slowness, too, allowing Sandra time to sit
and talk with some of the customers.

It was during such a lull that Sandra landed a
job at Robbins and Robbins Construction Company as
a personnel clerk. This came about through a casual
conversation with men at the hotel's bar. The few male
customers were mostly businessmen and they were
sitting at the bar discussing the requirements that they
found necessary to maintain the smooth operation of an
office filing system. While sitting there with them,
Sandra became involved in their conversation.

In the midst, one man in particular Trent
Robbins, began to verbalize his disgust and frustration
at the lack of proper filing in his office and the havoc it
had created. He became so impressed by Sandra's
input and suggestions for improving the filing system
and her suggestion of cross-filing personnel multi-
classifications, working status files, and other office
procedures that he offered her a job as a filing clerk.

Sandra's knacks for filing and organizing, which
she developed in church, were based on the same
principles but on a smaller scale. Although she was a
little anxious about what was required to work for such
a large company, she accepted the job offer.

Sandra's position at Robbins and Robbins
International Construction was a great challenge.
Compared to this vast construction business her family
business and church operation were minute. Working
with Raymond and the church organizations Sandra
had acquired extensive people skills, as well as a few

business skills from her family business and the church.

Robbins and Robbins' office staff constituted entirely of stateside employees like herself. However, the majority of the personnel were white. On the various work sites all of the unskilled and skilled workers, and a couple of foremen, were West Indians from various islands. Most supervisors were white Texans with limited or no understanding of the islanders. This resulted in a lot of confusion and work interruption due to their lack of sensitivity towards the islanders and their culture.

Sandra's position in the office afforded her the unique opportunity to meet and develop an inherent relationship with the islanders. She quickly learned the art of intervening between the men and their supervisors'. So Sandra had made herself a valuable asset by subtlety defending the worker's rights and respecting their culture and effectively promoting companies polices, she prevented a lot of unnecessary misunderstandings between the supervisors and the West Indian workers, eliminating many hours of confrontations that saved Robbins and Robbins time and money.

When she wasn't working, and didn't have classes, some of Sandra's favorite pastimes were indulging in the local food, swimming at the beach, conversing with tourists and sipping on icy pina coladas to combat the Caribbean heat. It didn't require much practice to acquire the habit of lounging around the beachfront bars or lulling on the sun-drenched beaches. Meeting the tourists upon their arrival on the island meant getting first hand information about places that she had or had not heard of, and sometimes there was even news out of North Carolina.

Whenever some tourist with an envious eye leered curiously at her leisure lifestyle over a glass filled with crushed ice and fruit punch or a frosty glass of pina colada and asked, "Why did you decide to come here to live?"

Sandra smilingly replied, "The weather is great, and right now it suits my needs."

Sandra's easy relationship with white tourists on the beaches was quite different from her relationship to whites on her job. The whites in the office were much like the West Indians, polite but clannish. The whites' desire for separation was very apparent, especially after five. They maintained their own communities apart from those of the West Indians. The whites seldom gave any indication or desire for any social contact with their employees after work except for special occasions.

The West Indians were of little difference. They laughed and talked with everyone all of the time, but to the discerning observer there was always the reality of worlds within worlds. Islanders mostly clung to their own country's people, speaking their own language, eating their provisions and observing their customs. There was an invisible force that binds islanders together, first as countrymen, then as West Indians.

They included you by allowing you to eat their island's food and imitate their dress, hairstyles and language. However, penetrating their intimate circle for anything other than business contacts was impossible unless they chose you as a trustworthy friend and deemed you worthy. All invitations had to be initiated by West Indians. Once you were trusted and accepted there were no boundaries to their friendship and devotion. When you were accepted into their homes and allowed to observe their customs and join in their family functions: weddings, baptisms, and celebrations of various types, the relationship was binding. It wasn't long before several different West Indian communities graced Sandra with such acceptance.

Eventually, Sandra found herself living in three different worlds. There was the world of racial integration from nine to five in her office, the world of middle class relocated stateside friends on evenings, weekends and some holidays; and then, at their choosing, there was her entrance into the world of West Indians' and their deep rich culture and devoted family life.

Each of these three worlds danced on the edge of each other, barely touching in their struggle to remain vastly independent and protect themselves by design, beliefs, and taboos. Sandra's access to each world permitted her to find a profound degree of satisfaction, a wealth of knowledge, and deep devotion in the midst of it all.

As Personnel Manager Sandra's days were filled with a variety of responsibilities, but after the initial experience of beach clubs, hotel musical bars and exotic restaurant hopping, the excitement wore off and there wasn't much else left to do.

Even the social and charity work in which she became involved included mostly daytime, weekend or annual functions. There was the governor's wife's

Children's Fund Raising Committee, the Hospital Fund Raising Committee, the Handicapped Children's Programs, and anything else to which she could contribute effectively. But when there weren't any classes, seasonal or annually scheduled affairs, Sandra found herself with empty time on her hands. Sandra began to toy with the thought of a business to consume some of her free time.

About a year after Sandra joined the staff of Robbins and Robbins the firm decided that it would no longer complete bonding papers for the bonded workers. The company claimed that too many man-hours were being consumed by providing this service to the alien community. Therefore, these workers were forced to find someone else to do this service for them to keep them immigration acceptable when they applied for a job.

Until the company quit filling out bonding papers, Sandra had been the person doing the paper work for the company's intended employees as part of her job description. It was only natural that the workers began coming to Sandra during her lunch break to ask for help with their papers. When Trent, the company owner, learned that she filled out papers during her lunch hour he ordered Sandra to immediately discontinue all such activity on company property. Then workers began coming to Sandra's apartment. At first there were one or two, then as word spread that Sandra would help the bonded workers, everyday, upon arriving home she was met by a line of people in need of help.

At first Sandra was reluctant to place a fee on her service. Then a St. Lucian named St. John said, "Sandra you do good work, man. You ain't robbing anyone to charge us. It's not right to do all this paperwork without being paid. Say what you wan' and we will pay. You'll see nobody will mind."

The bond paper was a necessary requirement by The Department of Immigration and Naturalization Service in order for these workers to obtain work permits, and the workers had to be assured of a job. If for any reason they became unemployed, they had sixty days to find more work, or were deported if they couldn't get an extension.

Before the former Personnel Manager retired and returned to the states he taught Sandra most of the immigration procedure. However, there was still a lot she did not understand. Before coming to St. Croix, the only aliens she ever heard of were those on television and came from outer space. Then Sandra learned to despise the word 'alien' because of the negativity some choose to attach to it.

Fortunately, an immigration officer whom she had to deal with quite often took time to teach her everything else that she needed to know about filing the papers. In a very short time Sandra became proficient on immigration laws and papers. Her relationship with the men, along with her undeniable skill of running the office and her stanch ambition were all valuable tools that worked well for her in the office and in her home business.

Before Sandra realized it a business had fallen into her lap. Due to her lower fees licensed business owners experienced a loss of revenue and rose up against her.

One of Sandra's friends, a government employee, warned Sandra that business owners intentions to bringing charges against her for doing business in her home without a license and offered to help her acquire the license needed to operate. Sandra didn't hesitate. After getting her business license, due to her excellent work and reasonable fees she became very successful in a very short time.

The island was good for Sandra and good to her. Each day she felt herself growing in strength and knowledge. Night courses at the local college and joining some local organization for charity fundraising added momentum to her energetic quest for self-esteem, Sandra discovered her ability to be creative and entertaining, enabling her to become a worthwhile contributor to the community.

For the very first time Sandra began to become fully aware of her own self worth. With each passing day the deep-seated fear of abuses and rejections began to fade into the background of her new life. Often she thought of home and sometimes even cried, but without any desire to return there.

CHAPTER-NINE

Mark Landers

Blessings and Curses

Born an only boy and the youngest in a household of three women, not including his mother, Mark Landers was blessed with a strong, loving father who made sure that he embraced all of the necessary elements required for complete manhood. Especially since Mark was always showered with the smothering love and protection of his mother and his sisters.

Mark was a bright child with many talents that he was allowed to pursue at his own pace. This resulted in Mark becoming a musician and mastering a number of instruments, including drums, saxophone, marimba and steel drums. But his favorite instrument was the electric guitar.

Mark's father was a master carpenter and from Mark's early childhood his father began teaching him many carpentry skills, especially the craft of furniture making. His father made sure that Mark grew into a strong, honest, reliable human being. He taught Mark to love and respect family, the love of work and creativity, hoping that he would one day follow in his footsteps and run their furniture shop. By the time Mark became a teenager, he was a craftsman who was recognized in his own right.

Mark's mother, a piano teacher was an attractive brown skinned Haitian, and his father was a very fair-skinned Trinidadian from whom Mark inherited his height, good looks and graceful attitude. When Mark was seven years his family moved from Haiti to Trinidad, but his maternal grandmother, whom Mark adored, remained in Haiti.

When Mark grew older, sometimes during the school year, on weekends, and a few holidays he went to visit his grandmother. Otherwise, most of Mark's free time was spent working beside his father in the furniture shop making sets of furniture and other pieces, as ordered by customers.

When Mark was fourteen he began spending his entire summers in Haiti caring for his grandmother, and helping out around the house, yard and fields. On one of his trips to Haiti, Mark saw Mira, a young girl who lived next to his grandmother's place. She never meant anything to him, other than just someone that he occasionally saw. But Mira had a cousin Twila whom he first met when he was fourteen. Twila was a beautiful, happy, warm, and friendly girl that had come to live with Mira and their grandmother. Twila made his heart leap at the first sight of her. Mark knew that he loved Twila when he first laid eyes on her as she passed his grandmother's house going into town to take produce to the market with Mira. Mark had never seen a girl so lovely, and also at twelve years of age, Twila fell in love with him as he stood leaning on a rake in his grandmother's yard mesmerized by her.

On her way back home Mark waited by the roadside and introduced himself to her. From their very first meeting they became inseparable spending all of their time together. To all that knew them, they became an expected pair around town. They were seen holding hands, sharing food, sipping from the same glass of soda or just sitting and talking. They soon declared to everyone that they were in love. Since they were both kids, friends and family teased them about what they called being in love. They were told that it was puppy love, fascination and infatuation, but no matter what anyone said, Mark and Twila insisted they were in love.

Twila never knew her father. He was a white English sailor that landed on the island just like many had and used whatever words, gifts, and idle promises required to trick her young, naive mother into seduction. The relationship lasted until Twila's coming was made known to him, then he hopped the first ship that was sailing back to England, leaving Twila's mother to fend for herself. Carrying the seed of a white man caused her much hardship. She became an outcast among her people. She died when Twila was six years old. At age seven Twila went to live with Mira and her grandmother Mrs. Arrington, who was also Twila's grandmother.

Although Twila and Mira looked alike they were as different from each other as cotton is from pure silk, with Twila being the silk. They had nothing in common. Twila was like the name that was given to her to mock her. Her skin was soft, creamy and her complexion was the color of goldenrods. She was bright, vigorous, petite, smart, and pretty. Her laughter was like tingling silver bells, her hair was like fine-spun copper, and her eyes sparkled with light like bright shining stars.

She enjoyed life's littlest treasures: birds, flowers, and soft helpless animals. On the other hand, Mira was also very pretty, but beneath her beauty she was dark and ominous presence. She had intense, deep brown eyes that always seemed to be staring straight through you. She seldom smiled, and she moved like a shadow, sinister, quiet and elusive. You never knew when she was near until you nearly fell over her. Mira's entire attitude was weird. She found pleasure in destroying things, such as plucking flowers just to throw them away, trapped honeybees in jars just to laugh at their frustration, stoning turtles because they were slow and kicking cats to hear them shriek. Most of the time Mira was a wilting, miserable person that never seemed to attract anyone to her.

At times when Mark worked in his grandmother's garden, upon hearing a cracking branch or seeing a shaking bush, he would look up to see Mira staring at him from some hiding place. He hated the way she stalked him. She made him feel that he was always being pursued. He had an overwhelming fear of becoming her prey. Mark resolved to stay as far way from her as possible.

However, the girl's grandmother, Mrs. Arrington, adored Mira and resented Twila, because Twila refused to believe in or take part in those queer religious rituals that she always considered very special ceremonies. Mira, on the other hand, loved those services and became an ardent participant as well as a devoted student of her grandmother, always being right in the middle becoming involved in everything her grandmother performed that was surrounded by an atmosphere of weirdness and mystery.

When Twila turned sixteen, life with her grandmother became unbearable and she struck out on her own. She went to Trinidad. About the same time Twila left Haiti, Mark's grandmother died. After her funeral there was no further reason for Mark to go back to Haiti.

Upon arrival in Trinidad Twila wanted to marry Mark right away, a desire that Mark whole-heartedly endorsed. Even though Mark and Twila still clung to the belief of their love for each other, Mark's family decided that they needed more time to grow up before making such a serious commitment as marriage. So they took Twila in to live with them and sent Mark to England to live with his married sister for two years and complete his education there. After that he went to New York to visit his other sister for another year.

By the time Mark got back to Trinidad, Twila had finished school and had gained the popularity of a Carnival Queen. Every up and coming young man was practically camping on Mark's family's steps in hopes of winning her affection. Mark decided that the only way to put an end to their behavior was to immediately announce their engagement and follow it up with a well-publicized engagement party.

Upon his return home Mark's father was very impressed by his behavior and the remarkable extent of maturity that he exhibited. He viewed Mark's forthcoming marriage, with his desire to settle down and raise a family as the crowning point of his manhood. His father gave Mark the business as a wedding present. Then he agreed to stay on and help Mark, giving him self something to do while he anxiously awaited his grandchildren's arrival.

CHAPTER TEN

Strange Proposal

About five months after Mark and Twila's engagement and two months before their wedding, Mark was in the shop working feverishly to complete an order for some counters that was almost due for delivery, when an old woman came into the shop. A shy young woman trailed silently behind her. Mark looked up and found them standing there silently staring at him. Somehow they seemed strangely familiar. There was a bizarre vibration surrounding him that seemed to be coming from them. It repulsed him, but he tried to maintain a business-like attitude.

The old woman inched toward him and said slyly in a calculated pretentious Haitian voice, "I done need a bed made fo my granddaughter."

Although he felt somewhat stifled by his intuition Mark stopped what he was doing and went toward the woman and politely said, "Well! You've come to the right place.'

"Young man," The old woman spoke in a

crackling, shaky voice, "I see in yor eyes dat yu is lookin' but yu still don't see, yu don't 'member me now, do yu?" Her voice was chilling and accusing, " I can tell by yor face dat you don't 'member Mira neithe'."

Completely surprised, Mark gasped, "So that's who you are. I thought you were familiar, but it's been years since I've seen you ladies."

"Yes, dat is right! But I'm still the same old Mrs. Arrington, 'member?" giggled the toothless wrinkled old woman, speaking with a thick Haitian accent.

She said, "Look at my Mira. She done all grown up, now. She is a real lady. Just as pretty or prettier dan Twila'll ever be. My Mira is a real princess, she is."

"Yes, she has changed a lot!" Mark confirmed.

"Now my Mira needs she own bed. It's for she weddin' yu kno'. I wouldn't be here in Port-au-Prince, Trinidad, 'cept to make Mira happy. She loves yor carpentry work. It makes she happy. It always has. She never talk of nothin' else," the old lady cunningly said.

Then she turned to the girl who cringed behind her and said, "Com' on Mira, honey, now dat yu is her', de cat done stole yor tongue? Com' on, tell Mark what tis dat you really want. Tell him," commanded the old woman.

Mira remained speechless as the old woman began moving about the showroom, crowded with furniture. Her trembling hands stroked first one piece of furniture and then another. Occasionally the crackling voice inquired of the mousy girl, "Mira, do yu like dis one?"

Mrs. Arrington's old, leery eyes moved slowly around until they became fixed on Mark. After being continually egged on, Mira said, "Yes Grandma, I do like this one. I want dis one."

All the time Mira spoke she, too, was eyeing Mark. What appeared to be a knowing glance was exchanged between Mira and her grandma as the old woman asked, "Is yu sur', girl? Is yu sur'?"

She answered softly, "I'm sure, Grandma. I'm very sure."

Pointing to a teakwood headboard, chuckling in a very low, decisive voice the old woman turned to Mark, "Well young man my Mira done decided. She wants this one."

"That headboard belongs to a set," Mark informed her.

The old woman looked around the shop thoughtful, before asking, "How many pieces comes wid dat?"

"Nine," he answered as he began to make a failing attempt to go on with his work. Mark watched as they moved closer to the workbench where he was using wood glue to join a section of furniture together. They began to move around him in what seemed to be a slow ceremonial manner. Mark felt very uncomfortable having them so close, not speaking, and simply circling him. On what could have been one of the hottest days of the year, the entire shop felt cold and he had a strange feeling inside. A binding spirit enveloped Mark. He tried to convince himself that he was being over sensitive and rude, just because he didn't like

them. Telling himself that his personal feelings were no
excuse for unprofessional behavior, Mark dropped his
tools and went over to the headboard where they joined
him. He began to describe the handcrafted artwork on
each piece. He slid his hands over each design in the
wood not missing any of the clean cut grooves that
fashioned the designs, as he said, "This required a lot of
time and careful work to acquire such beauty."

"Tis nice, indeed," said the old woman, "Dat
floral like pattern sur' is pretty. My girl got good taste.
She always makes wise choices." Her voice trailed off
into a string of weird laughter, "Hee. hee.., hee...."

Mark watched as her entire body vibrated with
the chuckling chanting. When she finished she turned
to Mark asking, "Do yu deliver?"

"Depends!" he replied.

"On what?" asked Mira.

Stunned by her sudden inquiry, since she hadn't
spoken a un-coerced word since she entered the shop,
Mark instantly replied, "Where, when, and how much
you are willing to pay for my service."

"De where tis my house, de when tis one week
from today, how much is whateve' it takes to git de job
done by yu, no matter what," said the old woman.

Mark shrugged his shoulders. He was pleased at
what turned out to be an easy sell. He said, " In that
case, you have got yourself a deal. Just give me your
address."

"De address ain't changed none, tis still de back
woods, you kno' de place back in Haiti," gloated the old
woman.

Mark couldn't believe his ears. Had he heard right? He asked, "Haiti?"

"Yea. Haiti. De same backwoods "

"But I thought…"

"Yu thought I don' moved to Trinidad. "Hee.."Hee…Hee." she laughed. "I never tell yu dat. I tell yu dat we com' to Trinidad, not moved to Trinidad," she snarled. "Now, yu don'made a deal and I 'spect you to keep it. 'Member."

She moved close to Mark and looked hard and long into his eyes as she said, "One week from today, Haiti. Now name yor price, I don' already kno' mine. Mira and I'll be waitin'. Tis my job to see dat Mira has whateve' tis dat she wants, no matter what's de price, or what it take' to git it."

Mark stood confounded as he watched her move towards the shop's doorway. Mira followed behind her like her silent shadow.

Mrs. Arrington's words were so foreboding that they rang Mark's ears for days. He became so upset that he told Twila about it. At first she thought that it was a joke. After Mark convinced her that it wasn't, she became very fearful. Her eyes reflected the terror she had felt when she pleaded, "Mark don't go to Haiti. You will be better off if you just forget the whole thing. Please, for our sake don't go. I am frightened of those two."

Mark said, "Twila, I wish that I could forget it. But I made a promise. Now I feel compelled to go."

Twila asked, "What do you mean compelled? What did she say?"

"It is not so much about what she said, but it is the way she said it. It was mostly old Mrs. Arrington, the way she looked at me when she spoke, as well as the way she acted. It was like she was sizing me up or something, if you know what I mean."

Twila said, " I think I know what you mean. In truth they are really a crazy acting pair. They have some strange ways that I have never understood. Mark, I'm begging you, please don't go anywhere near those two."

"Twila, honey, I gave them my word. I can't break it just like that. It is my fault. I should have found out exactly what I was getting into before I made such a promise."

A week later, upon arrival in Haiti, Mark saw the place hadn't changed much over the years. The weather-beaten one story bungalow where his grandmother once lived stood completely engulfed by a wall of prickly shrubbery that grew right up to the door. The dirt road leading past his grandmother's house and down onto Mrs. Arrington's house appeared to have no end as it led through an almost impassable web of dense bush and entangled vines. Mark must have traveled that road to her place a hundred times before, but this time it seemed that the years had moved it even further back into those nearly impenetrable, thick dark woods.

After arriving at the house Mark knocked soundly on the door. Mira answered. When she saw his face, she literally glowed. Mark waited at the door until Mrs. Arrington appeared.

"I see dat yu made it. Com' on in," said the old

woman.

Mark cautiously stepped inside. The musty room was polluted with an earthy smell and fumes of different herbs and other strange odors. Mark's eyes began to burn and his nose twitched. For a short while, it was difficult for him to breath. He hastily said, "Your furniture is at the dock, but I can't unload it until tomorrow. It's too late for custom clearance. So, I just thought that I would let you know that I'll do that the first thing tomorrow morning."

The old woman spoke very quiet-like saying, "Now dat yu her' der ain't no mor' need fo yu to rush off. Sit down and make yorself at home while I git your payment. How much it be?"

Mark said, "Here is your bill."

He handed her a slip of paper. After examining it closely the old woman went into a cloth sack that she had hanging on her side and pulled out a wad of bills. After counting off the amount required she handed the money to Mark.

Then she said, "Sit, and I'll make yu a fruit drink. How was yor trip from Trinidad?"

"Ummm…. no, I don't care for a drink. I really must go," said Mark. " And my trip… my trip was fine…just fine."

"Yu seem a mite nervous maybe yu need a bite to eat. Taint nothing like a good meal to calm one's body down. Since I know dat yu comin' today I took de liberty of havin' Mira prepare yu a little dish of food. She make yu some fish and fungi. I know yu know fungi, tis cornmeal boiled and cook up with some nice green okra. I hope dat living high on de hog in Trinidad ain't kilt yor taste fo dat kind of eatin'."

Mark gazed at the woman wondering how did she know that he was coming today? He hadn't written her or had any form of communication with her since she left Trinidad. He wondered how did she know that he would be there? She was really giving him the creeps, and that place didn't help any.

He said, "No thank you, Mrs. Arrington. I appreciate your concern, but I'll just wait until I get back to my hotel room, then I will order in and get right to bed."

The old woman eyed him narrowly as she softly asked, "Do yu want to hurt Mira's feelin', Mark? After all, she don' clean dat fish wid he' own little hands. She don' took much care to see dat twas fresh and cook up exactly right. Now yu say dat yu don't want to eat it."

Then she grumbled something to herself as she turned to walk away.

Mark found himself on the defensive and he quickly said, " I never said that I didn't want to eat it. I just said that I would wait until I reached back in town. I really don't want to put you all to any trouble."

"No...tis no trouble," rallied the old woman. "It gives my little girl pleasure, great pleasure, don't it Mira?"

Mark felt like a helpless minnow dangling from the end of an expert anglers fishing pole. Self-preservation became his great concern, so being steeped in proper protocol he heard himself saying, "Well, if you insist."

"We do insist," giggled the old woman with her lips drawn tight over her toothless gums in a deceitful smile. " Yes we do insist. Jis sit right dar at dat table," she said pointing to a far corner of the room. "Make yorself comfortable. I'll have de table all set in jis a minute."

It required all of the inner strength that Mark had to keep from bolting out of that place. His nerves were taut, his stomach churned, and the short hairs on the back of his neck stood up. As many times as he had been to this house when Twila was living there, it never affected him like this before. Everything about the place felt strange. He just couldn't figure it out.

Since Mrs. Arrington was Twila's grandmother, and a friend and neighbor of his grandmother, a reluctant Mark, didn't want to appear rude or ungrateful and above all reveal his foreboding reservations.

It wasn't long before the table was made ready. The big dish of steaming fish was placed in the middle of the table before him, beside a large bowl of hot yellow and green fungi. The pungent aroma of the food filled the room, overriding the already existing odors. Just when Mark thought that things couldn't smell worse, just before the two of them joined him at the table, the old woman lit some foul smelling incense. Mark began to cough. He felt like he was being stifled to death. Mira and her grandmother seemed completely at ease without exhibiting any reaction to the thick fumes.

Mrs. Arrington went on talking as if nothing was happening, as she said, "Jis 'cause yu lives in Trinidad, ain't no reason why yu can't visit de home folk no more. My Mira don'took to yu a lot when yu used to com' here. She talks bout yu all de time wheneve' yu left, now even moreso since we git back from Trinidad. She fretted so because she thought dat yu had changed your mind about comin' here. But I know better. I know dat yu would be her' tonight. I neve' had no fear 'bout you not comin'. Yu see, I know what Mira really wants, and I am sure dat yu do too." Then the old woman slyly grinned at him.

"That's well and good," said Mark, " but if you don't already know I'm getting married in two months. Therefore, I don't go calling on other young ladies, even ones as pretty as Mira. However, if Mira needs any more furniture I'll be glad to accommodate her."

An emotional Mira leaped up from her seat at the table and ran to where grandmother sat and fell crying into her arms, saying, " He is getting married grandma, he is getting married."

Mark replied, "Yes, I am. To Twila, by all rights we should have already been married but my parents insisted that we wait."

Mrs. Arrington proceeded to pat Mira on the head. "Don't fret yor head wid dat my child," cautioned the old woman. "All in due time…all in due time," she whispered to the sobbing girl.

By then Mark had finished eating and was looking towards the door, when the old Lady asked, "How yu like yor dinner? Maybe it would make Mira feel better if yu give her a few kind words."

"The food was delicious," Mark said. "What kind of fish was that?" he asked.

"So, yu liked it, huh? The old woman gave out the most repulsive laugh that Mark ever heard in his life. On she went with her wanton laughter,

"Ha...ah...ha...ah....ha...ha. Well, well, well my son, yu just eat de Doctor Fish." Then she went on laughing.

Instantly Mark recalled the age-old tale about the Doctor Fish and its strange powers when it was dressed at hands of a voodoo priestess. It became a powerful potion that stripped a man of all his free will and placed him completely under the spell of the one that served it to him. Then Mark recalled hearing those old wives' tales about the power of Doctor Fish, especially concerning marriage. It was said when a woman fed a man the Doctor Fish, no matter what, he had to marry her. He angrily leaped up from the table and stepped backward shouting, "Feed me all the Doctor Fish you want too, I'll never marry Mira. There is nothing to that stupid nonsense anyway, nothing at all."

"Oooooh! Nonsense yu say. Well we'll see. We surely will see," she declared, slapping her big black lips together and staring at Mark with cold, hard, narrow eyes, she said, " Yu done eat yor belly full of the Doctor Fish and twas good. Now the Doctor Fish will eat his belly full of yu. Den we see what tis what? Ha...ha...ha..."

Mark took another quick step backward, turned and dashed out of the door. Her laughter followed him out into the night. Everything around him seemed to resound with the mockery of the old woman's laughter. It required every bit of courage that he ever had as he fought his way back in the dark through the jungle-like woods. The thick brush cut into his flesh, snagged his clothing and blocked his way. Mark realized that coming to Haiti was probably the greatest mistake that he ever made. There was something very wrong with

Mrs. Arrington and Mira. All he knew was that he never wanted any part of them again.

It was late into the night when Mark arrived at his hotel. He was not a drinking man, but he stopped at the bar and downed a couple of stiff shots of rum and went straight to bed. There, he spent the rest of the night fighting his way through nightmarish dreams of thick brush, haunting laughter, and the staring eyes of Mira and the old woman.

Early the next morning as soon as the custom office opened, he signed the bill of laden, had everything unloaded and paid a local trucking company to make the delivery for him. All Mark wanted was to get out of Haiti.

CHAPTER ELEVEN

Mark's Decision

A few days after returning home still haunted by the events that took place in Haiti, Mark decided to tell Twila everything that happened there. In an effort to make it easy on the both of them Mark decided to take Twila to the Crimson Flamingo Club and discuss it over dinner. Twila always loved going to the Crimson Flamingo Club. It was one of her favorite places. The club was located high on the mountainside overlooking the city of Port-au-Prince. From its location the city streetlights of Port-au-Prince could be seen gleaming below, like strings of hundreds of little flashlights darting back and forth in crisscross rows.

At the Crimson Flamingo, surrounded by lighted paper lanterns, the dancing lights of flaming torches and the rhythmic musical sound of steel drums, they dined on lobster for Twila and steak for Mark, along with tossed salad, baked potatoes and chilled wine. They danced, embraced and reaffirmed their love. After being at the Crimson Flamingo for a while, Mark decided that their evening was too lovely to spoil with the horrible details of Haiti. Following Mark's decision they continued to dance until late into the night. Their closeness, the romantic atmosphere and a little wine swept their emotions out of control.

When Mark took Twila into his arms for their last dance, he said, "Twila, look we have been in love forever. We have been pleasing everyone except ourselves. I need you Twila and I want you now. Why must we keep on waiting to have each other, when that's not what we really want to do?"

"Mark what are you saying?"

"I am saying that I want you right now, tonight."

"But Mark it's only a little while longer before I'll be your wife. Your family has made so many plans for our wedding. They will be so hurt and disappointed, if we didn't wait. Shouldn't we just wait and not disappoint them?"

"No, because I can't wait anymore," Mark said. "I love you Twila, and I need you to be my mine, right now. We can still go on with the wedding just as planned. No one else ever needs to know. Let's do it tonight. We will go before a Justice of the Peace in Rema and make it legal, but we will do it now. No one will ever need to know and we won't feel guilty, but tonight it will be right in every way. I need you now more than I ever needed you before in my life."

Sensing the urgency of his words Twila reached out and took Mark's hand as she said, "I have never denied you anything and I won't start now. I love you far too much for that. Let's get out of here."

She went back to the table, picked up her purse and thin silk stole. Twila finished her drink, then looking at Mark standing beside her said, "Let's go!"

Mark said, "Oh my darling, you will never regret this night. I swear it." Standing beside their table Mark took Twila in his arms and kissed her from the depths of his soul. Then they headed for the door.

Once inside of Mark's car they embraced and Mark kissed Twila with a fury that she had never felt in him before. After a while, they realized that the night was slipping away, they began driving down the mountain heading for Rema, a small town on the other side of the Island.

The weather was dry, the air was crisp and cooling. Twila pulled the thin stole tighter around her shoulders.

The moon was almost as bright as the noonday sun. Mark's car top was down and his beams were on high, because the mountain road was treacherous. This was something that Mark was well aware of because he had driven that road a number of times. There were deep curves, and in some places there were sheer drops of hundreds of feet, straight down the mountainside.

Due to the lateness of the hour everyone except for the employees had left the club. It had closed while Twila and Mark were still fooling around in the parking lot.

There was no traffic as Mark drove with Twila's head resting on his shoulder. Twila seemed to drift off to sleep. Her perfume filled his nostrils and the warmth of her closeness was comforting to him. As much as he enjoyed fantasizing about possessing Twila within the hour, he had to drive carefully always being

Ophelia M. Turner

mindful to keep his eyes focused upon the winding road.

Midway down the mountain there was a very narrow stretch of road with a sloping downhill section leading into a stiff curve. Mark was really concentrating on what he was doing as he approached the curve. No matter how often Mark has driven that road he never lost respect for its treachery. Halfway through the curve Mark yelled out, "Oh my God."

Twila never stirred.

Right in front of Mark, sitting on the top of a big black car that was parked across the road, was a huge, old, black woman, naked from the waist up, wearing a colorful voodoo mask. Her large arms were folded across her enormous, bare breasts, as she sat grinning at him in raging madness, with the longest and biggest green serpent he ever saw, coiled around her shoulders. The serpent's long, large head shone like polished brass, as it weaved around striking at him. Mark was frightened senseless. Thoughts filled with fear rushed through his mind: fear of the serpent, fear of colliding with the car, and fear of that horrible black woman, causing Mark to swerve his car, sending it careening off the road and smashing into a tree. The impact threw Twila out of the car, killing her instantly. Mark didn't receive a scratch.

Someone must have heard the crash because the police arrived almost immediately. They found Mark almost out of his mind with grief as he cradled Twila in his arms, sobbing uncontrollably, "My Twila, my beautiful, adorable Twila, speak to me. Don't leave me! Please, Oh God, don't let her leave me in a loveless world. I need you. I need you, Twila."

Her lifeless body lay limp and warm in his arms. The police had to fight hard to make him release Twila so they could take her to the hospital. They asked Mark to explain to them what had happened. Between convulsive sobs he told them everything to the best of his ability. After they listened to Mark's strange account of events they didn't believe him and accused him of being drunk or hallucinating, or maybe both.

Mark yelled, "I am not drunk. I only had a glass of wine. I have never been drunk in my life, anyone can tell you that, and I know what I saw."

"Well if you are not drunk, and not hallucinating, then you must be crazy as hell," said one of the officers. "There was no car on this road tonight or we would have passed it coming up. There are no turn offs and you said that it never passed you. So make us know what happened here tonight, because all we have here is a dead woman and an accident that can't be explained. Now you tell us."

Having just lost the one person that he loved more than life itself Mark was out of his mind with grief and his body was numb with disbelief. He began wandering around in circles in a complete state of confusion. A deep fog closed in on him. Every word anyone spoke to him was disturbing, distort and seemed to be coming from some far away place, voices seemed to be slow, sluggish and dragged out. Try as he may, he could not focus, think or speak. He was void of feeling, all he was aware of was that Twila was gone, and nothing else mattered. Not even the fact that he was being taken to jail for manslaughter and drunken driving. All he knew was Twila was placed into an ambulance and taken away from him forever.

For the rest of the night Mark was taken from room to room in the local police station and harassed with the same questions over and over after being tested for blood alcohol. This went on for thirty-six hours. The investigation proved that Mark was not drunk, there was no mechanical failure in the car, and there was no recklessness involved. At a court hearing it was decided that the accident was results of an unavoidable accident that cost Twila her life.

A few days after the accident an investigative reporter went to the strange scene seeking some clue that could possibly unravel the mystery of the strange woman, strange car, and the large serpent. The investigator didn't find anything unusual, except a garden hose rolled up near the tree that Mark had struck. Since in all possibility it could have fallen from a passing farm truck he didn't see any point in even mentioning it.

From the day Twila died Mark stopped eating and sleeping. His mind was anesthetized. Mark became as a sleepwalker, meandering through life. As Twila's next of kin Mira and her grandmother hovered over and around him haunting him through his worst nightmare. Everything in Mark's life became one big blur. He saw Twila's funeral preparation and the funeral service through a haze of fog. Tears and pain filled Mark's entire existence. Everything else seemed to escape him. He was beyond reality. His world was completely empty to the point of nothingness.

CHAPTER TWELVE

The Awakening

Two months later Mark partially aroused from some seemingly long horrible sleep that had been filled with a continuous flood of endless nightmares, awful dreams, and events in which Mira and Mrs. Arrington played major roles in everything that seemed to be a part of his existence. He awoke to find that his life had become a living hell.

Mark learned that over a month ago, just seven days before what was suppose to be his and Twila's wedding day, he had married Mira before a Justice of the Peace. She had told his family that she was pregnant. Mark couldn't recall ever sleeping with her or anything else much less having married her.

Upon learning what had happened Mark was humiliated, devastated, and confounded. He couldn't face himself or anyone else. No one understood or accepted his marriage to Mira, especially so shortly after Twila's death, for which some people still blamed him.

Mark took Mira and moved into seclusion on the

island of St. Croix. He couldn't bear anyone that he knew and loved seeing her grow big with the child she said she was expecting. Every one voiced their disbelief when Mark swore that he never slept with Mira. Mark, who had been so loved, respected and admired, as an upstanding young businessperson became a scorned man.

In St. Croix, Mark and Mira took up residence just beyond the edge of the rain forest. Mark opened a small workshop to support them until he became hired a first class carpenter and latter became a foreman at Robbins and Robbins.

After months, there was no baby. There never had been one, just the two of them. Mira idolized Mark and tried to cling to him like a leech whenever he was around. Otherwise, she always remained at home living in the background and staying to herself, working occasionally like hired help in the store cleaning and putting away stock.

Mark sorted out a separate life away from her during all of his waking hours. Deep inside of him was a constant struggle to get as far away from her as possibly, but like a man stuck in quicksand, with each effort, he seemed to be drawn in deeper. Feeling physically hindered and emotionally negated became a way of life for Mark except on very rare occasions.

At the first sign of Mark's distraction, Mira devoted herself to working obsessively in her herb garden. She cherished her herb garden and its tools, particularly the hose that her grandmother bought her from Haiti. It held special meaning for her, and she guarded it well. She even transported it back and forth with her on her frequent trips to Haiti.

For three long years life for Mark was less than mediocre. He had no friends in St. Croix. Everyone else that mattered to him was in Trinidad, Europe, New York or dead. Otherwise, Mark held most people at a distance. But he often spoke with Lola, an employee at a firm that Robbins and Robbins sometimes did business with. Their paths crossed quite frequently and eventually they became quite friendly. Even with Lola there were some things that he would not share, especially the fact that he was married. This was something that he refused to admit even to himself.

For those years the only pleasure that Mark knew came late in the night and lasted until just before dawn when Twila appeared to him in his dreams. These dreams began in Trinidad right after Twila's death and continued from then on. Even, in the midst of his bewildered dreams, she was more woman than any woman he ever hoped to know. Other than his confused dreams of Twila, nothing really mattered to Mark. He found satisfaction in his craft, his music and comfort in his dreams. For Mark, daylight was like being forced to walk through death's valley in the heat of the day. There was no hope and no joy in it. Therefore, he welcomed the night it bought the answered to his prayer for Twila's return.

About three years into his marriage, Mark's dreams of Twila began to grow further apart. Life was cutting him off without hope when he accidentally met Diana Taylor.

After Twila's death, and his marriage to Mira,

Mark had become like the dead among the living, as he
went about life in a perfunctory manner. He was
handsome, pleasant, polite, considerate, and
industrious, but he exhibited no interest in anything or
anyone except his craft and his music.

Diana was a very stern, beautiful young police
officer who was assigned to patrol downtown
Christainsted. She was a no-nonsense officer who
despised the use of flattery, as a distraction to keep her
from doing her job.

"If it hadn't been for Diana's line of work I may
have never met her," Mark had once mentioned to Lola
over a drink during one of his breaks during a musical
session, while they were indulging in causal reflections.
"I met Diana in the damnedest way you could imagine."

Mark proceeded to tell Lola how he had gone
into Christansted early one Monday morning to pick up
some supplies for the shop. There was no parking space
anywhere near the store where he had to go for the
pickup. The things that he bought were on the heavy
side, and very bulky, so he decided to Double Park for a
few minutes in front of the store. When Mark came out
of the store carrying a portion of his supplies there was
this female police officer putting a ticket on his truck.
As he approached her, she loudly asked, "Is this your
truck?"

Seeing the ticket book in her hand angered him,
and Mark answered promptly, "You are damn right it
is. Do you have to ticket everything that is standing
still?"

"Yes! If it's in the wrong place like this blasted truck," she shouted as she handed him the ticket almost ramming it into his hand. In a loud commanding voice she replied, "Now you get that thing out of here!"

Mark stood and watched her step off in a lively and very sassy way with ultra confidence as she returned to her patrol car. He may have sweltered in his anger for hours had it not been for the fact that when Diana reached her patrol car it had a flat tire. He reared back his head and tried to laugh himself into hysteria.

Diana stood and looked first at the tire, then at him. Her dark eyes narrowed with the contempt that she felt for his disgusting behavior.

The morning sun was climbing high into the clear Caribbean sky. The air was still, the heat had reached an all time high for early morning, and the street was almost deserted except for people that were on missions of personal or business nature with no interest in anything else.

After Diana allowed him his moment to indulge in deep laughter she walked over to him with tongue in cheek and pertly inquired, "Are you going to keep on standing there all day laughing like a park ape or are you going to give me a hand with this tire?"

Mark could barely stop laughing long enough to answer her. But, he saw the slow flame of vexation consuming her features. He decided that teasing her any longer would be a big mistake so he swallowed his laughter, got the jack out of his truck and promptly began changing the flat tire. All the while that he was working; Mark kept glancing up at her. There was no hint of laughter in her lovely, intense, brown eyes, or any trace of it upon her serious pretty face, that was being done a great injustice by the ball of jet black hair resting at the nape of her neck. Her hard brim blue cap resting on her forehead said 'business as unusual'.

After Mark had finished changing the tire he mustered up enough courage to ask, "Does changing this tire square away that ticket?"

"No! No! Not at all," she flatly answered.

Mark decided to cut his loss and go on his way. As he started to get back into his truck he was surprised to hear the very placid voice call out, "Hey you."

He was almost afraid to turn around. Yet, still slightly smiling, Mark looked back at her not knowing what to expect. He was even more surprised to see that she was smiling at him as she said, " But it does get you one free dinner on me."

Mark turned and walked back to her car, quipping, "You don't say?"

"I do say, Mr...???"

"Landers! Mark Launders. And you are?"

"Diana Taylor. As you see I'm a police officer."

"And I am a furniture maker among other things. You are almost as bad as scrooge you know, but I guess that one dinner is better than nothing."

Diana said, "You got that right, especially since your one free dinner is at my house. In the end, you may consider my cooking a new form of corporal punishment. But, you can decide that later tonight."

Then she winked her eye and started up the patrol car. Putting the patrol car in gear and it began to inch forward. Mark called out, "How can I come to dinner when I don't know where you live?"

Diana continued smiling as she put her hand out of the car's window. Dangling between her two fingers was her business card. Mark eagerly grabbed the card. On the front of it was official identification information on the back of it she had written her home address. After looking at the card a broad smile covered his face as he waved her on calling out, "I'll see you tonight."

When Mark arrived at Diana's neat one story bungalow, located in a small community just outside of Christainsted, he open the gate of the white picket fence and walked up the pebble covered walkway leading to the partial glass door. He rang the door chimes while looking around at all of the beautiful flowerbeds lining the walkway. Within seconds, Diana came to the door wearing a white v-neck blouse and fitted white pants. She greeted him with an upturned smiling face. Her long black hair hung loosely over her partially exposed back. Her lovely flesh was like liquid honey glistening under the light that hung above the entrance. She smelled like his grandma's flower garden, all sweet, fresh and pure. Her body, which was so well hidden by her uniform, was one that rivaled any model: slender, solid, curvy in all of the right places and perfectly proportioned. There was no trace of the callous uniformed officer that he had encountered earlier that day ticketing his truck.

"So you made it, I see," she said.

"Did you think that I wouldn't? Did you?"

"Never can tell about law breakers these days," she teased. "Come on in, dinner is almost ready."

"I'm in no hurry," Mark said as Diana escorted

him into the coziest living room that he had ever seen.
High backed wicker chairs stood on each side of a large
picture window. Throw pillows lined the floor in front
of the window. A long floral sofa with a matching chair
was along the wall, and there was a floor model stereo,
tables each with a lamps, vases filled with tropical
flowers tastefully placed around the room, and a
colorful area rug on the floor in front of the sofa.
Everything in that room communicated gentleness and
tranquility.

"I hope that you are hungry. I cooked a lot of
food. I am not accustomed to cooking for men," she
teased. "I hear most of them are big eaters while some
are picky."

"Well you heard almost right. I don't usually eat
a lot, but tonight I am very hungry. I'm certainly not
picky, but I don't eat fish," he said. "I wonder why?"

"Huh! I wonder why, myself?" she gave a slight
giggle as she led him into the living room.

Mark commended her on her home saying,
"You have a lovely place, Diana."

"Thank you. It is a place of comfort after being
in those streets all day."

It turned out that Diana was an excellent cook.
There was plenty of roast beef, baked potatoes, tossed
salad and asparagus, with home made chocolate cake
and fresh perked coffee. Mark had no qualms about
eating his fill.

For the entire occasion Diana had managed to
capture all of the magical essence that was required for

an intimate evening, right down to and including the
flickering candlelight, the pleasing seductive scent of
slow burning incense, soft music, and great
conversation that added the final touch.

Being with Diana was a soul reviving experience.
It was a lovely dream that Mark feared would vanish
with the close of their evening. He couldn't bring
himself to leave, but in fear of wearing out his welcome,
he was forced to call it a night.

Then Mark finally brought himself to the point
of saying, "Good night, I really should go, each of us
have a job to face tomorrow. But, it's been a very long
time since I've enjoyed an evening so much. I really
hate to have it come to an end. But, I don't want to
become an unwelcome guest."

To his surprise he heard Diana say, "I can say
the same. We must do this again real soon. I have had
a wonderful, wonderful time."

Mark heard himself asking, "Why not
tomorrow night then?"

She immediately agreed.

Mark said, "This time the dinner is on me. I
hope that you won't mind if we don't go out. I'll have
caterers bring over everything. Okay?"

That sounds really good," said Diana. "Tell them
to be here at seven o'clock, you come at eight."

"Fine by me."

With an even bolder move Mark kissed Diana
on the cheek and she allowed it to happen.

When Mark arrived at Diana's the next night at
eight, nothing had changed except the menu, which he
had seen to, and her outfit. Diana was dressed in a soft

light blue rayon dress that clung to every curve of her upper body like scotch tape to wrapping paper, hung free below her hips and flowed with each of her steps. Looking at Diana, so sweet, so kind and considerate made Mark remember that once, all of his life hadn't been bland, tasteless, loveless, lonely and hard. There had been some soft sides, there had been some beauty and surely there had been some love. Mark saw in Diana the possibility for him to find that soft side again.

After dinner in the cool of evening they danced to romantic music, sat and talked openly about themselves, then danced and danced again. Each time Mark held Diana in his arms, she provoked an emotion in him that he thought had died with Twila. The miracle of Diana's closeness resurrected the broken bits and pieces of his shattered emotions and slowly weaved them back together. Tenderly, she took each tiny fragment, piece-by-piece, and generated new life into it.

He felt her breath flowing warm and gently against his neck as she moved freely in his arms, giving birth to a new life, setting off little flames one by one until they became a bonfire of passion that ignited his very soul turning it into a searing blaze. When he drew Diana closer he felt no resistance in her. Mark kissed, caressed and fondled her as she fed his increasing desire. With each caress she willingly allowed him to mold her to the passion that she had created in him until he too created in her a wave of fiery emotion. With no desire to restrain their longing, the flame quickly became a raging inferno in which they were completely consumed.

Even though their instantaneous lovemaking was exemplary and far beyond his greatest expectation, Diana was not an easy casual affair. They met in early summer; by midwinter Diana had become everything to Mark except the wife he once dreamt of having. She became the one thing that he really wanted more than anything in the world.

Mark went to Mira saying that he wanted a divorce. He made it known to her how much he loved Diana and that he had no intention of being without her. Instead of facing reality and accepting the inevitable Mira retreated into her darkest mood. She became very secretive and very mysterious, always slinking away when Mark came around. She seemed to live in the garden, even though planting was mostly out of season. Three days passed before Mira packed her bags and went to her grandmother in Haiti.

Since Mira never gave Mark an answer and didn't discuss her plans with him in response to his request for a divorce. Mark had no idea how long Mira intended to be gone and he refused to put his life on hold until she returned. The only thing that Mark was sure of was that he loved Diana and wanted to be with her all of the time, so he moved in with her in order to spend every possible minute with her.

Three weeks later when Mira returned, Mark confronted her again demanding an immediate divorce. He made it clear that he did not intend to return to her. Mira responded with silence as she sat in a living room chair listening to him. She could have been mistaken for store window mannequin if not for the slight movement in her clothing above her chest cavity. It appeared impossible for Mark to get through to her.

Ophelia M. Turner

He became infuriated and left the house in a huff, slamming the door behind him, as he headed for Diana's place.

Two days later, just before the shop's closing, Mark got a telephone call from Mira frantically pleading with him to come home, informing him that she was very ill and had no one to help her except him. Remembering the state that he left her in Mark felt obligated to go and see about her. When he arrived her body was hot with fever. She was tossing and turning while speaking incoherently. He began applying cold towels to her body, gave her an alcohol bath and he drenched her insides by forcing her to drink large glasses of cold water. Her temperature eventually began to fall. Within a few hours she was sleeping peacefully and her body temperature was almost normal.

Mark had no way of reaching Diana since she had already left the station hours ago and her telephone went unanswered. He knew that she would be expecting him to be there when she arrived home. Since he was sure that Mira was getting better, he decided to take a few minutes to see about Diana and to let her know what was happening. Mark had never told Diana about Mira, but tonight he made up his mind that he would. Tonight he would make her know that no matter what, come hell or whatever, he intended to marry her.

When Mark arrived at Diana's the house was dark. He rang the doorbell but she didn't answer. He used the key that she had given him to get in. Once inside stillness surrounded him. Mark flicked the light switch beside the door. There was no indication that Diana was even home. He thought that she should be since it well exceeded her quitting time. Mark moved down the hallway on into the living room putting on the lights as he went. Diana's uniform was laid out on a chair. He went into her bedroom to find the bed turned down and a radio playing so low that it could barely be heard even though he stood beside it. Mark began looking through the rest of the house. He found Diana lying in a pool of blood on the bathroom floor, beside a tub filled with water. There was a large gash in back of her head. She was nude and the blood cushioning her buttock indicated that extreme violence had been done to her lower body. Her thighs were ringed with bruises and bruises covered her battered raw breast.

Mark's terrifying screams brought people from the neighborhood rushing to the door. They found him kneeling beside Diana's mutilated body. His body shuddered with sobs as he tried to shake life back into her. Refusing to believe that she was dead he caressed her cold nakedness as he screamed out her name over and over.

Only when the police arrived was anyone able to pry him out of the room. At the hospital Diana was officially pronounced dead. The medical examiner established her time of death as being around five-thirty that evening while Mark was still at the shop. She had lain there until after nine on that night when mark arrived. The cause of her death was listed as murder during a sexual assault.

The autopsy showed that the rapist had been so

brutal that he had ripped Diana's insides apart. Trying to imagine any male organ huge enough to do such awful damage was impossible, unless he was like a bull or an elephant. Diana's broken neck resulted in instantaneous death. Upon hearing that from the medical examiner, Mark prayed that she died before being subjected to the awful assault that she had undergone.

There was no evidence to be found for a murder that was committed behind locked doors. There was not a fingerprint, a pubic hair and not even a trace of semen or any other clues. The killer or killers were never found. There was a door leading to the little outer room, just off of the kitchen, where Diana kept her garden supplies, it too, was bolted from the inside.

Everyone knew of Diana and Mark's relationship. Diana had no family, just co-workers and very close friends. Despite Mark's loss, he insisted upon making Diana's funeral arrangements.

Mark stood beside the yearning hole that waited silently to receive the remains of his brief happiness. Grief put a chokehold on his heart and Mark bid it to stop beating, but it didn't, and the pain went on. He placed a rose upon Diana's coffin and watched as it took a descending ride to the bottom of the grave and disappeared beneath the clods of falling dirt. He felt his emotions being buried with each thudding sounds of falling earth. Once again his world was shattered for no apparent reason, so once again Mark retreated into nothingness.

For over another year his very soul went into hibernation in a tomb of dead emotion. Mark slipped back into a world of meaningless gestures and learned behavior, letting each day pass as it may, not really caring about anything or anyone. Mark found himself back home and drowning in hopelessness and the heartbreak of his living hell not caring about anything. It was this same attitude toward life and people that landed him in the personnel office of Robbins and Robbins to answer for his irresponsible behavior to the new Personnel Manager, Sandra Lee Hayward Dubois.

CHAPTER THIRTEEN

Stimuli One-on-One

After one year and three months of being promoted to Personnel Manager for Robbins and Robbins, and almost three years of being employed there, Sandra Lee Hayward Dubois had an occasion to encounter another employee named Mark Landers. He began employed there about six months or more before she had as a carpenter, but now he was classified, as a multi craft employees, carpenter, welder and pipe fitter.

Once Robbins and Robbins stopped filling out immigration papers for employees, other than office personnel, field supervisors and other top management, no employees had business in her office unless she sent for them. When she did send for them it was to hire them, fire them, or handle emergency family, personnel or personal problems. Otherwise all other problems were handled by an appointment made by the employee or at her request. Everything else was handled on site by the supervisors or in field offices.

Therefore, Sandra had sent for Mark Landers for being absent from work for more than three weeks without filing the proper notice or submitting a written explanation to her office. Reviewing his personnel file she saw that this behavior was somewhat habitual for him. As she sent for him, Sandra was seriously entertaining the idea of firing Mark. However, she was required to inform him of the possible consequences he faced for such violation of company and union rules.

Upon meeting Mark, who was also a foreman, Sandra was instantly impressed by his neat attire despite the laborious work he was required to do. His carpenter's uniform was crisp, clean and neat. He remained respectful, subdued and was handsome to a fault. However, despite the serious charges he faced, Mark didn't appear to be the least bit perturbed at being summoned to her office. Sandra detested the indifference and lack of interest that he blatantly displayed. It really irritated her.

Once in his presence for some odd reason Sandra's palms began to sweat. Her legs felt wobbly and her throat became dry. Suddenly she realized that she hated the way this man's physical appearance had reached out and grabbed her mind with such a magnetic force and sent her emotions crashing into the Caribbean sun searing her very soul. He caused uncontrollable heat waves to radiate through her being, threatening to incinerate every rule for self control that she had embraced for a lifetime-- that is what was really irritating her. The most disturbing part of it all was that she didn't really know or understand why it was happening.

In order to deal with her emotions, Sandra

Ophelia M. Turner

arose and walked leisurely about the room as she slyly observed this man wondering am I simply irritated by the way this man has sauntered into my office, leaped into the middle of my life and is standing here like he is King Solomon himself, staring down his generous, well-fashioned nose, with those dark brown, smothering eyes. Or is it his broad smile and the unwavering way he stares at me with his smug, 'all-so-knowing' attitude, just looking through me like I am made of glass, with a 'I don't give a damn look on his face?' Whatever it is, he is really irking the hell out of me."

In order to justify her confusion and sudden weakness from being in his presence, Sandra instantly makes up her mind that Mark Landers was a carbon copy of some cheap, no-good New York city con artist that she once heard of; or even a flesh demon from hell which Raymond had always warned her of. Sandra became convinced that Mark had come, like the serpent in Eden to make her the devil's proposal and he was aiming to tempt her into lust and steal her soul. She realized that she had to pray hard and long against him.

Just as if he was reading her thoughts an even more impertinent smile danced on Mark's well-shaped, full lips, turning up the corners of his neatly trimmed, thin-mustached mouth as he conspicuously eyes her.

Highly motivated by the emerging force of her resentment towards him and even more contempt for herself for even entertaining any lustful thoughts of him Sandra was swayed to act on her first thought to discharge him.

Sandra minced no words as she sternly said,

"Well, Mr. Landers, please tell me why I shouldn't fire you or put you on a two-week suspension and thirty days probation for being absence without permission in violation of the union contract?"

His polite response was, "First Miss Dubois, I am deeply sorry for any problem I may have caused you."

Sandra thought of all the gall. She snapped, "Excuse me Mr. Landers but the only problem here is the one you have caused yourself. Unless you have a legitimate excuse for your absenteeism such as sudden death, a paralyzing stroke, or alien abduction, no apology can help you. Since you're standing here before me that's proof that none of these occurred. Do you acknowledge that?"

Willfully intending to further provoke her, Mark smiled condescendingly, saying, "You're right, Ms. Dubois. None of those things happened as you so aptly put it."

Mark exhibited even more of that 'I don't give a damn' attitude that exasperated Sandra very soul, as she exclaimed, "How someone as irresponsible as you are ever became a foreman is well beyond me?"

In a passive voice Mark readily replied, "I didn't say that I disagree with you, Miss Dubois, but I do have my moments, besides, I had to leave suddenly. I didn't have time to contact this office, but I did give my written request for a leave of absence along with the required proof to my supervisor at Hess Oil."

"Well where is it?" she inquired, as she went back to her desk, walked around behind it and thumbed threw the papers on it, saying "I certainly don't see it here."

Attempting to patronize her, he said, "For some reason beyond my understanding it didn't find its way to your office, and I'm truly sorry. If you'll allow me the opportunity to do so I'll investigate the matter. If not," he said as he stretched his arms outward with upturned palms as an act of surrender, smiling, Mark said, "I'll have to take my punishment won't I?"

Upon entering the personnel office of Robbins and Robbins Mark had expected business as usual, which was the cussing out always given by Jason, or anyone else along with threats that were never followed through on and sent back to work.

The pretty face named Sandra Hayward Dubois was unexpected. Her luscious demanding pert lips were complimentary to her hard, blazing, eyes and stern words of confrontation. She completely disarms him, as well as gave him some well-deserved jabs to his faltering ego, but she also jump started his anesthetized heart and made it beat with a rhythm it had almost forgotten. He felt immediately helplessly drawn to Sandra making him practically unable to take another breathe and left him without any desire to defend himself.

Mark tried to avoid accepting his feeling for her, because long ago he realized that love and happiness was not on life's agenda for him. Recognizing the attraction that he had for Sandra, Mark determined that in order to protect her as well as himself from the pain of losing, he must become repulsive to her and stay his distance.

Sandra can't concentrate on a word that Mark

Landers was saying. Whenever his eyes became fixed on hers, they were as flaming erasers, eradicating her every thought. Without reason or explanation, this man had crawled inside of her, captured her senses, completely disorganized her thought process and she was on the defensive.

Sandra didn't dare to speak another word to Mark fearing that her voice would either betray her instant desires, extreme dislike, or even her fear of the man that stood before her.

With a half mind and divided attention Sandra attempted to listen as Mark rambled on about his reason for being absent. Her thoughts kept racing back to the enormous amount of emotional guilt she experienced at the first sight of him.

It required her entire reserve of professionalism to calmly accept what she imagined that he said and stamp his pass with her approval, allowing him to return to Hess. As Sandra handed Mark his stamped pass, his unrelenting eyes continued staring into hers. He took the pass without looking at it, allowing her shaking hand to quickly fall to her side. Trembling, she watched Mark Landers saunter back out of her office.

Once the door closed behind him Sandra collapsed into the swivel chair behind her. A few minutes where required for her to compose herself. Afterward, she rushed to the personnel filing cabinet and pulled out Mark's master folder.

To Sandra, Mark appeared to be six feet tall and about one hundred and seventy five well distributed pounds, pure muscle and certainly a few years older than she was. His deep glazed-brown complexion and athletic appearance made him too damn good-looking to be any good. His entire being had a magnetic force that she had to fight to escape. Her only refuge had depended upon how quickly she could get him away from her.

Opening Mark's file she said, "Here it is. He is thirty-five and single. He is a little over two years older than I am." Then she thinks, so what? Who really cares?

Feeling flustered and foolish because of her behavior, especially for talking to herself, she slid his folder back into the filing cabinet drawer and unsuccessfully tried to erase Mark Landers from her mind. But somewhere deep inside of her he has taken root. Sandra sat down and closed her eyes only to have Mark Landers face float before them. For an instant, he became the fairy tale prince of her childhood. She imagined his lips upon hers as he gave her an awakening kiss. The intense desire to be in his arms forced Sandra to whisper, "Forgive me dear God, for I have greatly sinned."

CHAPTER FOURTEEN

FACE TO FACE

A formal introduction to Mark, for Sandra came a few weeks later on a Wednesday morning. She was sent to work on the job site at WAPA in Port Richmond. WAPA, The 'Water and Power Authority' plant was located on the back road that ran behind Harbor View Apartments.

Robbins and Robbins bid the job to do their major repairs and were awarded the contract. Supplies for the job arrived early that morning at the Port Richmond Docks from Puerto Rico.

The supplies came in at the docks by oversea freight and had to be off loaded before noon the next day. Robbins and Robbins had to get the job done without stripping the worksites at Hess or Martin Marietta of manpower. There wasn't enough unassigned regular employees available to handle a job that large.

In order to unload immediately the unusually large shipment Sandra had to hire a crew of temporary workers. To protect the company on all fronts Sandra had to disregard the 'no immigration papers' rule and hire new skilled workers and their helpers, especially laborers. She had to check out everyone's working papers to make sure they were in order with proof they were either citizens, green card holders whom could go directly to work, or legal aliens who in some cases required filing papers with immigration to obtain working bonds. Every skilled man, such as carpenters and backhoe and crane operators had to be screened and tested for experience, certification and license, union membership, and other credentials pertaining to their crafts as well as tested. Mark Landers was sent down to the work site as one of the foreman to assist Sandra with the screening of the men and to administer tests.

This rush for temporary hiring was not a new occurrence for Sandra. She often came to the Port for such emergency assignments. Sandra had found a good friend at the dock in Lola Fleming, the executive secretary for I.I.T.C. (Island International Transport Company), the shipping company that handles the imports for Robbins and Robbins, and other local companies.

Lola looked forward to having Sandra there and spending time with her, especially for lunch. During working hours, Lola's world, like Sandra's consisted of one hundred percent working males. For Lola, Sandra's coming to work there was always a bright spot in any day.

Lola and Sandra first met when Sandra began work at Robbins and Robbins's. Lola was older than

Sandra. Her warm nurturing nature and easygoing spirit drew Sandra to her. Before long, Lola became somewhat of a mother figure to Sandra and her best friend. Without intent or realization Sandra began sharing little intimate portions of her life with Lola, even some of the intimate facts about her married life. Lola became a good listener and sympathized without getting involved. They grew very fond of each other and shared a closeness unlike any Sandra ever had with any other female.

A former New Yorker, Lola, was a very sophisticated, pretty woman with butterscotch complexion and satiny soft skin, came to the islands twenty-seven years earlier. After graduating from a New York college and becoming his secretary, she married Pierre Fleming, a high profile, white Canadian lawyer with a very lucrative practice. A long line of unpleasant circumstances on the mainland arose out of their racially mixed marriage that influenced their decision to move to the islands.

Lola and her husband built a beautiful home high on a mountainside on the west end, overlooking the Federicksted harbor. There they became the parents of two girls. Pierre established a law office in Federicksted, and for a short while before deciding to become a full time mother, Lola continued to be his secretary and office manger.

Years later, when her husband died, Lola went into seclusion. After her children grew up and left home, she decided to return to the same line of work that had brought her and Pierre together years ago

A little before ten o'clock that morning, Sandra completed the task of checking out the paper work of potential employees. This meant that she had plenty of time to make the trip to the Department of Immigration to obtain bonding papers for some of those men, while Mark took all of those men that were cleared to work and begin administering their tests. Upon completion of their testing he would give each of them their assignments and break them down into crews.

As it stood everyone was looking at an all nighter at the dock and several long days of hard work, which included inventorying, delivering and storing the material at Robbins and Robbins work site inside of WAPA.

Sandra returned from immigration to the port to find Lola and Mark sitting together in the employee's lounge of I.I.T.C. happily involved in deep conversation. When Sandra entered the room Mark's eyes met hers with such intensity that her body shudder. His smile mocked her. Sandra attempted to avoid having any eye contact with Mark but his attraction was too great. Mark's eyes were so penetrating that she had an impulsive urge to flee the room. Emotional bands seized Sandra, binding her very soul, filling her with an uneasy sensation that slithered up and down her spine. Fleeing became her only thought, but her feet refused to move. All she could do was to helplessly stand there.

Slightly smiling as she gazed at Sandra, Lola's curiosity was piqued by the expression on Sandra's face. With a curious glitz in her eyes and a nod of her head in Sandra's direction she asked, "Do you two know each other?"

Fighting for composure, Sandra softly

whispered, "We've talked, somewhat, but we've never really met."

"Well it's time you did," said Lola boisterously. "Especially since you both work for the same company."

As Lola spoke Mark rose to his feet and faced Sandra. Sandra's face smarted at the onset of a slow burn that crept over it, mostly from the embarrassment of her secret guilt and partly because of her private fantasies. Sandra hated herself for even entertaining any thoughts about this man and she hated him even more for fostering them.

Lola's words recaptured Sandra's attention as she said, "Sandra Dubois, this is Mark Landers. Mark Landers, meet my friend Sandra Dubois."

Mark smiled. Sandra nodded. With an extended hand he approached Sandra. They shook hands. Mark's grip was firm with confidence; Sandra's was soft, shaking and limp with anxiety. For Sandra their encounter was brief but highly infectious.

Suddenly realizing it was time for him to return to work Mark cast a nervous glance at his watch. Smiling he said, "It's that time. Ladies it's been a real pleasure. Please excuse me, but I have got to run."

Before Mark reached the door he stopped long enough to say, "I am playing at a dance at Pelican Cove Beach Friday night, why don't you ladies come on down and check out my band?"

Without waiting for an answer, Mark winked his eye, smiled teasingly, turned and immediately left.

A strange silence filled the room and lingered momentarily between the two women, broken only by the fading thuds of Mark's footsteps, as he disappeared down the hardwood hallway. Then, Lola stared at Sandra asking, "Am I missing something here? What in the hell just went on between you two?"

Sandra met her question with silence.

Lola cocked a quizzical eye at Sandra searching her face for some revealing clue to answer her question before asking, "Are you going Friday night?"

"Of course I'm not going," snapped Sandra. Then she rudely asked, "And why do you think that you are missing something between that man and me, or that something is going on between us?"

"I haven't decided on an answer yet. But you two got awful strange there for a minute," said Lola.

"Well I can assure you that there is nothing for you to miss," said Sandra. Then she asked, "Are you going to hear him?"

"That is partly what we were talking about when you came in," said Lola. "Mark was telling me about his interest in music. He also talked about some of the acts that perform with him at some of the places where he entertains. He said most of the time when he performs, there are fire eaters, limbo dancers and glass eaters along with his steel band."

"His steel band! Is he the leader?" asked Sandra. "Is he West Indian?"

"He sure is on all accounts, sweetie," answered Lola, "But you would never know he is West Indian by his looks, his dress, and certainly not his speech. He has no accent even through he was born in Haiti, partly grew up in Trinidad and received some of his education in England. If that isn't enough he even once lived in

New York for a short time."

Sandra's recalled her first impression of Mark as being a New Yorker slickster, she whispered, "I knew it."

"You knew what?" asked Lola.

"Oh, nothing. I was just talking to myself," murmurs Sandra.

"Huh!" said Lola, as her twinkling eyes gazed at Sandra. Indistinctively she softly mumbled, "That's a damn bad habit."

"What else can you tell me about this Mark fellow?" asked Sandra.

"Well, let me see...he is a naturalized citizen, that's why he can travel so extensively. Rather than being called a West Indian he prefers to be called a world citizen. Once, from what I have been told he was always traveling."

"I knew I smelled New York all over him." Sandra added with sarcasm. "Too New Yorkish for me. He looks and acts the part."

"Oh...come on, Sandra," teased Lola. "Give the guy a break. The man is okay. Besides he plays a mean guitar, as well as beating the hell out of a bongo. Let's go to the dance Friday night the outing will do both of us good."

Sandra tossed her head objectionably causing her dark auburn hair to swing loosely from side to side, and said, "I have no intentions of going. After a day's work in that sweat box of confusion called an office the last thing that I need in my ears is the loud pounding of steel drums and bongos."

"Well suit yourself, girl," Lola said. Then converting to the West Indian dialect which she has mastered very well, saying, "As fo' me mi'son, I goin' liming Friday night. I gonna jam'it up, den some." Rising to her feet, Lola began winding her behind around outrageously and festively flinging her hands above her head.

Sandra gasped as she watched Lola wind her way out of the employees lounge.

Hours later, long after Sandra and Lola returned to Lola's office and Lola had settled down and gone back to work, Sandra sit looking at Lola through critical eyes. She had never seen Lola behave so frivolously before. Finally she couldn't resist curtly asking, "What's up with you Lola?"

Surprised by Sandra's unexpected question as well as the tone of her voice, Lola queries, "What do you mean, what's up with me?"

Sandra firmly replied, "I mean what's wrong with you? You are acting sort of wild and loose."

"Wild and loose? What in the hell do you mean?'" asked Lola with a resentful attitude.

"Lola please don't get angry but I only mean kind of sinful like, you know," said Sandra.

"No! No, I don't know. What? What? What are you talking about sinful like?" repeated Lola.

"I mean the way you were talking and the way you were moving yourself, you know, shaking your behind part, that is all acting sinful-like," she said with all sincerity. "In all the time I've known you, you've never before acted like that."

Lola looked at Sandra as if she cannot believe

what she was saying. However Sandra's face portrayed her sincerity.

Lola burst out laughing as she got up slowly and begins walking erratically around the room, and then with an arched eyebrow, she looks at Sandra and asked, "Where have you been all of your life child? Girl do you really know what sin is?"

Sandra groped for words before finally answering, "Yes! Yes! I do."

"Well," said Lola as she began to flail the air randomly with her opened hands before pointing her index finger at her chest repeatedly saying, "Will you explain sin to me, please?"

"There isn't much to explain. It is more like what you do or don't do," answered Sandra.

"Well then, explain to me what I should or shouldn't do," insisted Lola, with her hands placed firmly on her hips.

"Well, for an instance, you are not suppose to shake your behind, especially in public, like you just did," said Sandra, looking down toward the floor.

Flinging her hands upward, laughing uncontrollably, Lola stumbled backward onto her chair. It required a few minutes before she recovered from laughing long enough to ask, "Who in the hell told you that shit?'

"It is true enough. My husband told me that it is a sin. It's in the Bible," said Sandra.

"What Bible has he been reading?" asked Lola

"You know the Bible, the Holy Bible," answered Sandra.

"Well damn, I thought that he had found a new one because it certainly isn't like the one I read because

mine told me to make a joyful noise, sing and dance
before the Lord," said Lola. Then, still giggling, she
asked. "What else did your husband tell you is a sin?"

"Lust and sex! Sex is a sin," said Sandra.

"Sex is a sin," repeated Lola. "Well now tell me
how in the hell did you get two children, Immaculate
Conception?"

With naive sincerity Sandra said, "No, that was
different. We were not having lustful sex. We were
fulfilling God's purpose for mankind by mating."

Furrows of frowns covered Lola's forehead as
she attempted to wrap her mind around Sandra's
words before asking, "What is fulfilling God's purpose
for mankind if it is not sex? The purpose of every man
I know is to have sex. The more the better," said Lola.

Sandra said, "No, that is not God's purpose.
That is man's sinful purpose. God created all males to
mate with females for propagation only and man is the
only animal that disobeys him. That is written in the
book of Genesis. He said be fruitful and multiply, that
means to mate only once in season, then wait."

Now completely baffled, Lola asked, "What
damn season and what in the hell are you waiting for?
As a matter of fact what in the hell are you talking
about?"

"The season is what you are supposed to wait
for. It begins ten days after the issue of life has flowed,"
explains Sandra. "Every woman has an issue. It is her
body's cleansing period. When she is clean her time is
right for her husband to mate with her. Afterwards, he
waits to see if she is with child. If not, after her next

cleansing they mate again. When they succeed and she is with child she will go forth to have their baby without any further mating. They don't have unnecessary lustful sex. When they mate according to God's Word, they are doing God's Will." Sandra proudly informed Lola saying, "To have sex, just to have it, is lustful and a terrible sin."

"What the hell is this you are saying, girl? Somebody has fucked your mind up good and proper. No wonder you damn near piss your pants every time a man like Mark look at you or even come near you. So, which is it, are you afraid of sinning or afraid of really having sex with a man? You are really all fucked up, child," said Lola.

Almost crying Sandra asked, "Why are you talking to me this way? I thought we were friends. I've told you all about myself and, now including this, all I believe in. I've told you things I never told anyone else, including why I came here. Now you are talking to me like this. Why, please tell me why?"

"I'm doing it because I am your goddamn friend, Sandra. That's why. I love you girl, I wouldn't be your friend if I didn't tell you the truth. I had no idea that somebody has mind fucked you child, you are damn near nuts. They mind fucked you up really good. No man can come near you, girl much less think about fucking you. You've been brainwashed with a lot of down right shit. My God, that kind of shit just isn't normal," declared Lola, as she rushed over to close her office door. Then she went and sat down behind her desk opposite Sandra.

Sandra was crying uncontrollably. Folding her arms on the desk in front of her she put her head down on her folded arms and wept bitterly.

Looking at Sandra's body shake uncontrollably with each sob, a sorrowful Lola said apologetically, as she reached over and took her hands. Holding them tenderly she said, "You know, Sandra at first this whole conversation seemed like some sort of stupid, joking sort of thing. But now, I don't see anything funny about it. You are for real. There is nothing at all funny about this shit."

Sandra stood up to leave but Lola stopped her by reaching over and taking her by the arm as she said, "Instead of going out Friday night I want to come over to your place and explain a few things to you that you really need to know. You are damn right pitiful."

Sandra resisted Lola as she continued to weep. Lola quickly walked around the desk and went over to Sandra, putting her arms around Sandra and drew her close saying, "Sandra you are a very beautiful young woman and an extremely caring person. There is no need to live your life under the influence of a lot of misinformation served up in God's name. God never meant to enslave nobody's body or mind. There is a right and wrong way for everything. What you have been led to believe about sex is all wrong, believe me. Please let me come over and talk to you. I love you and I hate seeing you hurting like this."

Sandra sat back down still crying and shaking. Deep down inside she wanted to know what Lola had to say, but the wall that Raymond had built in her mind began to rise up between them.

Then Lola said sympathetically, "So that is what

I saw whenever Mark came near you. I mistakenly thought you and Mark was having secrets, when in truth your inhibitions were flaring up, but oh boy was I wrong. You alone have got the secret."

The mere mention of Mark's name by Lola began to lower those walls of Sandra's objections and curiosity became strong enough for her to step over them and consider Lola's offer. Sandra wanted to know why Mark affected her on so many emotional fronts. Those feelings that he arouse in her were so like those that almost surfaced when she first met and married Raymond, before he surrendered her body to God's Will. They were feelings that became smothered by fear and shrouded in righteousness, perfection and brutal possession. They were now buried under a hoard of Biblical threats that had frightened her into numbness. She heard herself saying, "Alright Lola, come on over on Friday."

CHAPTER FIFTEEN

Delivering Sandra

Around seven o'clock Friday evening Lola arrived at Sandra's apartment. Sandra appeared awkward and nervous with a certain amount of resentment evident in her behavior when she invited Lola into her apartment. Consequently, Sandra was aloof and cool. Her reception obviously lacked the warmth that they always shared.

After the strained greeting Lola attempted to loosen Sandra up by complimenting her on the appearance of her apartment, saying, "You have such a neat and lovely place. I love it. For so long I have known you, but this is my first time for coming here. Your apartment is really beautiful and so modern. Your choice of furniture is great. I really love it, especially your white carpeting, it adds such a tranquil effect."

"Thank you, I'm glad you do," said Sandra, "This is my first time for having a really personal friend here, if that's what we still are. I live alone and I have to be careful about people. You think that you know them only to learn that they are much different than you first thought."

Ignoring Sandra's sarcasm, Lola said, "You have never had any other friends here at all?"

"No!" Sandra said. "Not friends just people I do business with like you. I see all of my so-called friends at the club or the beach, someplace that is not too personal."

"I'll be damned," said Lola. Pretending density she asked, "What about boyfriend?"

Sandra said abruptly in an irritated voice, "You know that I don't have any."

"None? Not even one?"

"None! You know that. Why are you continuing to ask?" She said angrily.

"Just wants to make sure," said Lola. "So why not?"

"I've had a husband and two sons. I've done God's Will. So what do I need a man for now?" asked Sandra.

"Oh! Now I suppose that your life is over," said Lola mockingly. "Is a has-been husband all that you want or need for yourself?"

"Oh no, I've found work to do," said Sandra firmly. "Besides, I've become an excellent friend with solitude."

"Work! Work! Child, there is more to life than just work, haven't you heard, Sunday is a day of rest. Sometimes even a maggot gets tired of working all the damn time and falls the hell off his shit. And there is certainly so much more to be friendly with than

solitude. Damn! Everybody needs somebody at one
time or another. Even God boast of having rocks to
sing his praises if men don't, meaning that even he
don't intend to be lonely. Once in a while you need a
man, child, if to do nothing more than just to hold you,"
said Lola.

Sandra asked, "How can you say that after what
I told you on Wednesday? I have no intentions of
sinning, not even in my mind, much less in my body."

"I can say this because of what you told me on
Wednesday. The only sin here is to let your life become
wasted, when you have so much to offer," Lola told
Sandra.

Sandra turned her back on Lola and moved
nervously around the large living room. Lola walked
over to the sofa and took a seat. She looked at Sandra
as she went and stood facing the huge sliding glass door
over looking the lawn. She was so small, so restless and
completely trapped by her emotions.

In a placid voice Lola said, "Sandra baby, it is
no sin to want and have a man or to be loved. You
haven't lived yet little girl, until a man fucks your ass
senseless. You haven't lived until you want a man
inside of your stuff so bad that you can taste him in
your mouth. But you would not know anything about
that. In reality, you have never really been fucked yet,
have you? According to what you've told me, you
certainly haven't been loved. You are a misused virgin
and I bet by now, how long have it been, let me see,
your oldest son was born just after two years of
marriage, then your second son came almost four years

later and he never touched you again. Then after being married for ten years he left you. During that time he only tapped it just long enough to make two babies and that stuff haven't even been hit on since the beginning of your last pregnancy. I'll bet by now, you're so tight that it hurts you just to piss."

Filled with embarrassment Sandra placed her hands over her ears and cried out, "Lola I never dreamt that you talked like this."

"Talk like this! Talking like this," said Lola. "I don't just talk like this, Sandra, I do like this."

Lola got up and went over to Sandra and placed her hands on Sandra's shoulders and pulled her around to face her as she said in a low, firm voice, "When I need a good fuck I go out and get one. My husband is dead, but my behind isn't. It is very much alive, and it still needs a good hard ramming every once and awhile. When I get that kind of urge churning around inside me only a king size prick with lots of stamina can fix it."

Sandra hung her head shaking it vigorously from side to side she and said, "I can't even think like that. I certainly can't feel that way. It's too worldly and it's too shameful; besides men's parts are more like terrible weapons. They are painful and debilitating."

"I guess so when you been mated like you was a beast, by a beast, you are allowed to say that. But child, don't knock what you don't know anything about. Sandra please don't keep a closed mind, certainly since you have never tried it.

"Tell me Sandra have you ever thought of trying a good and proper fuck with a loving man? Have you ever dreamt of having a man finger fuck you until inside your hole turns to whip cream? Have you ever

Ophelia M. Turner

imagined a man gliding into you like a warm knife through soft butter, so smooth and so soothing? That shit can happen you know, when you are in love."

Sandra was fidgeting around like the carpet beneath her feet was on fire. She looked in every direction except at Lola who held her firmly as she asked, " When was the last time a man 'passion-kissed' you? You know, stick his tongue half way down your throat and tickle your tonsils. Have you even let a man kiss you, period? When was the last time a man sucked your tits until you wet your pants?"

Now beyond being thoroughly embarrassed, Sandra indignantly replied, "I haven't been kissed since my husband, then that was on my cheek. No one ever touched my breasts except my children when I nursed them. That's what a woman's breasts are meant for."

"A peck on the cheek over three years ago, damn," said Lola as she released Sandra and walked back, sloping down on the couch, leaving Sandra to stand and stare back out the plate glass door.

"Shit," said Lola. If I don't have me a man all up in me for three weeks I would lose my fucking mind. There is something about fucking that makes life so damn sweet, child. You can fly without wings. Try it."

"How can I try it when I just can't accept that way of thinking," said Sandra. "The kind of mating that you are talking about is something that I have never heard of. It's far too sinful to even discuss. Maybe you had better just leave, now," she said without looking back.

"Leave? Leave? Does the truth hurt you that

much, or are you just afraid of the truth?" Lola asked.

She walked over and stood beside Sandra and calmly said, "Sandra I am not going any place, that is too damn easy. Look, I have seen your behavior around Mark, the way that he makes you feel scares the hell out of you. It shows all over you. Why not be honest and tell me the truth or at least to yourself. You have been thinking something or feeling something, or maybe even dreaming of that man, haven't you? You may or may not have heard of good sex, but you damn sure do want to have it or at the least know what it is all about. Whatever happens to you when you are around him is saying just that. What in the hell do you really think it is that's happening? Be real, Sandra and face facts" said Lola. "And for God's sake don't tell me nothing. I'm not blind."

"Nothing! Nothing!" Protested Sandra as she moved away from Lola.

Lola grabbed Sandra and dragged her over to the sofa and pulled her down on it and declared. "Look Sandra, we really need to do this. But we can't do it if you don't tell me the truth. You said that you thought that I was your friend. I am your goddamn friend, the best one that you will ever have, so just tell me the damn truth. What happens to you when you are around Mark Landers?"

Sandra hung her head and tearful whispered, "I just feel so funny."

"Funny how?" asked Lola.

"Just really funny. Like I don't understand kind of funny. I get warm, shaky, hot sensations racing throughout my body and I get all nervous and jittery inside. I get scared. I just feel funny," moaned Sandra.

"That's not funny, honey. That is your body
sending you a message. It's talking to you telling you
that you want that man to fuck you. You feel him
tingling between your thighs, don't you? It's nature's
way of telling you that you want Mark. Sandra I know
that you don't want to admit that, you certainly don't
want to hear it and you probably can't even accept it.
But, you've got to let up and stop punishing yourself.
Give yourself a break. Let your body and mind work
together and instruct you in what to do with your life.
You've spent years listening to your crazy ass husband.
Now hear yourself, especially when your body is
talking. Let loose and get loved," beseeched Lola.

"Don't you think that sometimes I have wished
that I could, but I know that I am just reacting to the
lust of my flesh. Raymond warned me about the sin of
flesh a long time ago and I can't give in," said Sandra.

Lola looked into Sandra's childish eyes and said,
"Flesh is all we have, do you see anything else? The
spiritual things come from the inside and how can they
be good if everything that you are feeling is so damn
bad? Life is not like that and neither is God. Get real,
girl. Give life a chance and you may find some real
pleasure floating around in it."

"I don't know how," cried Sandra. "I'm afraid
to try because I just don't know how."

"Look Sandra, that screwed up, misguided
husband of yours has only introduced you to a man's
penis in the worst damn way possible, but he never
really loved you. He propped your ass up on the edge of
a bed and bored into you like a jackhammer drilling

into concrete causing you undue pain, traumatizing
your body and mind. He was probably only good for
forty seconds once a month and he laid his
shortcomings at God's feet. His viciousness left you
fucked over, abused and as ignorant as hell.

"For years, Raymond kept you on a moral leash
by putting all of these crazy inhibitions in your head.
He never prepared your body for sex or let you feel any
enjoyment. He made no attempt to tenderly nurture
you into satisfaction. That was not real sex that was
hell.

"You need a man with a free mind and no
agenda except making you happy by making tender
love to you the way that you were really meant to be
loved. I'm not saying that it will be easy for you to
move on with your life. You were so mentally and
physically abused and emotional barbed wire fences
were put in your mind, tearing them down is going to
hurt just like hell. "Besides, it won't be physically easy
the first time you really try to let a man love you. By
now you are a recycled virgin. The fact that you've
been traumatized makes it worse."

Sandra sat with her hands clasped over her
mouth as she rocked back and forth shedding silent
tears that flowed from her closed eyes. Each of Lola's
words became a bullwhip, intent on lashing her
distorted ideology to shreds.

Lola went on saying in her own nurturing way
what she felt needed to be said, "Sandra, a loving man
will help you through this mess, not hurt you. But with
your experience, shit, at the first hint of pain you'll
probably freak out. But oh my God, Sandra please
don't, I beg you Sandra, please don't. If you just trust a

little, yield a little and endure a little it will get better with each new touch. After a while it will become so damn good you will always want more. Real good sex is like that."

Sandra sat listening, trying to open up her mind to understanding, as Lola went on, "Mark is a nice guy. I've known him a long time. Even though he tries to hide it, I believe that he likes you and that is so unlike him. He is not known for fooling around. If you have feelings for him give him a chance. Who knows, maybe he will be just the one to change your life or you his."

The past rose up and disgust filled Sandra's voice as she said, "Lola, I had my first chance with Raymond and I prayed to God to let it be my last. When my husband told me that if I got with child he would stop mating with me, long after he withdrew himself from me and left, I lay for hours with my knees raised against my chest and my legs clamped tight holding his seeds inside me, sucking up my breath hoping to make a difference, begging God for a baby. But God didn't listen he let Raymond keep on coming back measuring out misery thirty-nine blows at a time. When Raymond said that we didn't need more children, I thanked God for the blessing of not having to do his or God's Will anymore. Why should I even want that fate again?"

Sympathetically, Lola listened as she stared at Sandra's pitiful face before saying, "Sex is not a fate, Sandra. It's a choice that is meant to enhance relationships, not destroy them. Raymond was more animal than any sinner man that I know. He took your innocence, ignorance, your virginity and he molded you to his fanatic will. Then he sacrificed your body and mind to some unrealistic cruel God. I will swear that he got more than his nuts off with what he was doing to you. I will almost swear that you weren't the only one, or the first one, or even the last one that he has pulled that God's Will shit on.

"No man in his right mind will lie beside or be anywhere near a willing, young virgin that is pure candy, night after night unless he is plowing in or sucking on some other kind of forbidden ground. That is probably why he never really looked back when he left you. He was more likely ministering to his flock of rams."

Sandra shrieked, as she cried out, "How can you say that Lola? You don't know Raymond." Tears flowed even faster down her face.

"No, I don't know Raymond," said Lola, "But I do know sanctimonious mother-fucking sadists like him. He'd fuck a coke bottle lying on its side, 'cause he likes tight holes that much. Then, if he gets caught at it, he'd pretend that he stumbled and fell into it"

Looking Sandra directly in the eyes, Lola said, "What I'm saying is that he targeted you from the beginning to be his front, because he knew that you would accept any damn thing that he told you. He knew that you would. He also knew that if his ass got nailed, you'd go to hell defending him as a good and faithful husband. He was as queer as hell, Sandra. But whatever happened, he wasn't going to shit in his own nest. You were his prefect cover, you were obedient, innocent, beautiful, sweet and believable, he trained you well. He trained you really damn good. That God's

Ophelia M. Turner

Will business was to keep you off his ass."

Sandra cries, "Lola, you are wrong! You are wrong!"

With palms facing outward, Sandra began waving her raised hands from side to side in front of her face in a protesting manner says between her sobs, "There was nothing morally wrong with Raymond except he was just human. He proved to me that he was right in doing God's Will. He read it to me in the Bible and acted accordingly. He took care of me. He didn't beat me, or anything like that, just because he kept God's Word about mating. God never said that mating was painless. In fact a woman is cursed with pain. So you shouldn't talk like that about him. Lola you shouldn't, you just shouldn't."

"See! See! Just as I said, you are defending him. You will go on defending him." Lola stood up, displaying her annoyance at Sandra's persistence, saying, "All Raymond proved to you was that he was not a man. He was too gutless to admit his sexuality. He wanted it all. He wanted the respect, the prestige and the financial security of his chosen profession. In the church of his choice, where he and others like him preached love and tolerance, 'saying come as you are' there was no place for him, so he used you. When the fabric of society was woven no strand was included to represent him, so his guilt and God forced him to use you. He had to prove his penis power to a segment of the world that only had contempt for people like him and he needed a fine, young, tight-little thing like you to do it.

"As a friend you were perfect. You were congenial, submissive and very willing. You two were friendly, not friends, but you called it love. In bed, Raymond was a real woman hater. He hated you as a woman, because God ordered him to have a woman in order to prove his manhood and satisfy God's Will. He was angry with God because he did not believed that God did not sanction his freedom of choice for a sex partner and he hated himself for being too weak to openly make his own choice. That is why he hid behind God's Will to punish you for being there and for being God's choice for him. God demanded that only through a woman could Raymond prove his penis power by fathering a child. Your mind and body were fertile grounds and he exploited your body and mind mercilessly, while stamping out your natural feelings and destroying your emotions because you weren't a man."

Sandra flinched and retched, as she attempted to close her eyes, ears and mind against a truth that for years she had rejected. In an instant she relived the scene that confronted her when she dared to go into Raymond's bedroom. She had buried that day deep in her mind and had never dared to revisit it again. In a moment Lola had yanked away the cover and made her face the unspeakable. For the first time since that morning, Raymond and the young elder appeared clearly before her face. Before this time, she had never allowed herself to really see them. Suddenly she was forced to accept the truth, which was something until then she had refused to know or believe. It was easier to blame herself, rather than seeing Raymond for what he really was.

Sandra bended over, wrapped her arms about her waist and began screaming out in agony. She struggled to push the truth back into that dark secret corner of her mind where she had buried it for so long, but it had become to tremendous and awful to remain there. She was being purged. She began slobbering and almost foaming at the mouth. She cried out as the pains of truth ripped through her. Sandra made a finial attempted to hold onto the scales that had covered her mind's eye so completely by yelling out to Lola, "No! No! Lola you are wrong. You are so wrong, Lola. It's not true. Raymond was only doing God's Will. He took his instruction straight out of the Bible. We were going to have more children. He said as much. Raymond is not like that. Lola please tell me that you believe that."

"No! No! No! Neither do you. If you had lived with Raymond a thousand years there would have been no more babies," said Lola. "No matter what the hell he said. His manhood was established, and he didn't need you anymore except for show.

"Raymond didn't learn that shit by his self. His father taught him and his mother condoned it. She too had been in your shoe that is why Raymond is an only child, and why the propagation gown was almost new. She may have gotten lucky and was fertilized the first go around. Besides, unlike Raymond's prick, his father's may have been a wiener, who in the hell knows? His father got him and then he quit. Maybe he hit Raymond's mother stuff once, and while stuffing her ass with Raymond, he probably rammed all of the feeling out of her ass at the same time. His mother's pain was short lived, and she forgave and forgot. That's why they appeared so happy to you. But you, you were ruined. You were mutilated for a solid year as Raymond went for a second child to prove his manhood beyond that of his father's by out doing him."

Still attempting to evade the truth, Sandra cried, "Oh, my God, Lola how can you say that?" But the severity of Lola's words left her no place to run and hide. Her mind floundered in shock. She wanted to cry out, Lola you are right, but pride would not allow her to, but she accepted the truth in the privacy of her mind. Sandra endured her pain, knowing that in doing so meant the end to what her life was suppose to have meant with Raymond, so she went on crying.

"Look," Lola said, "I've been around and I've seen the Raymonds of this world. They are selfish self-serving bastards that hide the truth from themselves and the rest of the world. They are much too cowardly to stand up for their beliefs. Instead, they prey on other people's weakness and shatter their lives as well. I am saying just be whatever in the hell that you are. That's your right and your life, and you don't need anyone's approval except your own. This world is large enough for everybody that's in it, and there are enough ways in it for all of us to have our own. Why screw up other people's lives?

"That's why I screw whomever I want to, when I want and I don't give a damn what other people think about it. Even if I wanted to make love to a woman I'd do that too. But it just so happens that I love a long stiff prick, the longer and bigger with durability the better. If a man wants to piss me off, by going on and finishing, leaving me hanging and unfinished that kind of selfishness is damn near as bad as Raymond's shit."

Missing Lola's smattering of humor, Sandra
cried herself sick before she allowed herself to really
hear Lola. Afterward, more over Sandra's hearing was
no longer impaired by a multitude of lies and her mind
longed for the fresh warm milk of truth with a deep
desire to accept the fullness thereof.

Hours later, Sandra sat with blank eyes and
emotionally drained as she stared at Lola wondering if
she realized that she had been forced her to accept the
truth. She when she realized that she could no longer
live in denial did the pain begin to lose its edge. Sandra
felt the knots in her nerves as they unwind and her
mind began to unfold. As it opened up to all the truths
that she had closed up inside for so long, she took a deep
breath and looked pathetically at Lola and asked, "How
long have you been like this, Lola?"

"Like what?" asked Lola?

"So loose. So free, so wild," said Sandra.

Lola answered, "I'm not wild. I'm just not
stupid. I learned everything I need to know from the
beginning. When I first learned a boy had a prick and I
had a hole, I wanted to know why. When I was
fourteen I made a boy bust my cherry in the school's
bathroom and I've been fucking every since. I learned
how not to get pregnant until it served a purpose.
When I got married it served a purpose."

"My mother never told me anything," said
Sandra. " Not anything, she just said I had womanhood
in me."

"Yeah! I believe that she never told you anything," said Lola, "Your mother created in you the prefect setup for Raymond. She kept you as dumb as hell and your every word made you a target."

Lola and Sandra talked late into the night. Lola compelled Sandra to examine all of her many feelings, thoughts and desires. So many closed doors in Sandra's mind were breached before they finished. She tried to fathom everything that Lola had said, but it was all too new, confusing and hard, especially accepting the truth about Raymond. All Sandra knew was that Mark kept walking around in her mind, keeping her thoughts turned upside down. She had warm thoughts of him and she feared him. Still, she wondered about the effect that he had on her and what it would do to her life.

CHAPTER SIXTEEN

TRIAL BY FIRE

Several weeks passed since Port Richmond and Sandra's lengthy talk with Lola. Lola's words, along with thoughts of Mark, still haunted Sandra. Nightly she drew Mark into her dreams where he stood over her with that arrogant smile on his face as she trembled before him. Often she woke up in a panic and cried.

It was a Sunday and Sandra was restless, totally bored with her apartment, she donned her bathing suit, grabbed a beach towel and in haste she fled her apartment. She jumped into her convertible, let down its black canvas top and headed for Pelican Cove Beach.

Sandra parked her car near the beach, but away from the beach club section. That end of the beach was usually unoccupied, that Sunday was no exception. Sandra got out of her car, grabbed her beach towel off the seat beside her, pulled off her sandals, tossed them into the back seat of her car and walked barefoot towards the sea.

Her skimpy, floral bikini provided the prefect exposure to the cooling sea spray and hot tropical sun. The soft breeze filled with mist from the sea caressed and soothed her hot skin.

The combination of sun, sea and moistened warm wind was so calming that Sandra decided to sit on the long reef extending out into the water and enjoy the moment.

There she spread her beach towel on the reef, laid back in the sun and watched fluffy white clouds form pictures as they drifted lazily across the light blue sky.

The sea was a transparent azure blue and calm, but the air was alive with the sound of surf, squabbling sea gulls and rustling palm leaves. All of these sounds swirled about her in various irregular volumes.

She watched a land crab scamper for cover beneath a moss covered rock. From time to time, a fish leaped up out of the water to capture a floating tidbit. Placid waves wash upon the beach making a tranquilizing swishing sound as it drenched the base of the reef of surging sea water. The peaceful surrounding fitted her free flowing thoughts. She felt very content and uninhibited. Sandra smiled.

"What a marvelous life," she whispered.

Slowly Sandra closed her eyes and allowed her mind to freely soar. Without warning, the sea stealthily lulled her to sleep. Later she was awakened by a brand new sound creeping into her environment.

From somewhere in the distance, the sound of sweet island music fell gently upon her ears. The light pianissimo sound of the music penetrated her mind, ejecting all other thoughts.

Slowly rising up, satisfying herself that she was
not dreaming, Sandra whispered, "That sounds almost
like a Marimba. I wonder where it is coming from."
The magic of the music washed all traces of
listlessness away from her body, soul and mind. Sandra
immediately forsook her intention of relaxing on the
reef. As if in a trance, she began walking in the
direction of the music. Sandra dismissed the stinging
pain as her bare feet tread upon the white, hot, sandy
beach. The overgrowth enclosing the beach club
property began to thicken as she neared the edge of the
palm tree grove. The palm trees and undergrowth
wove a curtain of seclusion around the club's beach.
Sandra had to carefully fight her way through the vine-
covered underbrush in search of the tinkling
instruments playing the melody that beckoned her.
After a short walk through the bush, Sandra
stood at the edge of an open courtyard filled with people
clad in bathing suits, shorts, evening attire or island
garb. They sat around tables, sprawled out on lounging
chairs, or were seated in the sand sipping drinks and
engaged in deep intimate conversation. Some people
were immersed in the sound of the music performed by
a five-piece band on the outdoor stage.
The entire engaging scene was as enchanting as
the music that had lured her there. Walking slowly,
Sandra gradually made her way to the outside bar.
There she ordered a rum punch. With drink in hand,
she went over and took a seat at a table near the band.
Sitting there in the high backed cane chair,
Sandra listened intensely to the band's rhymmic sounds

as they rose and fell with the gentleness of the breeze around her. The tranquilizing sound took her mind on an appeasing surf ride upon an invisible wave of rhythm. Her spirit glided gaily upon the flowing billows of perfect harmony.

Sandra closed her eyes enabling her to enjoy the uninterrupted experience of becoming completely absorbed in the musical excursion. Having fallen so deeply into the pleasurable mood, Sandra failed to notice the tall, handsome man staring at her from the stage.

Then suddenly as if on command, Sandra's eyes flew wide open only to find they are locked into those of the man smiling at her from behind his sparkling guitar. It was Mark Landers.

Becoming aware that she had finally noticed him, Mark flashed an even broader smile. Sandra nodded her head in his direction and raised her glass in recognition. The music and the booze had made her mellow to a point beyond precautious.

Having seen Mark's smile, Sandra wondered aloud, "How long has that been going on?" Then she muttered. "If this is his band, it's not the least bit primitive. The music is absolutely outstanding."

The delightful flow of music, the sips of rum punch and the fabulous influence of the tropical setting created an air of serenity that was absolutely captivating.

The blissful scene was so alluring that an hour passed before she noticed it. The band played continuously through the hour before finally taking a break. Sandra watched Mark as he leaped off of the stage and leisurely walked towards where she sat lying back against her chair.

As he approached Sandra he called out, "Hi there!"

Sandra tried to conceal the feathery feeling in her head, caused by sipping down several rum punches and the pounding of her heart caused by his nearness. She somehow managed a crisp, "Hi there yourself. Refreshment time I suppose."

Extending his hand in greeting, Mark quipped, "You supposed exactly right. It certainly is about time. I am glad you finally decided to check out my band."

As a greeting, she placed her hand in his. At Mark's touch, warm waves vibrated though her body. Somehow Sandra managed to give him a brief handshake. A nervous smile danced around her lips, as she mouthed, "Yeah! Finally!"

The guilt of knowing none of this was intentional was tugging at her conscience, when she heard him asked, "Can I get you anything from the bar?"

Smiling she answered with a low drawn out, "No...! I am just fine, but help yourself."

Leaning over, Mark reached over her shoulder and placed his hand on the back of her chair. For Sandra, time momentarily froze. His dark brown eyes gazed into her staring wide eyes, suddenly transporting her to someplace serene and beautiful.

After a fraction of a second, as if from somewhere beyond a swirling mist, Sandra heard Mark almost pleadingly asking, "May I join you when I get back?"

Then, as if an after thought, he timidly asked,

"You aren't expecting anyone or anything?"

He paused uneasily as he awaited her answer.

"Yes, you may join me, and no, I am not expecting anyone or anything," she cheerfully replied.

His eyes twinkled with joy when he assured her, "In that case, I'll be right back." He called back over his shoulder asking once again, "Are you certain I can't get you anything?"

"Yes! Very certain," she called back, slyly feasting her hungry eyes on Mark's departing body. She was fully aware that he had disturbed an illicit consciousness in her.

Sandra lazily leaned back and took a long, slow sip from the tall glass of rum punch as she stared at Mark. The lingering fragrance of his sensuous masculine aroma hypnotized her. Sandra was once again brought face to face with the exciting feeling that he aroused in her at another place and time. Seeing Mark now caused this feeling to stir even deeper within her, forcing her to give it a proper name "lust and desire."

Sandra allowed her eyes to trace every inch of Mark's fabulous body from his neatly trimmed hairline across the back of his sun browned neck to the snug fitting beige nylon shirt that cuddled his broad athletic torso, as the highly visible muscles of his shoulders flexed through it. She observed how Mark's narrow waist tapers off perfectly, accenting his full, firm shapely buttocks that slightly rotated with each step. Mark's head was erect, his body was flawless and his legs were long, strong and perfect.

As if she was unable to control her thoughts, Suddenly Sandra sat up straight and in an emotional outburst, she heard herself say, "What the hell, he is such a gorgeous sight."

Humiliate by her behavior, consequently, Sandra looked around to see if anyone heard or noticed her action. Assured that no one had, she eased back against the chair chastising herself, saying, "Now girl you better watch out, you are getting like Lola, lustful, sinful, and horny. You are none of those; besides, you really don't want to get involved with any of these local men. You have been warned already that to stateside women they are bad news. They can get in and out of your stuff with the quickness. So you just watch it. Whatever happened to your teaching?"

To counter act the self-warning that had ran through her mind, Sandra instantaneously recalled every word that Lola had said to her.

For the first time Sandra accepted the truth of all she had fought so hard to deny. Mark excited her tremendously. The thought of being possessed by Mark caused her throbbing body to draw her into a world of what could be.

With her eyes closed, reclined in her chair, Sandra became lost in day dreams filled with heated thoughts. She did not see Mark as he approached and leaned over her. She only realized his presence when she inhaled the masculine aroma of his body and heard him softly said, "You make a pleasing portrait. You seem like you haven't a care in the world."

"I haven't, that is none to speak of. How about you?" she quizzed.

"None that can bother me right now, anyway.

Are you glad you came out?" asked Mark.

Glancing at him through curious eyes Sandra replied, "Very glad."

She watched Mark as he moved his chair close beside hers.

"Well, how did you like my band?" he inquired.

"It's really great. I really like it," approval seeped into her every word. "I had no idea that you or your band played so well."

"I'm glad you like us. We try hard to please the tourists with our special brand of music. It really is very different from what they are accustomed to hearing from most steel bands. Just to let the tourists know how versatile we are, we play jazz, rock, polkas, waltzes and sometimes classics."

"That is a unique twist-a-bout, rock, polka, waltzes and classics on steel drums of an island band," said Sandra. Then they both laughed.

Mark was such delightful company that it seemed that only moments passed before he had to return to the stage. In reality, it had been forty-five minutes since Mark first sat down beside her.

Intermissions, Mark, the music, rum punch and the intimate setting sent time quickly leaping off into eternity. Before Sandra realized it, the evening was spent and the night was almost gone. For the last time, the band stopped playing. People were leaving in small groups.

Sandra sat there with half closed eyes trying to prolong the night filled with lovely intervals and secret dreams of ecstasy. She tried to harvest every last minute of the night's mesmerizing events. Mark's voice penetrated her steamy thoughts saying,

Ophelia M. Turner

"It seems like you are tired. Can I see you home?" he asked.

"No, I am not tired. Quite to the contrary, I feel so marvelous, so fantastic, that I could just stay here all night," she sighed.

Laughingly, he playfully reminded her by replying, "But you can't." Then he repeated, "Can I take you home?"

"I have my car," she said.

"Where is it, out front or in the side parking lot?" he asked.

"Neither," she answer. "It's parked somewhere further down the beach, behind the palm tree groove."

"Well...I see," concern etched Mark's voice. "I hope that you locked it."

"No, I didn't. I didn't intend to come this far and I certainly didn't intend to stay this long," she said.

Mark laughed, saying, "I just hope that by now you still have a car. Anyway there is no way that I will let you walk back there alone this time of night. I'll give you a lift. Come on. Let's go."

Guitar in hand, Mark walked through the club towards the parking lot; Sandra strolled behind him. Mark went to his small yellow Volvo and opens the door. Sandra was glad to get inside of Mark's cozy little car. The night air was chilly and her floral bikini barely covering her body offered very little warmth or protection against it. "I wish you weren't driving,' Mark said, "Then I could take you home instead of just a few yards down the beach."

Sandra whispered an assurance, "There will be

other times."

"Is that a promise?"

"It's a promise."

"When?"

"Next time."

"Does that mean that next time you will leave your car at home?" he asked.

Slightly smiling, she said, "That means that next time I will leave my car at home and then you can drive me home."

CHAPTER SEVENTEEN

Prelude to Sin

That night at the beach club marked a new beginning for Sandra. With each passing day being around Mark became much easier. She often allowed Mark to drive her home after a day at the beach. She learned to relax and share some of her feelings with him. The exciting months that followed swiftly moved Sandra and Mark into a poignant relationship that slowly began to transcend their emotional barriers. On some occasions these emerging feelings still frightened Sandra and worried Mark.

When Mark and Sandra were not working, they spent their evenings playing on the beach, laughing, dancing, swimming, boating, fishing, or drinking coconut water, sipping rum from tall glasses and enjoying being alone in a crowd. For over two months, like children playing hooky from school, they enjoyed their lives.

All during those times Sandra and Lola often

talked. Sometimes Sandra shared her deepest feeling concerning Mark with her. She reveled in his tender kisses to her cheek. She spoke of how it felt to have her head resting upon his chest. She even admitted to wanting him to really touch her, but she was afraid of what might happen. At all times, Lola encouraged her to live life freely. Whenever Sandra was with Mark she tried to keep everything that Lola had told her in the forefront of her mind. Little by little, Sandra attempted to build bridges over everything that Raymond had taught her.

Each day Sandra trusted Mark a little more. She began seeking short intimate moments such as being held close and caressed.

Despite the fears of his own past, Mark found himself becoming, lost in his emotions for Sandra. He convinced himself that he would just be with her because he liked her and cared about her but he was not going to fall in love with her. Yet the more time he spent with her, his emotions thickened, until all of the vows and promises he made to himself become completely meaningless. All he could see, all he wanted, all he needed was Sandra. Soon he began speaking to her of his growing affection for her.

Within those times when she allowed herself to hear his words and spoke of her past, Mark was made aware of some of Sandra's life before him, but she withheld so many things. She thought it was not wise to tell him everything, especially concerning Raymond's treatment of her. But Mark learned enough to know that it required patience and time to fully gain Sandra's trust.

Mark was apprehensive of Sandra's lingering

emotional restraints and was very happy when she showed signs of departing from them. On a number of occasions they embraced and lingered in each other's arms. Sometimes when apprehension made her tremble, Mark gently pulled Sandra even closer and caressed her adoringly. Still, Mark remained careful not to allow his acute longing to rush carelessly over her feeling.

After a while his lips went from a slightly brush against her cheek to her lips without upsetting her. Whenever Mark felt the slightest resistance in Sandra, he whispered phrases of love into her ear until it passed. As time went on, he was permitted to freely kiss her lips, neck and ears while holding her tight against him. Often, when they lay on the beach or watched the sunset from the front seat of his car, she eagerly responded to his display of affection. Mark felt Sandra becoming supple in his arms. Still day after day Mark played the waiting game patiently biding his time and continued speaking to Sandra of his unwavering love.

The keener Mark's affection for Sandra became, the more he feared sharing any of his past with her. It was too sorted, too unbelievable and totally unacceptable. Besides, sharing his past with Sandra may require him to pay a price that he was not yet prepared to do. From the first time he saw Sandra, he did everything possible to avoid these moments of caring. Now that he had totally surrendered to her sweetness and acknowledged his longing for her, he was in no way ready to relinquish his feelings in anyway or risk anything connected with it.

In mid-July, late on a Sunday evening, they were frolicking at the beach, engaged in swimming and long hours of languishing in each other's arms beneath the tropical sun. Towards night, Mark and Sandra found themselves alone near an inland cove at the east end of the island. Totally isolated, they lay embracing on a mossy plot of ground that they had covered with a blanket making it serve as the perfect place to get lost in each other. Before they realized it, they are surrounded by darkness, with only stars and the emerging moon to observe them.

Even though they had made tremendous advances in their relationship, Mark had not touched Sandra in very intimate ways, except to share a passionate kiss. Whenever they were on the verge of going beyond such a moment, she would freeze up.

Mark knew that Sandra preferred more open places with other people around them, but miraculously, unscheduled this night had happened, and he cherished it. In all of their time together, Mark had never had an opportunity for such a privileged moment with Sandra, especially when she seemed to be feeling so free and relaxed. Lying there in his arms she felt warm and comfortable. He dared a quick kiss on her lips and she eagerly accepted it. Encouraged by her response, Mark promptly pulled her closer and crushed his mouth harder onto hers. Every fiber of his being trembled and the world around him screamed with emotions.

At his touch her blood rushed to her head and her heart beat erratically. She became engulfed by a gigantic heat wave. Her entire body burned and her mind reeled out of control. When his lips covered hers, a sensational sweetness invaded her mouth and flowed throughout her body. She clung to Mark.

Caressing her tenderly Mark felt her shaking in response to his embrace and held her fast. He cradled Sandra in his arms, rocked her gently and kissed her even more passionately. Once again she doesn't resist but did begin to squirm. He detected an emerging passion taking control of her body and was manifesting itself throughout her body.

Mark hugged Sandra as if his life depended upon it. His lips smoldered with desire that he had smothered for so long out of fear of rejection was released, as he pressed his mouth against hers.

Sandra's head spun. Her quivering lips submitted beneath Mark's. His hot tongue parted her soft, wet lips. Her open mouth allowed his seeking tongue to smoothly glide in and out of it. She tasted him, and he was delicious. The rising heat consumed Sandra's body and sent her helplessly swirling into a world of overwhelming, unexplainable desire. She wanted him yet fearfully she trembled.

Mark put his lips next to her ear and softly whispered, "I want to make love to you. Don't be afraid my darling, free up yourself. I will not hurt you. I promise that everything will be all right. Just let me make love you."

Sandra gradually surrenders into Mark's arms.

Bursting with longing their entwined bodies tossed feverishly around on the blanket cushioning them against the soft patch of dew drenched moss. The cooling mist of the falling dew was no match for their sizzling desire.

For the first time, Mark's hands moved freely over her soft thighs. His touch generated an invasion of countless flaming sensations that caused her to twist and turn enthusiastically.

Mark held his breath as his hand inched aside the crotch of her snug fitting bathing suit and he slipped his hand between her quivering thighs. When he touched her warn, soft, silky flesh his mouth flew open and he inhaled deeply to keep from losing self-control.

When Mark invaded the delicate area between her thighs Sandra flinched and slightly drew back.

Kissing her passionately, he pleaded with her, "No! No! Baby, please don't be afraid. Trust me!"

His advancing hand moved further on until his fingers completely entered her moistened warm chamber. Ever so sweetly he said, "I love you so much. I want you more than life itself."

Very gently, his fingertips perused her insides and caressed her slender folds as he manipulated the softness of her, and begged; "Please let me make love to you."

As a sign of consent Sandra held her breath as his probing fingers moved deeper into the velvet interior of her tightness. She twitched at the discomfort nonetheless his actions provoked a craving in her.

With deliberate rhythmic strokes his fingers began moving in and out of her until he felt her wetness increase. With his lips pressed against hers in a lingering kiss, excitedly Mark shoved his busy fingers further down into her, thrashed them in, out, around

Ophelia M. Turner

and about, as his rigid organ straining with desire lunged against his swimming trunks trying to break free.

Kneeling upward, Mark leaned over Sandra, rolling her onto her back and removed her swimsuit bottom. He spread her legs and placed his hand beneath her hips, elevating them. With his other hand, he freed his impatient prisoner from his swimming trunks and placed its moist crown against the rim of dampened softness between her thighs. Upon contact with her bare flesh in its passion the eager organ leaped and pounded wildly against her.

Feeling the massiveness of him Sandra lay still, shaking inside. Her hips quivered. Her limbs grew taut. Her throat closed up and dryness sealed her lips. Tears welled in her eyes. She was torn between fear and desire. However, her twitching channel was beyond her control. It seemed to grope at Mark's organ with an increasing snatching movement. Not understanding the way her body was reacting, panic like a blanket of began to enclose her. A rush of awful conflictions swirled inside of her head. She fought hard to free herself of dreadful fears and concentrate only on wanting Mark. As a defense against the guilt attempting to ensnare her, Sandra softly repeated Lola's words, 'whipped cream, whipped cream, whipped cream.' "

Feeling her trembling in his arms, Mark kissed her heatedly and murmured, "I'll not harm you, my darling. I'll not harm you. Please, just let me love you."

Mark proceeded to inch down slowly into her primed opening. With only required pressure and patience he began to gradually forge his way through her tightness.

As he descended the increasing pain terrified Sandra. Suddenly Raymond was there over her with his thirty-nine horrendous strokes. Panic-stricken, Sandra gave Mark a tremendous shove and sent him tumbling backward onto the ground, and she leaped up screaming and crying, saying, "I can't do this. Oh my God, please don't make me do this. I just can't."

Confused and completely distraught Mark didn't know how to react, Mark lay there staring up at Sandra, as she leaped around screaming and clutching her bare crotch with both hands. She had become completely hysterical and was sobbing profusely.

Mark body ached. He was uncertain as to how to approach her. He could not find the right words to say that would make a difference.

Sandra kept repeating, "I can't. Oh God, I just can't."

Mark repeated over and over, "You don't have too Sandra. You don't have too."

Finally Mark was able to make her understand.

All the way home, silence hung heavily between them, until Mark finally found the voice to say, "Sandra, I promise you that I will never attempt to advance our relationship into any intimate stage unless you initiate it and is completely ready and willing to freely surrender yourself to me. The pain of disappointment is far more agonizing than any longing that I've ever had for you."

Ophelia M. Turner

Sandra sat silently beside him.

From that night on, Sandra spoke more openly to Mark of her life and feelings. She shared her up bringing, her relationship with her mother and the brutality that she endured during her marriage. Before, Mark had never quite understood the reason or the extent of Sandra's behavior. But now the picture became focused and he gained a deeper understanding of the fears that ensnared her. Mark became more attentive for her feelings.

Even so, for Mark, many times their constrained relationship made being around Sandra almost unbearable. At the end of each date, at her door Mark kissed Sandra good night and walked away in agony. Every emotion in Mark called out for her until he was nearly mad. Still, Mark determined that no matter how long it took, he would wait. Mark held fast to his intention of leaving that moment of readiness to her without trying to force her into submission.

The more Sandra thought about Mark the more she desired him and longed for his closeness. He no longer engaged in deep heated kissing or passionate lengthy embraces. Not only did she miss these moments, but she also began to fear losing him.

During lonely nights, hot tears burned her eyes as ethical and religious conflicts ran rampant in her body and mind. She had to find a way to release herself from the physical and emotional pain of her yesteryears. No matter how wrongly she had been taught, they were firmly anchored deep in her mind. Had living with the artificial moral standard that Raymond brainwashed her into nullified every one of her natural desires? She knew that she had to overcome his deceptive and wrongful use of God's Will.

Mark was offering her a new life and a new awakening filled with strange new desires. She wanted to know the truth of real love and have a loving sexual experience. But her desires were always overshadowed by the horrible legacy of agonizing physical pain that Raymond left in her mind that made her believe that she had to go through hell in order to get to heaven.

CHAPTER EIGHTEEN

Lessons Learned Behind God's Eyes

Six weeks later on Labor Day weekend, as a special favor to the governor, Mark and his band were entertaining a tourist group of New York politicians at the Fedricksted hotel. They were the governor's guests for dinner, including a show that evening, and a quick tour around the island the next day. Mark invited Sandra to join him for dinner and he asked her to stay on until he wrapped up the show for the night.

Despite the fact that Mark spent most of his time on stage, Sandra enjoyed the event. She met a lot of interesting people and indulged in stimulating conversations, ranging from life in New York to life on the island and everything else in between.

The governor made a brief high, profiled appearance, but discreetly disappeared after the sit down dinner and show was over and the dancing began.

Afterward on the long drive home, Mark and Sandra's excitement overrode any fatigue they may have had. They laughed, talked, touched, and exchanged stories about the events of that night.

A light tropical breeze came sweeping in from the south shore filled the night with the scent of sea and salt water that blended with the sweet smelling blossoms of flamboyant trees and aroma of ripping mangoes. The continuous vocals of night birds furnished a low but lively enchanting symphony. The pale moon cast a shimmering blanket of silvery moonlight over the island, creating a natural wonder giving everything about the night an illusion of paradise.

Sandra found herself remembering the night on the beach weeks ago when Mark attempted to make love to her. She remembered the warm sensation she experienced when Mark's body touched hers and the fire that he ignited in her. Momentarily, she delighted in the pleasure, forgetting the pain and fear. Recalling that night generated a pulsating throbbing between her thighs. She tried to flush the feeling from her mind, but her body disregarded her feeble intention.

Arriving at her doorway, Sandra handed her key to Mark and stood looking on as he unlocked her door. With the door unlocked, she quickly flicked on the light switch located on the wall just inside of the door.

She turned to him for their usual goodnight kiss. As always, Mark slipped his arms around her tiny waist and drew her to him, saying "Goodnight."

When Mark attempted a lightly kiss her on the cheek, Sandra quickly turned her face to received Mark's lips fully upon hers. When their lips met, his lips were softer and warmer than ever and filled with urgent, wet longing. Sandra eagerly pressed her

Ophelia M. Turner

deprived body hard against his. She opened her mouth
as an invitation to Mark's tongue. His warm tongue
filled her mouth and she gasped uncontrollably. She
breathlessly murmured, "My God. Oh my God."

Sensing her passion, Mark began slipping his
tongue in and out of her puckered lips, further
inflaming the euphoric feeling that rushed throughout
her body.

Sandra didn't struggle against her need for him.
Deciding no matter what it required of her psyche or
what immortal price she must pay for her sin, she
couldn't just kiss Mark and watch him walk away
anymore. Sandra determined, no longer would she toss,
turn and cry another night away, wondering what
might have been if she had the courage to say yes.

Sandra gave her body an impulsive lunge and
sent it pressing hard against Mark's, as she raised her
leg and rubbed it in between his whispering, "I want
you, Mark. I want you."

With an automatically reflex he responded by
tightening his arms around her and pulled her so close
that his painfully engorged manhood poked solidly
against her body. Unbelieving of what she said his
words challenged her, saying, "Prove it to me."

Sandra's placed her hands firmly on his buttock
and pulled him hard against her. In the heat of her
passion, she solemnly promised, "I will. Right now if
you will just please come in! Come on in Mark."

Still vaguely doubtful of what he heard Mark
paused a moment. His body ached with a desire to
believe her as he asked, "Sandra do you know what the

hell you are asking?

She quickly replied, "Yes!"

"Do you really mean it, Sandra? Please don't start this if you are not ready to finish it. Lord knows I can't stand it anymore."

"I am ready! Mark I need you. This time I am begging you, you are not asking me."

Kissing her heatedly Mark said, "Do me a favor and send me away right now rather than later, that's all I am asking."

Sandra murmured, "I remember what you said. I'm ready. Take me now and don't stop no matter what until you are satisfied."

The surging heat radiating out from the center of her, causing Sandra to tremble. She placed her shaking hands on Mark's and moved them to her hips, pleading, "Come on Mark and give me a chance to prove myself, please. If you don't let me I'll...I'll..."

"Shush, sweetness! Shush!" whispered Mark as he held Sandra. "Hush baby"

Mark tried to seal her lips with a kiss, but Sandra went on pleading, "Please Mark! Please just come on in."

Still somewhat reluctant he paused before obeying. Then Mark's hands firmly closed about her hips as he walked her backward into the apartment and kicked the door shut with his foot.

Behind locked doors, Mark bit his lips in guarded anticipation. His sweating hands fondled Sandra's clothed body like a curious child fingered a tightly wrapped gift.

Sandra's body twitched and shook beneath his touch. She experienced a hunger that she had never known. Her blood was hot and her head reeled.

The months of waiting had created in Mark an excessive craving. The fire in his loins commanded him to dispense with all customary protocol and elegant procedures and immediately satisfy his needs. Mark agonized with the urge to rapidly possess her. He felt driven to rip at Sandra's clothes until she stood naked before him. But Mark knew that he couldn't, shouldn't and wouldn't. Initiating extreme self-control, he whispered frantically, "No! No! No! Mark no."

Instead, Mark slowly caressed her and explored her clothed body inch by inch. Meticulously he passed his hand over each of her covered openings, protruding bulges and vivacious curves that represented her hidden treasures. During his guarded advances, he thoroughly kissed every luscious part of her that was available to him.

Sandra's body became swollen with desire. Her breasts grew firm, and her blood become effervescent with titillation. A new heartbeat developed between her thighs, giving life to an alien nerve in the center of her that twitched and quivered, her longing increased causing her to plead, "Take me, Mark. Please take me, now."

Mark took a step backward while appraising her loveliness and regrouping his emotions while fighting to maintain self-control.

Almost breathlessly he declared, "Oh God, Sandra darling, you are so damn beautiful, even more so tonight."

With parted lips and short rasping breaths she

softly pleaded, "Please... just hurry up, Mark. Hurry up and take me."

Recalling the night at the beach, in spite of her pleading, Mark refused to rush. He had no desire to generate any panic in her when he was so close to paradise. Until this moment, the freeing of Sandra had appeared an unobtainable dream. But now at last, he had it all. This was his chance to open every closed emotional crevice obstructing their lives, freeing Sandra's mind, body and soul from behind a wall of imposed ignorance and reveal the woman that he knew she could become.

Leisurely and carefully Mark began to unwrap her in sections. He unbuttoned each of the four buttons on her soft cotton blouse. Steeping with impatience, Sandra readily assisted him with her blouse removal.

With her blouse gone, Sandra closed her eyes as Mark unhooked her bra releasing her breasts from their satin prison, bountiful, free, so agile and completely accessible they bobbed up and down before Mark's beaming eyes.

Impulsively, Mark cupped Sandra's breasts in his trembling hands and gently crushed them against his moistened face. They were warm and comforting, the size of silk covered grapefruits and smelled as sweet as the light fragrances of fresh, spring flowers.

He whispered, "My beautiful, flawless darling, they are lovelier than any early morning sunrises on a prefect summer's day."

When Mark's hands enfolded her loveliness Sandra became slain with pleasure. He repeatedly massaged her nipples between his enthusiastic fingertips until fully extended and they stood erect.

Adoringly securing Sandra's breast in both hands with the tip of his wet tongue, he repeatedly massaged each of the projecting nipples until they throbbed.

Beneath Mark's proficient manipulation the great sensation stirring in Sandra's most sacred chamber caused it to constrict, vibrate and pulsate uncontrollably, as her additional heartbeat gained in momentum. The feeling was so intense that it forced her to promptly perform an impromptu series of little dance steps in place. This was the only emotional expression that she could make in response to Mark's introduction to such new and wonderful sensations.

As Sandra danced, her bouncing breasts, vigorously slapped against Mark's face. He attempted to restrain her by enfolding her in his arms, as he tried to contain his own immeasurable pleasure.

Sandra cried out with joy, "Oh Mark, my baby, my darling Mark, you are making me crazy but it feels so good. I love you so much."

Absolutely immersed in his own pursuit of pleasure, he whispered, "Easy baby, easy, the best is yet to come."

Holding Sandra close, Mark's hand moved down her spine until it touched the waistband of her skirt, un-zipping it, he rolled it down over her shapely hips, letting it fall on the soft, white carpet. He whispered into her ear, "Step out of it, baby"

Sandra immediately obeyed and kicked her shirt aside. Mark stooped down before her and with light flicks of his hands he began to roll her panties down over her hips, but Sandra had no more patience. She grabbed the band of her underwear and ripped them apart. He helped her to finish it and tossed the garment away. Sandra grabbed his hands and guided them between her wide spread legs. As she did so, he dropped to his knees saying, "I am going to love you baby, in ways that you have never dreamed possible."

Mark sent his tongue racing over the smoothness of her alluring belly. Sandra was completely surprised and became tense. Before she could fully grasp what was happening, Mark had wedged his head between her legs and sent his tongue darted around inside of her quivering thighs, caressing them in unspecified patterns. Each brush of his tongue created countless tracts of heat. Sandra trembled.

Still kneeling Mark grabbed her nakedness with overwhelming enthusiasm. He spread her unsteady legs and pushed his head between them, as he drove his tongue into her center and began caressing her newest heartbeat. Sandra shrieked from shock and almost fainted from sheer delight.

She felt the heat of his breath searing her inner tenderness as his nimble, untamed tongue went surging into her, generating even more energy to both of her heartbeats. Her shaking hands clutched Mark's thick black hair, as she tried to balance herself while she stands wide legged and reeling with emotion. She refused to think, she willed herself to only feel, allowing Mark to created even more uncontrollable longing in her. The heated movements of the unprecedented unification aroused unfamiliar desires in Sandra that lay lifeless beneath a blanket of taboos and religious doctrine. The sudden awakening caused her to inhale deeply and hold her breath until the indescribable sensational of the thrill peaked, forcing her to shiver, sob and whimper hysterically.

Between tears of joy Sandra begged, "Oh Mark, please keep on doing what you are doing to me. I need you so much. I can't wait anymore. I am ready for you to take all of me like you tried to on the beach. I will let you do it, but please do it now! I want you to do it."

"In a minute baby. In a few minutes you will get it all."

With his head wedged between Sandra's thighs, Mark placed his hands on her hips as a means of control, crawling he pushed Sandra backward toward the bed. He only stopped when she stumbled backward falling upon the bed with her legs spread and her feet off the floor, while his tongue continued to caress her inside.

Mark held her magnificent body close. Clutching Sandra's calves, he pushed her legs skyward, making her fully accessible as he nibbled her into madness.

With dreamy eyes, high on passion, Sandra breathed in his intoxicating essences, basked in the abundance of adoration that Mark showered upon her, Sandra, no longer resisted the ride on the forbidden excursion that Mark provided for her. Locked into a hallucinating trance, she floated toward the prefect power of raw passion.

Removing his head from between her thighs, wrenching and twisting his body Mark managed to rid himself of his clothing. Once nude, he stood over her, pausing just long enough to allow his starving eyes to

savagely ravish her. Before he once again granted
himself the pleasure dipping his tongue into the stream
flowing from her secret garden, not an inch of her
shapely body escaped his famished, psychological
possession. As Mark indulged in the luscious flow, he
knew there were still demons lurking in the background
that demanded defeating if they ever expected to fully
enjoy their lovemaking. He slowly withdrew his mouth
and called softly to her, saying, "Sandra, come on baby,
it's now time for you to look at me."

Sandra struggled to endure the frustration of
feeling the sudden withdraw of Mark's hot mouth from
her starving orifice, leaving her throbbing space empty
and cool. She laid moaning, trembling and rolling from
side to side. She vibrated from the lack of his presence
and its affect to her entire system just when he had
begun to provoke her into yet another emotional
breakthrough. Hesitating, she sucked in short rasping
breaths between clenched teeth.

Once again, in the same soft voice, Mark insisted
on her complying with his request, as he firmly
repeated, "Open your eyes wide, Sandra. If we are to
go on you must look at me right now. I want you to
look at all of me."

Mark was determined to destroy all of Sandra's
old taboos. He knew that he had to create new
memories in her to set her mind free. In order to do
this, starting now, he had to begin with what she sees,
touches, tastes, smells, and feels. So once again he said,
"Sandra, open your eyes wide, now."

Hesitantly, she attempted to obey his persisting
voice. But slowly she allowed her eyes to nervously drift
away from him and said, "Mark, I can't. I don't want

to look. Why can't we just make love without all of that?"

Adoringly, Mark looked at her as he insisted, "Darling, it's the only way. You must look directly at me, not away from me.

With lowered head and timid eyes, Sandra pleaded, "Don't make me do this, Mark. Don't make me do it. It is a sin."

Mark said, " Darling, there is no sin going on here. You have kissed my lips and felt my arms embracing you. These are the only parts of me. Now I want you to look at all of me. I want you to see all of the man that loves you, and it not shameful or sinful, its loving and being loved. So look at me now! Look at all of me, Sandra, please!"

After wavering in indecision for a few moments, Sandra reluctantly began by first focusing on top of Mark's head for a moment. Then Sandra's eyes slowly moved to Mark's face. One look into his adorable eyes set her head reeling. Thoroughly emotionally intoxicated, she allowed her eyes to slowly drift to the nude body of the man standing before her. They peruse over the remarkable skin of his broad chest and his magnificent shapely body and continue down until for the first time she gazed directly upon the forbidden sight of manhood protruding from between his well-built thighs. There was nothing to obscure her view, like the full, round cheeks of the young priest that swallowed up Raymond's manhood. Mark's immense form was erect, smooth skinned, poised, wonderfully embellished and truly an incredible sight.

Mark stood facing her, gazing into her eyes, elated by the amazing look of innocence reflecting in them. In an attempt to further convince her, he whispered, "Touch me my darling, I won't shrink away and die, neither will you. Touch me, Sweetheart."

She moaned, "Oh God, must I, Mark? Must I"

"Yes, you must, you can and you will. Touch me."

"Mark..."

"Touch me! Share in me. I'm all yours. Touch me."

With a timid outstretched hand, Sandra slowly leaned forward, placing her trembling fingertips on his warm hardness. For the first time, she knew the reality of the apparatus that at one time had only made her its victim.

Mark said, "That is my flesh and there is nothing sinful about looking at it. It is yours to touch, feel, and love as much as you want to, it was made just for loving you."

Somehow seeing and touching Mark's instrument of God was not frightening to her anymore. The way it leaped with Mark's every heartbeat made it appear hospitable, humane and seeking her attention. It amazed and hypnotized her.

Now, boldly, Sandra's slender hand reached out and made an unsuccessfully attempted to encircle the thickness of him. It was only with overlapping hands that she can completely enclose him in her sweaty grip. Mark flinched from the pressure that she applied.

Placing his hands over hers, he said, "Take it easy honey. I can be hurt, too."

Sandra relaxed her grip, saying, "I'm sorry. I

didn't mean to hurt you. Its all so new and so
wonderfully exciting."

Leaning forward, smiling, Mark pressed
Sandra back onto the bed and lowered his damp body
down onto hers. Elevated by her willingness to try, with
his hands still placed firmly over hers, Mark initiated a
stroking rhythm and together they slid their hands up
and down his eagerness.

Hand over hand; together they guide his eager
member toward the place in her that anxiously awaits
it. For the first time, Sandra could comprehend the
firm instrument that would be positioned into her and
she spread herself wide in readiness. Wide eyed and
breathless, with over whelming excitement Sandra
allowed herself the thrilling expectation of experiencing
Mark.

Mark fought to restrain his eagerness.
Clenching his teeth and flexing his jaw in great
anticipation, Mark cradled himself firmly in the niche
leading to the center of Sandra. Upon touching her soft
moist, opening, a raging longing stirred in his loins
pushing him to the point that he can barely wait. But,
patiently he attempted to gain entrance into the
precious vessel that she willingly yielded up to him.
Mark slid his hand under Sandra's slender hips
grasping them firmly he drew her close. With his
manhood securely in place, he momentarily entertained
an out of control urge to plunge into her. This thought
produced a brief downward thrust, causing her to
cringe.

Suddenly her fears appeared vivid before

Mark's face. He managed to gain control over his impulsive desires and began to gradually meter out slight, little nudges, while constantly reminding himself easy does it. Mark, easy does it. Don't blow it now.

With each endeavor to penetrate Sandra, Mark felt her flinch, but she sustained her courage.

Slowly, Mark pressed deeper into her narrow space demanding its unyielding barricades to relinquish all their objections. Despite Mark's gentleness, the progressive descent into her delicate vessel forced Sandra to emit short series of sharp outcries like those of an immature virgin.

With the increasing pain, Sandra began to push against Mark and tug at him trying to dislodge him. She struggled to squeeze her legs shut. As he continued to press down tears welled up in Sandra's eyes, overflowed and streamed down onto the crumpled sheet.

She cried, "Ohoo...Mark, please. Oh, please, you are hurting me. Mark it hurts. It hurt so badly. Let 's not do it now."

Her crying tempted Mark to lean towards her request. Reluctantly he proceeds to withdraw from the snug velvet channel that had just begun to receive him. Then he recalled her beseeching words in the beginning, when pleadingly she had begged him saying, 'Don't stop no matter what until I'm all yours.'

Knowing it was now or never, Mark renewed his challenge, refusing any further denial from his reluctant host. Neither Sandra's silent tears nor her tightness could any longer deter his slow, progressing descent. Inch-by-inch Mark compels the walls of her taut channel to finally totally surrender their resisting hold on her delicate sanctuary.

She bit her lips, swallowed her tears and as Mark conquered the depths of her. Once she overcame the initial pain, despite her brief moments of attempted rejection, Sandra had accepted the fullness of Mark.

Once firmly anchored into her innermost part, Mark's throbbing manhood took on a life of its own and began expanding until it filled her to capacity, touching her very soul.

With a low continuous simultaneous flowing of mixed sounds of both joyful sobs and painful whines Sandra soulful moans echoed softly throughout the otherwise silent rooms, as the stinging sensation of bittersweet pleasure of having Mark buried so deep inside of her was completely overwhelming.

Unbelieving that at last he had actually secured his most sought after dream, and the warmth of Sandra's pulsating velvet walls were tightly enfolding him. Mark marveled at being so properly mounted between the soft cushioning of her lovely thighs. In deep gratitude for finally achieving such good fortune, Mark paused briefly to authenticate the reality of it all and to exist of such a wonderfully satisfying and rewarding moment.

Feeling Mark's sudden stillness transported Sandra back into another time and place to different pause. Mark's paused once again triggered her past and bought it rushing to the forefront of her mind, overwhelming her. Suddenly the experience of Raymond overshadowed her and she expected Mark to deliver the first of thirty-nine devastating, merciless blows into her.

Her low whines that she uttered as she hovered on the edge of undefined pleasure became panic outcries of, "No, Mark, no, please don't do this to me. You promised never to treat me like Raymond did, not thirty-nine blows, not thirty-nine blows, please. I'm begging you, Mark please don't."

Shocked by Sandra's outcry, Mark shouted, "Oh my God. My poor, little, frightened, baby. Oh my God, what are you thinking, Sandra? What in the world are you thinking?" Mark said, "Look at me, I'm not Raymond. I am Mark the man that loves you. The God I serve does not demand punishment of me. He made my body just for this moment and loving you. I thought you knew that by now. God left our loving to our will, all I'm going to do or ever will do is love you baby, love you, as tenderly as I can."

Sandra's past now surrounded them and her fear disrupted the world that Mark had just created for them. Mark kissed her tear covered face and caressed the smarting perimeter of the precious little vessel that fully sheathed him. With nimble fingers, Mark worked feverishly gently massaging her, as he manipulated and loved her back into calmness.

After successfully satisfying Sandra there is no danger in him. Mark reaffirmed his position between her trembling thighs and got a mental grip on his urgent desires, as well as a firm control on his impulses. Then with compassionate, repetitive glides, Mark began to take a weeping Sandra's on a slow triumphant journey through her many anxieties, whispering, "I love you, darling. Oh how I love you and I will make everything all right for you, baby, trust me. Trust me darling."

Kissing, caressing and skillfully kneading her while with tender strokes Mark increasingly stimulated her latent passions.

Beneath Mark's continuous pampering Sandra gradually relaxed and freely surrendered to him, becoming a supple and eager participant. Sandra's sobs became verbal out cries of pleasure. In a soft passionate voice she moaned, "Oh Mark. Oh my wonderful Mark!"

She placed her hands on Mark's rotating hips pushed him further into her. Her arms and legs embraced him, holding him tightly in an effort to receive even more of him. Hovering on the brinks of sheer ecstasy, Sandra incoherently began muttering over and over, "Take all of me."

No longer feeling restricted, Mark, honed his inflexible sword of fleshy sensitivity to its maximum. Clued by her action and encouraged by her words, no longer compelled to become subdued he gorged his famished beast of desire upon the abundant feast Sandra heatedly served up to him.

Mark strived to eliminating her fears, nullifying her emotional pain and to force her reservations to disappear beneath smoldering flames of desire that he fueled in her.

Mark's unbridled procedures triggered a multitude of unfamiliar, spontaneous emotions in Sandra. Now with thrashing legs and shallow breathing only the feeling of sheer pleasures made her writhe beneath him. Feverishly she clawed, scratched, screamed, kicked and grabbed at him, desperately craving all the pleasure that Mark was delivering to her very core. She greedily demanded him to explore every dimension of the womanhood that she now certain was somewhere inside of her.

Sandra's suppressed sexual appetite had been released with an immeasurable fury and she was soaring out of control. The full revelation of sinful sedition had become the answer to her long lonely cries.

With her arms firmly imprisoning Mark and her legs draped over his shoulders and dangling wildly in mid air, Sandra bucked beneath Mark as he rode her like she was a spirited spring colt, flogging her from the inside with his superb rod. Mark whipped her like a jockey whipped his horse as he neared the finish line looking for that almighty win. Mark rode her so magnificently to where she once thought God had dared her to go and all the way she pleaded for more, saying, "Take me. I'm yours forever."

Mark's only response was to continue to perform magnificently at her demand.

At the height of their ferocious love making, the emotional flames inside of Sandra incinerated every inhibition that had loomed as barriers to all the unadulterated pleasure that she had never dared to seek. Sandra went into a frenzy of liberating bodily expressions, activating every nerve in Mark's sensual network.

Sandra's loud, feverish, shrilling cries announced that she was ascending to unfamiliar realms of sexual gratification. All of her bones seem to melt. The air around her grew thin, her breathing became shallow and her head felt like it was about to burst, as

her energy threatened to gush out through it. Her
eyesight dimmed and she almost passed out. Her
floundering legs went limp and her heart skipped beats.
She explodes emotionally to the point that she could
only react with continuous body spasms of flexing and
wrenching. She had never experienced such a moment.
Panicking and fearing death, she began shedding
uncontrollable tears. With eyes bulging, open mouthed,
gasping for each short, shallow breath, seized by the
thongs ecstasy she cried out, "Oh God, what is
happening to me, Mark? Tell me what's happening to
me. Have mercy on me. I'm dying. I'm dying. Oh
God, am I dying?"

Aware that she was experiencing a first time
orgasm, Mark whispered, "No! No! No, my precious
darling, you are not dying, for the first time you are
beginning to live. Free up yourself and feel it all. It's
your time and your pleasure, feel baby, feel all of it and
live."

Even as he spoke, Mark had not yet begun to
share in the height of her gratification. He tried to free
himself from her twisting body to prevent her from
forcing him into a premature ejaculation.

Sandra held on to him trying to prevent him
from pulling away, seeking to have him further appease
her insatiable desire. She feverishly begged, "Just a
little more, help me Mark. Baby, please, just a little bit
more."

Fighting Sandra's grip, Mark quickly
disengaged from her and pinned her firmly down
against the bed. He knelt between her spread legs and

slid his hands beneath her wrenching hips and pressed his mouth to the softness of her.

Almost as rigid as his efficient organ, Mark's flicking, intrusive tongue thoroughly manipulated Sandra in so many unfamiliar and unimaginable ways, as he continued with her as he guided her to the completion of her euphoric journey.

In Mark's skillful hands, Sandra wretched, moaned and groaned, with drowsy eyes she looked pleadingly at Mark and in a barely audible, slurring voice she pleaded with him for mercy without really wanting any.

Holding Sandra's winding hips securely in his hands, Mark relentlessly took her through the transforming experience, until suddenly with a long, shrilling, piercing cry she announced having reached completion and went limp in his hands. Mark released Sandra's hips and sprawled out on his back beside her.

The flame of irrepressible passion had consumed most of the lies and imposed biblical taboos allowing her mind and body to experience the reality of natural, raw sexual freedom and Sandra had endured.

Mark had succeeded in stripping away almost every root of the propaganda that had her imprisoned. Now Mark needed to achieve his own satisfaction, as well as accomplish his ultimate goal on the road the to of completion of Sandra delivery. In order to do so he had to dare to risk it all, because there was no turning back.

After a few minutes, Sandra began to slowly stir out of a trance alike serene motionless state. Drowsily, she began quivering and twisting in an indecisive display of unique physical expressions, as every newly found emotion resurfaced and vibrated throughout her body.

Turning to lay on his side, Mark placed his hand beneath her unsteady head and turned it until Sandra was facing him and he kissed her hard on the lips. Her hazy, unfocused eyes gradually opened and she smiled at him. Continuing to kiss her, Mark slowly pushed her head downward until her face was level with the mass of hardened flesh that danced and leaped before her misty eyes. With his other hand Mark stabilized his lusty offering and held it out to her. Its miniature jerks made it appeared to beckon her. Mark said, "It's all yours. If you are willing to go all the way, take it baby. It belongs only to you."

Although weak, spent, and barely functioning, Sandra no longer had any trepidation of being face to face with Mark's bountiful manhood. Eager to endorse her newly found freedom, Sandra lovingly reached out and accepted his dancing wonder with both of her unsteady hands and timidly she gently pressed its warm hardness to her cheek and tenderly massaging it. In complete awe she thoroughly observed Mark's offering. Its stout, solid surface was satiny and warm with an earthy aroma. Then, surprisingly everything concerning it suddenly became very clear and with great adoration Sandra excitedly shouted out her great revelation, she cried out, "This is truly what "God's Will" really looks like. It 's beautiful and its all mine."

Filled with relief of her acceptance and high on satisfaction, smiling, Mark held his breath, as he aimed her gaping mouth to his pulsating member. The leaping muscle was too portly for her lips to encircle. In eagerness, Sandra's perusing tongue explored every inch of Mark's skin that her hands held. Sandra's inexperienced attempts aroused an incredible degree of excitement in Mark, sending his passion soaring to the highest peak of soulful bliss unlike anything he had ever experienced.

Mark grew weak beneath her inexperienced passionate performance. Her uncoordinated manipulations stimulated him beyond his wildest dream. Not even within his most racy imagination could he have prepared for the immense pleasure that Sandra bestowed upon him.

Sandra's unwavering effort to become the willing source of his every desire and to fulfill his every need, confirmed his belief that she was worth every minute that he spent waiting for her.

Reaching down, Mark gently placed one hand under her chin and the other on the sides of Sandra's face and her drew to him, leaned over and firmly kissed her velvety lips.

He said, "I love you so much. You are everything that I ever dreamt that you would be and even more."

He caringly rolled Sandra onto her back and once again pressed his lips onto hers, as he slid his hands between her legs and under her hips lifting them upward. At his touch she readily responded, spreading them wider allowing him to quickly fling himself between her welcoming thighs. In that second Mark triggered an incredible longing in her that instantly consumed her. Sandra knew words would not suffice during these profound moments, so she opened her mouth and deeply inhaled as she surrendered her all to Mark.

Driven by the carnality that Sandra aroused in him, Mark's electrifying, rogue like stamina becomes irrepressible. Enthusiastically he skillfully molded their bodies into a single unit of tumultuous action. The slapping echoes of pounding, perspiration soaked, flesh filled the surrounding air. The cooling waves of the tropical night breeze could not rival their heat.

Emotions thrashed the lovers about like grains of dry sand in a whirling tropical windstorm. The vigorous rhythm of their magnificent performance of boundless pleasure moved them to the edge of infinity and blended them together in a spiritual oneness.

At last, the swelling of an unfathomable ocean of unstoppable ecstasy enveloped Mark. His eyes fluttered, as he reared his head back and hairs on the back of his neck bristled. With a long, throaty groan he plunged deeper into Sandra and called out her name several times and collapsed.

Within that exact moment, in a low, breathless voice she murmured, "Mark, Mark, my darling Mark." Sheer bliss sent Sandra sinking into a semi-comatose state.

At the completion of their incredible lover's feast, they wilted, him on top of her and their world stood still. At last, Sandra knew in her heart of hearts that she had truly discovered the meaning of 'God's Will,' and it had embellished every fiber of her very being. Now having known real, guilt free love, she could look God directly in the eyes knowing that all else except real love had fallen by the wayside.

CHAPTER NINETEEN

Fallen Scales

Still sheltered inside of Sandra, Mark ushered in Saturday morning sprawled between her soft, warm wide stretched legs, as the bright rays of the morning's sun plucked at his cracked eyelids. Mark's body gave a sudden shutter, as his throbbing extremity began leaping back to life.

Awaking slowly, Mark rose up on his elbow and marveled at the woman lying beneath him. If the reality of her nearness weren't so undeniable, her sweet aroma weren't so intoxicating and the pulsating warmth that enclosed him weren't so stimulating, he would swear that she and all she had given him was just another wonderful dream.

Sandra stirred beneath the security blanket of Mark's warm body. She opened her eyes, smiled at him and enfolded him in her arms. Neither of them spoke, their bodies became the conversationalists. All he gave she gladly received.

Their day became lost in repeating their sensuous unions of the night before with no desire, what so ever, to control their passion. Except for the few brief moments taken to replenish their bodies with food and drinks, their entire weekend evolved into a marathon of exploratory sex for Sandra and extraordinary sex for Mark. They journeyed into worlds filled with unlimited feeling and physical indulgence, where untold satisfaction was revealed with eagerness and joyful exploration. Sandra happily pursued her greatest adventure with overwhelming enthusiasm. Mark was her personal tour guide through each new world filled with so many heavenly wonders and his magnificent lovemaking was the passkey to her new found paradise.

Immersed in happiness, Sandra looked up at Mark's smiling face as he hovered above her. She said, "Never before have I ever been so happy. I've never been loved. I've never known that anything could be so wonderful this side of heaven."

Mark looks down at her and said, "This is only the beginning of a lifetime of happiness, I promise you that. You're my every dream come true. I love you so much."

Mark's heart beats with gratitude. He had finally solidified the essence of his desire and there isn't any wanting to be found in Sandra. Although their needs generated from different places, their worlds collided and burst into flaming splendor capturing and fulfilling every longing each ever dared to have.

Late Sunday evening, Mark managed to separate from Sandra. Reluctantly he left her sitting in the middle of the bed, nude, and wide legged and tender, but tremendously happy.

After Mark left and closed the door behind him, she needed relief from the smarting and burning of Mark's magnificent pillage.

For an entire lifetime she had been led to believe the only acceptable use of her body was sanctioned by her husband and ordained by God. Now she knew her womanhood was not a curse to undergo endless pain and suffering, nor an artifact of forbidden sin. In reality, it was God's most beloved gift to man. It's God's smallest gateway to heaven's greatest pleasure.

Finally Sandra dragged off of the bed and walked wide legged to the bathroom and submerged her fatigued body in a tub filled with warm water, oil and a herbal bubble bath.

Lying back in the tub Sandra recalled Lola's every word. Had it not been for Lola she would have never dared to trust herself to Mark. If Lola hadn't encouraged her to see another side of life, what would've happened to her, certainly nothing like this?

After Sandra eased her body down into the tub and managed to find a comfortable position the soothing water lapped at her center with a soothing yet stimulating sensation. She freely fingered herself and guiltlessly experiences a tingling within her that causes her to wish for more of Mark. However, Sandra could only nurse her searing body with warm compresses.

Lola was right in saying that she'd only experienced a man's organ being brutally rammed inside of her and she had never had a man make love to her.

"Fucked," is what Lola called it. " Being fucked!" Just hearing herself say it made Sandra laugh.

"Mark, Mark, wonderful, good-fucking Mark," she whispered and laughed aloud saying, "Thank you Lola. Thank you! Thank you! Thank you!"

She had forced her to finally open her eyes to see Raymond for what he really was a pathetic, helpless, cowardly pervert and Sandra realized that there is no healing in denial. She admitted to herself all she had been denying. Especially that somewhere deep inside her there had been something urging her to face her feelings and experience the warmth she felt for Mark, but the fear of sin kept getting in the way of her desires.

Before Mark, pain was all Sandra had ever known. Not once was she given a kiss, a kind word, or even a tender look, for fear of sinning against God's Will.

She shuddered at remembering Raymond and "God's Will" and recall when all she could do was endure in silence and cry in secretly.

When Mark took her into his arms and together they went on their sacred journey to paradise, Sandra knew that at last she was being loved and pain was not a curse, but just a preamble to the beginning of the greatest pleasure that life could ever afford. As she happily massaged her tenderness, Sandra smiled. She had been embraced, kissed, fondled and made to feel absolutely adored. Besides knowing all of that, she cried "I've been wonderfully, wonderfully fucked Lola. I have been so well fucked."

Sandra laughed and cried all at the same time

with happiness, saying. "Oh my God, I've been so adoringly, so fabulously, gloriously, magnificently fucked and it was absolutely marvelous."

CHAPTER TWENTY

Confide and Confess

Carrying her purse on her shoulders and briefcase in one hand, Sandra bounced into the Water Plant with a stack of papers in her other arm. She zipped into the office happily shouting a bubbling, "Good morning to you, Lola."

Lola looked up and Sandra stood before her grinning. "Well what good fairy sprinkled your behind with stardust so early this morning? Or did you swallow a handful of happy pills?" Asked Lola.

Sandra replied, "Neither. It is just such a lovely day. Don't you think so?"

"It's not that damn lovely, now," said Lola with a sneer. "All morning this place has been as crazy as hell. Now here you come acting like goddamn Mary Poppin."

"Well, things do get like that sometimes. Lola, but come on, lighten up. It will get better, trust me," she said in a singsong voice, still smiling.

Just about that time, Mark walked through the hallway, smiling, as he paused just long enough to

Ophelia M. Turner

loudly called out, "Good morning ladies"

Sandra became flustered and could barely speak.

Grinning, Mark was almost salivating, as his eyes quickly scanned every inch of Sandra's body.

With a dreamy eyed, lingering look, Sandra stared back at him, even as he slowly strolled away. Minutes after Mark had disappeared down the hallway Sandra still couldn't turn away. After a long gaze down the hallway in the direction Mark had gone, smiling, Sandra heaved a low sigh and all but collapsed into her chair.

During the entire episode, Lola peered at Sandra over her gold-rimmed glasses with a smirk on her face. She watched Sandra as she melted like an ice cube in hell. Then when she couldn't take it anymore Lola slowly rose to her feet and walked around to the other side of her desk to the chair that Sandra had collapsed into and stood in front of her. She leaned over Sandra and looked her directly into her eyes and through clinched teeth, said, "I'll be damned. I'll be god damned." Then she bluntly asked, "You fucked him didn't you? You sure enough fucked him didn't you?" Lola repeated in a loud affirming voice, "You fucked that man! I know that you did."

Standing directly over Sandra, Lola gazed down at her so hard the Sandra became fidgety and disoriented. Lola's eyes didn't waver as she looked long and hard into Sandra's eyes. Then she glanced in the direction that Mark had gone and again back at Sandra, saying, "Shit, that explains why you sashayed your little fresh ass in here so full of sunshine and dripping with honey." She asked, "He have lit your little ass up, haven't he?"

Sandra felt like a child caught stealing candy. She was speechless with the expression of guilt written all over her face.

Even though Lola correctly read the look on Sandra's face and knew that she was right, she just wanted Sandra to openly confess.

"God damn, you sure enough did fuck him," shouted Lola. "I bet he showed you what God had in mind for your little ass didn't he?"

Shyly Sandra softly pleaded, "Please don't talk like that, Lola. You are embarrassing me."

"Come on girl, sex isn't anything to be embarrassed about-- especially if it's good. It's a part of life. Hell no, I take that back, it's life itself. Lord knows I sure do my share of living.

"Besides, I thought I saw an unfamiliar swing in your little ass when you waltzed in here this morning. Now I know where all of that sweet mush was coming from. That smile on your face reflected that smile that Mark put in your ass. Everything is suddenly becoming self-explanatory. Well, I guess I don't have to give you no more one on one sex education do I? Apparently, Mark has schooled your ass well."

Still blushing Sandra lowed her eyes and said, "Lola, it's not what you think. Mark taught me about making love, that's true. It did hurt some like you said, but it was well worth it. Once I got used to it, it was beautiful. It was absolutely beautiful. He is so... so... so...."

"So damn good in bed," teased Lola.

Ophelia M. Turner

Sandra replied, "No! Yes! I mean no! He is so nice and loving. He really cares about how I feel."

"I hope to hell he does. I heard that you two had been seeing each other quite often for sometime, but you were so screwed up I never thought that there was a chance in hell of him ever getting any of that ass. As a matter of fact, with all that shit you had been taught, I thought nobody would ever get any of your behind without a notarized note from God," said Lola.

"Sometimes I still don't feel right about it, Lola, but it feel so good. When I am with Mark I just plain forget about everything, especially sin," confessed Sandra.

"See! I told you if you ever got it done right you'd change your mind," boasted Lola.

Sandra bashfully looked away.

Tossing her hands skyward, with a slight smile on her face, Lola went on talking as she slowly walked around the room, "Look girl, I am much older than you and I have seen my share of shit. I'm not looking for love. If I meet a man, and we can get along better than two cats tied by their asses to the same rope and flung across a short clothesline, we will fuck. All I want is some good conversation, a quiet dinner and a decent lay. That's my comfort zone."

Then, she turned to Sandra, the sincerity in her voice was evident, kind and motherly as she said, "But you, girl...Sandra, you are young and pretty and you can use all that other shit. Besides you are a decent girl, raised up in a kind of crazy sort of way, but you are very decent. There's nothing wrong about calling it love. God knows it can be with the right man. So don't feel guilty about a damn thing," Lola instructed her.

Sandra said as she got up to leave, "Lola, you know, that's what drew me to you in the beginning, when we first met. It was the way you always put things. You tell a person the truth in your own kind of special way. I like that. I owe you so much."

"You don't owe me a damn thing. You owe yourself all of those years you were robbed of being a woman. Now enjoy the rest of your life, just like I hope Mark will."

"You said 'just like you hope Mark will.' What do you mean by that? Of course he will," said Sandra.

"I meant just what I said," answered Lola. "God knows he deserves it."

Sandra looked upset by Lola's remark, causing her to shout, "What do you mean by saying he deserves it? I suppose that means he deserves it more than I do? Sometimes I just don't understand you and some of the things that you say."

In a soft tone of voice, Lola said, "There is nothing to understand. If you had any idea what that man went through a few years back you'd understand exactly why I said that."

"Well I don't know what he went through and I don't understand what you are talking about."

With a surprised expression, Lola asked, "You mean Mark hasn't told you yet?"

"Told me what? What is there to tell me? What are you talking about, Lola?" asked Sandra.

"I talking about Diana Taylor, the woman that he was engaged to marry a few years ago."

"Engaged?" On the verge of panicking, Sandra repeated, "Engaged? He never told me anything. I don't know about any other woman."

With a puzzled look on her face, Lola said, "Well, I'm not surprised. It was so horrible it seems like the entire island deliberately chooses to forget. It generated a lot of pain for a lot of people. It was just too awful, just about the worst damn thing that ever happened here. So I'm not surprised that he hasn't mentioned it to you, yet. No one ever talks about it anymore. Who in the hell would want to talk about something so damned awful?"

With an air of distance concerning Lola's remark about Mark's engagement, Sandra said, "Apparently whatever they had doesn't matter, because now Mark loves me and I love him."

"You are right. It doesn't matter because she is dead."

"Dead? Dead how?" gasped Sandra, "What are you talking about?"

Sandra moved toward a chair and dropped down in it as she stared at Lola, standing with her back to the wall near the door.

Lola looked at Sandra for a moment before saying, "She was raped and murdered in the worst way possible. It was a hell of a ugly situation."

Sandra sank deeper into the plush chair and raised her hand to her opened mouth to hold back the gasp. She felt her body being drained of strength. A wave of shivers raced through her, as she whispered, "Oh my God."

Lola folded her arms and began pacing the floor, "The worst part of it was that Mark was the one to find her body. It was awful."

"How do you know so much about it?" asked Sandra.

"Good Lord, girl, I live here. Besides I was sleeping with one of the detectives assigned to the case."

For a few minutes no words passed between the two women. Lola paced and Sandra sat whimpering in shock.

Finally Lola said, "That was a sad time in St. Croix. Everyone loved Diana. She was such a pretty girl and so full of life. Every one knew Diana, from one end of the island to the other. I've never heard of anyone saying a bad word about her. That's why it was impossible to imagine anyone doing such a horrible thing to her."

"What about Mark? Was he involved?" asked Sandra, "How did he deal with it? Tell me something. Tell me everything," demanded Sandra.

"I can only tell you what my friend told me about the crime scene. He was one of the first detectives to arrive there that day.

"It was proven that Mark was innocent. But he couldn't deal with it for such a long time. He loved that girl. He became like a walking shadow. He was an emotionally wrecked that went through each day damn near on automatic control. He went through hell. Nothing seemed to matter to him after that, not until you came along. Knowing you as I do; and knowing Mark's story, as well as knowing that he is a damn nice guy, is why I wanted to see you two get together."

"Well! Thank you for being God Almighty, Lola

and planning my life at your discretion," said Sandra resentfully. "You could have told me all of this before now."

Taken back by Sandra's resentful tone of voice and rude attitude when she asked the question, Lola became irritated, and asked, "Why in the hell should I have told you anything when you were running backward from the man as fast as you could? What good was it going to do you to know that then?"

"Well, why in the hell are you telling me now?" screamed Sandra.

Half-heartedly, subdued Lola replied, "Damn if I know, except you asked, remember? Then Lola heatedly replied, "You asked! You climbed on my damn back and stayed there and kept pressing me for an answer. Now you've got your damn answer. Now, what in the hell are you going go do with it?"

Almost tearful, Sandra stared at Lola, who was staring hard at her. Sandra was shaken to her core by Lola's attitude. She suddenly realized that she had never given any thought of Mark ever having made love to anyone else. She had chosen to see herself as the only woman that ever mattered to him, now she had just learned that not only did he love someone else, but also had intended to marry her.

Sandra's mind kept forcing her to say, No! No! No! None of this can be true." She heard herself telling Lola, "I don't know. I just don't know anything anymore. I can't believe any of this."

Lola shouted, "Sandra, grow up! Grow the hell up! The man had a life before you. No one is prefect, no matter how much we want them to be. Mark didn't choose what happened in his life, no more than you did in yours. Shit just happens all of the fucking time. He is the one that was hurt here. All of this took place before he knew that you even existed."

Lola moved closer to Sandra and with heart felt compassion and said, "If you are smart you will go on with your life knowing that you have one hell of a wonderful guy. Pain is pain, whether it is your kind of pain or his kind of pain. It all hurts and who needs it? So, if you love Mark, just keep your mouth shut it's his past and it has nothing to do with you. Like I said before about your past, if Raymond had kept boring into you night after night, instead of once a month, you wouldn't had anything to offer any man except the beat up box that your cherry use to be in. For all the shits that you have gone through you are damn lucky that you were just screwed up with damn lies. Now look, you are as lucky as all hell, you've got Mark and he loves you. So, like I said, enjoy the rest of your life."

"What can I say to him, Lola?" moaned Sandra. "What can I say to him?"

"Not a damn thing! He will tell you in his own good time and in his own way. So, for now, give it a rest. Besides, whatever happened to that happy little ass that you switched in here just a little while ago? What has really happened to change all of that? Not a damn thing! So just back up to a while ago, remember that smile that Mark put in your little ass, flaunt it on your face and enjoy your life girl."

Sandra managed to squeeze out an insufficient smile and flashed it in Lola's direction as she remarked, "That's all I'll have to enjoy if I don't get out here and get those men signed up. Maybe I'll see you at the beach party tonight. Mark is playing at Hotel on the Cay."

"Maybe!" said Lola, "Maybe!" as she watched Sandra leap up and hurriedly headed for the door.

Lola smiled, as she watch Sandra's hasty departure, and whispered, "Damn if he didn't bust her tight little ass loose. Come hell or high water, damn if she is going to let anything get in the way of that."

CHAPTER TWENTY-ONE

Unconditional Love

For six months Sandra entirely entrusted her every emotion to Mark. Time dissipated into a cloud of bliss. They vigorously pursued life in unlimited, impromptu episodes of love and sex. In Mark's reckless attempt to solidify his relationship with Sandra, all during that time he hadn't dared to reveal the truth surrounding his life. Feeling thankful that they had come so far, he feared such a revelation would become a barrier to stand between them, or a wedge splitting them apart.

Soon after the beginning of their involvement, Mark realized that he did not dare share his life's story with Sandra. Not because of secrets, but because of pain.

After Mark learned of Sandra many fears and wrought beliefs, he knew there was no way that he would have made her understand anything that he had to say. Now Mark found himself hopelessly bound by his love for her and he knew that he owed her the truth. Becoming certain that Sandra really loved him, Mark realized that he had no choice but to take a chance and share the truth with her. But he questioned himself, asking, if I do will it cost me everything?

Previously, every time he made up his mind to tell Sandra the truth, his heart failed him. Finally, Mark decided to choose a time when Sandra could least resist him. He didn't want to take any unnecessary chances or add to the risk of losing her. To minimize such risk he had to carefully choose the right time and the place to tell her.

Sandra had to spend a working weekend in St. Thomas because she had steel workers' union meeting there on Friday and half day Saturday. This allowed her part of Saturday and all of Sunday to be off. She saw this as time that she and Mark could use for themselves. So she asked Mark to fly over to St. Thomas, Friday, after work and join her.

On his flight over to St. Thomas from St. Croix, Mark decided that being alone in a romantic setting might prove to be advantageous, as the prefect place and time to share the truth with Sandra. Mark has no choice except to put everything that he ever wanted on the line if he was to be honest with her. Yet, his troubled mind churned with anxiety and apprehension and his thoughts made him grow cold with fear.

Mark knew that what he was about to do was a tremendous crap shoot that he may very well lose, regardless, he had no choice except to come clean with Sandra and he knew every word that he used may well become his greatest enemy.

After the union meetings were over they spent

the rest of Saturday evening at one of their favorite places, the beach. Upon returning to their suite at Frenchman's Reef they decided to shower together. Mark sponged Sandra down beneath the flow of sprinkling warm water, with the bath sponge he toyed with her most intimate part while nibbling on her breasts and kissing her belly.

Mark's struggling thoughts were floundered in indecision and he began leaning towards once again prolonging the inevitable. He proceeds to slip his lusty root between Sandra's lathe slicked thighs. Her heart raced with excitement and her face glowed with expectation.

With her legs open and leaning closer to him with her gaping legs Sandra fished for Mark's elusive organ, only to have it repeatedly slip away. Unable to restrain herself any longer when she could not snare him, Sandra reached up and wrapped her arms around Mark's neck and clasped her legs about his waist and rode him out of the shower and into the living room. There she wrestled him until their drenched bodies tumbled onto the carpet in front of the wide-open sliding glass door. In the midst of the hot afternoon sun and gentle cool breeze they continue their love play of touching, caressing and speaking in low amorous tones.

Lying on top of Sandra, Mark held her winding body down as he purposely sent his moistened, roving hands to rushing over, under and dipping into her body. Sandra's arched hips were all set for another wonderful afternoon of a long love marathon.

Mark vigorously glided his rigorous apparatus back and forth between her legs, passing it over and around her ravenous opening, without penetrating her.

Ophelia M. Turner

He teased her until she was teetering on the edge of losing her mind.

As he watched Sandra squirm and heard her utter throaty moans while he teased her to the limits, guilt besieged him.

Suddenly Mark's thoughts become thieves, depriving him of what at any other time would have been an extraordinary happy moment. He realized that he was engaged in the most difficult moral battle of his life.

Nevertheless Mark knew that postponing the enviable any longer was no longer an ongoing decision and any further postponement was only going to make things worst.

Mark began to lose the war with his conscience on his thoughts of making love to her, as he became torn between two opinions. One reason being having her had become selfish. He thought that he may soften her up if he did, the other being after he tells her the truth it may be the last that he will ever have her again.

Then he agonized thinking yet another thought, tell her first and afterward chance letting their lovemaking become the ultimate tie that would bind them together forever, or make love to her first and weaken her senses to the point of forgiveness.

Although he was almost out of his mind with wanting Sandra he made his decision. Mark stopped his behavior abruptly, moved away from her and propping up on his elbow, he solemnly said, "I must tell you something, Sandra. If you hate me afterward, I'll never blame you."

Sandra slid almost under him and pushed her raised pelvic up toward him seeking the main source of her desired pleasure. She said, "Let the conversation wait Mark. Let's do it later, because there is nothing in this world that could ever make me hate you."

Sandra chose to envision what Mark had to say mostly because Lola had already told her about Diana, a woman who could no longer become a threat to her. Right now all she wanted was Mark. So, why at this time should she allow a meaningless conversation about Diana prevent her from having him? After all, she had made peace with his past and right now was all that really mattered.

Twisting as she rubbed her hand over his partially reclined body, stroking his inflexible erection stimulated her tremendously. With each stroke she begged him, "Put me out of my misery, baby, give it to me. There is no hate in me for you."

Clutching her winding hips with both hands, Mark pushed her away and held her at a distance, as he whispered, "Don't be too sure, Sandra."

"I'm sure!"

"I pray that you are right."

Impatient, Sandra opened her eyes and pushed Mark down flat and rolled him onto his back. Straddling him she grasped his tottering extremity, positioned it upright. Holding it tight she attempted to lower herself onto the thick, hardened mass, as she insisted, "I know that I'm right, so just stop talking baby and let's get really busy."

Mark quickly grabbed her around the waist and held her up preventing her from descending onto him. He said, "Please baby give me a moment. Before we do anything I must ask you something and I need to know your answer now. Do you believe that I love you more than any thing or anyone in this world?"

Sandra fought frantically to become impaled on him. Her throbbing body wanted him so badly that it burned. She could almost feel him entering her as she answers, "You know I do."

She began pleading with him, begging, "Give it to me Mark. Give it to me now. Why are we still talking? I want it now!"

Removing her hands from around his instrument, Mark lifted Sandra off of him and laid her on her side next to him, as he said, "I must have my say, baby."

For the first in their relationship Sandra was beyond frustration. She rolled over, looked into his eyes and asked, "What is so important?"

"Sandra if I don't say what I must now, I may not ever say it. I'm not a coward, but I have already waited too long.   If you know that I love you and no one else, what I'm about to say shouldn't make any difference in the world to you, as long as you know that I only love you."

Apprehension caused Sandra to sit up and look directly at him frowning as she again asked, "What is it Mark? You're scaring me."

Almost whispering he said, "I'm married, there is no other way to say it Sandra."

Not certain of what she heard Sandra just sat there starring at him.

When Sandra made no reply in a louder voice

Mark repeated, "I'm married!"

At the impact of his words all life drained out of her. Sitting in a paralyzed state Sandra could only stared at Mark.

Then Mark's words impacted her like a slap in the face and Sandra reeled from their effect. Doubling over as if she had suddenly been struck in the stomach by some mighty force, she gasped for air and inhaled until she almost passed out from hyperventilation. With her mouth wide open she continued gasping as she stared at him. She was totally speechless. Her glaring eyes are flooded with tears. Her head whirls with disbelief and her entire body shook as emptiness filled her being. She was emitting a stream of clear fluid from her opened mouth while kicking and scooting she scurried backwards across the floor to get away from him. Suddenly Mark is no longer there. Some stranger had invaded their world and was ripping it apart. She was unable to feel anything except deep-seated pain. She sobbed hysterically, as she wonders how could this be? Diana was dead. How can it be? What is he saying?"

Crawling slowly toward her on his knees, Mark reached out to touch her, but she slid even further away.

Mark tearfully moaned, "This is what I was afraid of. Had I told you this when I first met you we wouldn't even be together now. With your upbringing and the things that you were taught to believe and all those experiences you underwent, you wouldn't have let me near you much less let me explain. I thought that by now we loved each other enough to talk and I could make you understand. I guess I was wrong."

Despite every emotion that she had experienced with Mark all she could do now was become anesthetized while continuing to cry. Hours passed while Sandra went on weeping bitterly without saying anything to him. Like a hot poker, pain stroked her heart and her insides felt like everything had melted into nothingness.

Somewhere deep inside she recalled that Lola had told her about his engagement to Diana, but that was all that it was, an engagement. Now he was speaking of a marriage. If it was to Diana, that shouldn't mean anything to him anymore and why would it be so painful to her? Fear was telling her that there is something more.

There on the floor in the bright sunray, Mark sat helplessly by Sandra. Lines of sorrow and pain furloughed his forehead. His heart pounded with fearfulness, as he wondered had he lost Sandra? Had he lost the only person that he loved? That is the only question that he needed an answer to. If he had his life is over.

Time passed in loud annoying ticks from the small clock sitting in the table and evening dragged into night. Sandra calmed down enough to allow Mark to say, "Sandra, I told you something before I said that I am married. I said that I didn't love anyone except you. Sandra, you said that you believed me and remember you also had just said that you loved me too, baby."

Looking pleadingly at her he asked, "What happened to that?" Begging for an answer, Mark asked again, "Please tell me what happened to that?"

Between broken sobs, she whimpered softly, "Nothing! Nothing happened to that, except you lied to me Mark. You have been lying to me all of this time. I trusted you and you lied to me," and she began to cry again.

Mark leaned in close to her, saying, "No Sandra, you are wrong, I've never lied to you. I've always said that I love you. That's not a lie. If I didn't love you, why do I spend all of my available waking time with you trying to prove it? Especially in the beginning, when there were times when you wouldn't let me come anywhere near you except maybe for a casual kiss? Why didn't I up and go someplace else with someone else that was willing and able to have me? Why aren't I someplace else right now, rather than facing you with this agonizing confession," he reasoned.

"But you are married," Sandra repeated. "How?"

Mark replied, "Yes I am, but it's meaningless. I only love you. I never said anything about not being married or being single Sandra because you never asked."

"I've seen your personnel file remember? I have all of your personal information in that file," insisted Sandra.

"You don't have all of my information because I've never claimed my wife and I never will," he said. "I'm telling you because I don't want any more walls between us. Besides, I just want you to hear about her from me. One day when we least expect it, you will meet someone that does know and can't wait to tell you all about it."

She thought, why should any of this matter since Diana is dead? Then she asked, "Have you ever told anyone else about your marriage?"

"Only those that were there and everyone else was on a need-to-know basis," said Mark.

Resentment filled Sandra, angrily she cried, "Well now, Mark Landers, since you have decided that I need to know tell me. Yes, you are right, I do need to know everything about the woman that you really belong too!"

He said, "Sandra, you are that woman. I only belong to you. You are everything to me. I need you, and I swear that I love you and always will. After tonight, I don't want Mira, that's her name, Mira, in our lives any more than she was before."

"Mira? Mira?" Sandra gasped, as she sat already reeling from shock, trying to absorb and assimilate what Mark had just said. It was all so crazy. Old fears were rapidly surfacing. All of the guilt from her past began to crowd her mind. At last she is being punished for the sin of giving herself freely and so completely to a man that she was just getting to know. She was drowning in the lust of the flesh and she was being aptly punished. She cried out, "Mira? I thought her name was Diana. I was told that you were to marry Diana, before she was killed. Who...in... the hell is Mira?"

Mark is surprised to learn that Sandra knew so much about Diana. This too was something he had never shared with her, either. The effect of her revelation, in addition to the revelation of his own sent

Mark's mind spinning off in another direction. All he could say was, "Diana is dead. Yes! She is dead, and as far as I am concerned so is Mira, so just forget about Mira. She is nobody. She doesn't count."

"How can I dismiss this...this Mira person?" asked Sandra through her tears. "How can I make her disappear when out of nowhere she is suddenly here and she is your wife and her name isn't Diana? From the day that I learned about Diana, I accepted that, and I dismissed her. Now you are handing me this Mira, and you are telling me to dismiss her. What in the hell are you trying to do to me? What are you asking for? How can I forget anything? What in the hell do you expect me to do? She will always be here with us, between us, in bed with us. How could you Mark? How could you do this to us?" She shivered from hurt, fear and betrayal and shook like a water drenched dog.

The room grew cold and silent. Her heart pounded wildly. Rage, hurt and disappointment overshadowed her. She suddenly wanted to run as far and fast as she could. Forgetting that she was naked, Sandra leaped to her feet and attempted to dash out of the sliding door forgetting that it only led to a balcony. Her pain was overwhelming, so much confusion and grief had made her weak and her head spun rapidly. She immediately staggered and fell backward.

At that precise moment, Mark leaped up, reached out, grabbed her and pulled her to him. Sobbing, she wilted into Mark's arms.

Mark knew there were no words that he could say that would change anything. Handling Sandra like the fragile doll she had become, Mark carefully stretched her out upon the carpet. Sandra lay motionless as Mark proceeded to caress her. Mark's heated hands rapidly administer strokes of comfort, melting her into a quieter world as he prays for her understanding. Everything else between them is left unspoken.

Once back on St. Croix, Sandra retreated into her world of loneliness and misgivings. The ordeal with Mark had left her devastated. She requested a leave of absent from her job and spent her days crying and her night fighting her way through unending nightmares. She refused to see Mark or accept his telephone calls.

Mark buried himself in work and cursed himself for believing that he could ever make Sandra understand a part of his life that he did not understand himself. Once again his world was in shambles, leaving him shackled to a woman that he had never wanted and deprived of one that he loved with no solution in sight.

Two weeks pass and Sandra went back to work. Everything around her was familiar but nothing is the same. She welcomed mornings, dreaded nights and despised all the hours in between. Mark had filled every fiber of her life. Without him there was not anything.

A week later, on a Wednesday morning around ten o'clock Hess Oil called for a crane operator and two welders. Sandra immediately dispatched a crane operator and two young men, whom were not only excellent welders, but also her close friends. Their relationships developed through working together and weekend interaction.

At two o'clock the emergency alarm went off in Hess. There is an accident in which one welder fell to the ground from the personnel basket of the crane. The other welder's foot got caught in the safety strap and he was slammed into a tower repeatedly and was dead before he was rescued. Seriously injured the fallen welder died almost immediately.

Upon hearing the horrible death of her two friends, Sandra went into a state of hysteria. Knowing her relationship to the two men Mark rushed to her side. Taking her home Mark called her doctor and he gave Sandra a sedative.

Forgetting all else, Mark never left Sandra's side. Her friends death and her disappointment in him had become more than she could bear. For days Sandra slipped in and out of a world that has become too painful to endure.

Mark faithfully nursed her through those painful hours. Lola came over every day to stay with her, insisting that Mark take short breaks. It was during some of her times with Lola that Sandra divulges her soul and voices her pain.

Upon hearing all that has happened Lola say, "Sandra, had I known Mark was married I would have been the first to tell you. That the biggest and best well kept secret that I have heard of in years. All I can say is that there must not be anything to that marriage or someone would have said something about it before now."

"Mark swears that he doesn't love her. He said that he never has and never will."

"That maybe true, Sandra, but it doesn't make

him any less married. The point is where are you going
to go from here? Do you believe Mark? Do you believe
what he is saying?"

"I don't know. I just don't know anything
anymore," moans Sandra. "At times I think that I do,
then at others times I just don't know."

"Do you still love him?"

"That's the hard part, I love him so much that it
hurts. I want to believe him Lola. Lord knows I do.
But he has hurt me. He deceived me. He says that he
didn't. He says that he was afraid to tell me the truth,
therefore he didn't tell me anything, because he was
afraid of losing me."

"Well, did he?" asked Lola. "Did he lose you?'

"I don't know. It hurt too badly to think about
it," said Sandra.

"Well you are going to have to think about it,
Sandra," Lola said. "He has either lost you or he
hasn't; only you know the answer to that. Until you
decide exactly what you are running from, running
from him is not the answer."

"How am I suppose to know that?" asked
Sandra.

"The same damn way you know everything else.
Knowing Mark as I do, I am sure there is more to this
than he has told you. Go on Sandra give him a chance
to explain. Then if you are not satisfy with his
explanation you can walk away knowing that you are
not wrong. Talk to the man. How much worst can it
become. You are crying your eyes out day and night as
it is. Talk to him Sandra, talk to him."

Shortly after Mark returned, as Lola was leaving she walked over to the bed before she left and leaned over to kiss Sandra's cheek and whispered, "Remember, talk to him."

Upon returning, thoroughly exhausted physically and mentally, Mark collapsed into a chair near the bed where Sandra lies. He placed his head in his hands seeking relief from the driving pressure of the events surrounding him.

For days he had been at Sandra's side, not saying anything concerning their relationship, just attending to her needs. She was slowly coming around and he knew that it would be just a matter of time before she shut him out again. His only choice would be to do as she wished.

Mark closed his eyes and laid back against the chair just as Sandra whispered his name. In the quiet room the faint sound of her voice is just above a whisper, it is the only sound to be heard, yet Mark does not believe his ears until once again he heard her more clearly, saying, "Mark."

He sat up straight and looked at Sandra. She rested on her elbow with her hand cupping her cheek, staring at him.

"Did you call me Sandra?"

"Yes I did. Mark we need to talk."

"Sandra I have said all I know to say, which is I love you. There is nothing else that I can say."

"Mark this is about more than love. It is about us and our lives and what our realities are. I am learning things about you that I never imagined as being part of your life. How am I supposed to handle this, especially the part about your wife?"

"That's the least important part of my life. She is nothing to me Sandra. She never has been and she never will be. I told you about her because I want to be free. I didn't want her standing between us. I love you. For the time being can you just please accept that?"

Before Sandra could speak again, Mark informed her, "As a carpenter and furniture designer, I make furniture between times in a workshop in back of my house and sell it out of my store on the waterfront. Since I met you I got a salesperson to work in the store full time, which frees me up to do as I wish. My woodwork and furniture is the backbone of my livelihood. My pieces of custom furniture sell extremely well.

"I support Mira and the house. I always leave her allowance on the kitchen table. I've never loved or wanted her. I don't account to her and she doesn't account to me and we have never slept together, I have never physically touched her. The only thing Mira and I share is a meaningless marriage certificate. Please believe me Sandra."

Sandra thoughtfully said, "Mark, every since St. Thomas, I haven't been able to talk to anyone, not even you, about what happened until today. I talked to Lola, I told her everything. She made me face myself. In doing so I realized that I never gave you a chance, even as you tried to explain."

Mark sat astonished and amazed, completely surprised by Sandra's attitude and words.

She went on saying, " As I recall it you could have just made love to me without saying a word, God knows I begged you hard enough and I also know that you wanted to. But you chose to be truthful with me instead and I chose not to hear you. Everything that you said was true, had you told me earlier, I would not have let you near me. I would have run away just as I did when you finally did tell me, and I am sorry."

Her words surprised him to the point of almost weeping Mark said, "I can't believe the words that I am hearing. I thought it was all over, Sandra. I thought it was all over. I only came here to be by your side when you needed someone. Despite how I love you I never expected anything from you and now like always, you are giving me everything."

The only way that Sandra could express her feelings was by placing an assuring hand on Mark's cheek. The touch of Sandra's soft, warm hand went directly to Mark's heart. Mark was scared, excited and grateful. He thought, oh God, please don't let her change her mind.

Sandra said, "I love you Mark. I don't want to ever loose you. I heard everything that you said to me in St. Thomas, but when the picture was no longer near perfection for me, pride, prejudice and my holier than thou attitude made me close my ears, heart and mind to your every word.'

Mark said, "You don't have to explain, Sandra... baby. I am happy just having you back."

"Please, let me talk Mark," begged Sandra. "It will make me feel better. Today I got a lot of straight talk from Lola. I allowed myself to feel instead of think. I have done too much thinking, now I realize that the only feeling I have that really matters is my love for you. I don't know a lot of things but this I know, I love you, Mark Landers."

Mark closed his eyes and took a deep breath as if he was inhaling an answered prayer. All he ever wanted was to have Sandra to look beyond the harshness of reality and see the beauty of possibility and above all his love for her.

Sandra placed her other hand on the side of his face and drew him down within reach and kissed his lips, whispering, "Darling stop trying to explain any further."

Then she pulled him onto the bed beside her, saying, "All evening I have been secretly wondering if you would like a little closeness and a smidgen of a zesty love exercise? Instead of talking lest play some 'show me'."

Although it is what he needs so badly Mark hadn't dared hope for any physical assurance from Sandra so soon, but there it was within his reach. She was again committing herself to him.

Mark prayed that the flame that he once kindled so easily in Sandra still lay flickering just below her emotionally shattered surface.

He began to tenderly caress her as he kissed and touched every vulnerable spot on her. With deliberate strokes and words of adoration, Mark bestowed a series of little pleasure upon Sandra with every attribute that God had endowed him with.

His emotional nurturing thoroughly aroused Sandra quickly becoming accessible and responded with an unprecedented over flowing of emotions.

Trembling like a wounded bird in his hands she

clung to Mark, sobbing softly. There was no resistance in her.

Incapable of waiting any longer, Sandra slid her hands between Mark's thighs and began to massage him through his pants. He groaned with pleasure and spread his legs to her. Sandra slipped off her gown just as Mark stood up to step out of his pants and under drawers. Just as his pants were around his knees, Sandra gave him a quick shove and sent him off balance causing him to land on his back on the soft carpet beside the bed. She rolled out of bed landing on top of him and grasped his manhood she said, "I owes you all of this baby from St. Thomas and more. Now I will make sure that you get all that is due to you."

Sandra sent her tongue gliding into his ear, while her hand clutching his petrified organ, hurriedly struggled to freed it from his partially removed pants enough to lowered herself onto it. Upon impaling herself on him, squeezing her muscles as she forced him to deeply penetrate her. Then she moved her body upon his to suit her pleasure, wiggling and pressing down onto him. Mark closed his hands about her hips and shuddered with delight.

Yet, no matter how much pleasure she generated in Mark, it was not enough. In an instant Mark flipped Sandra over onto her back and showered her with swift deep thrusts. Like a flaming swords his fiery penetrations caused her succumb to screams born of pure happiness.

Between her energized thighs Mark sought total forgiveness as he skillfully and consistently vigorously kneaded her. He administered to Sandra

Ophelia M. Turner

until her soul exploded and she cried out, "I love you Mark. I need you, Mark! Oh how I love you."

Her cry told him that once again he was resting safely in the harbor of her love and the tide of emotional justice was flowing in his favor. With his life desire no longer drifting on a stormy sea of indecision his fondest wishes were fulfilled. It's with obliging enthusiasm that Mark finally escalated to the apex of satisfaction knowing that he didn't have to live without her. Firmly sheltered inside of each others willing sanctuary they drifted off into a perfect sleep.

Some hours later, toward the wee hours of dawn, Sandra was aroused to find Mark's pulsating body ardently caressing hers from the insides. Hovering between awareness and slumber from somewhere beyond the realms of reality, instinctively, she thrashed about beneath him in wild adoration. Sandra became so overwhelmed by his enthusiastic lovemaking that her breathing almost ceased.

Mark clung to Sandra in desperation. With each movement of his body and every flow of his breath, Mark constantly swore, "Sandra. I love only you, my darling Sandra. I'll never let you go no matter what."

Inundated by his heated thrusts Sandra's body vigorously response to Mark's every word sometimes moaning, sometimes crying and sometimes simply praying but at all times knowing life without him wasn't worth living. She cried out,

"Mark, I love you, too."

Sandra realized that she loved Mark totally and unconditionally to the point that she was pass caring about anything or anyone except him. She surrendered him her all with forgiveness becoming her only option.

CHAPTER TWENTY-TWO

Mark, Mira, Marie, and Things

After being at Sandra's side for weeks Mark returned to home to find Mira waiting for him. She was sitting in the corner of the dimly lit living room, her piecing dark eyes gazing at him shone like those of a cunning cat. He walked right pass her and headed for his room. He made no attempt to acknowledge her presence.

She spoke in a low, snarling voice. "The big man now returns. He gave her all. She took all without no shame. So now it's done, so you think,"

Making no reply, Mark went on his way. The lingering thrill of Sandra still stirring in his loins let him know that nothing else in the world really mattered now.

Almost hissing as she spoke, Mira said, "You think that you have it all now, huh, big man, as well as all of the answers, yes? Well, we'll see about that."

Mark went into his room and slammed the door

behind him. But Mira's voice rang through, saying, "The time done come for me to speak or forever hold my peace. The time is done come and this I tell you," she called out after him. "Remember this my love, until death do we part! It is until death do we part!"

Even though Sandra loved Mark, every day the thought of him being married to Mira became unbearable. She pondered, how could he have not shared this information with her before? Now that he had there was still so much that she had to know.

Her first mission becomes to see and know Mira. Early one Saturday morning she heads for the rain forest. She drove her car to the foot of the hill and parked it there. Then she travels by foot to the edge of Mark's property. In the background, Sandra saw a modest, white cottage that was almost concealed by large plants, running vines and bushes. The well kept and cared for plant life was dense. Off to the far side of the building Mira was working in a large garden. Sandra crouched down behind a bunch of aloe plants. Parting the tall aloe leaves with her hands, peeping through them, she took a long look at Mira. She is beautiful, thought Sandra. Her coco butter colored skin was protected from the morning sun by a wide brimmed straw hat that also shaded her cold black eyes. Mira's long black braids of hair dangled loosely in the breeze as she dug around the plants that sprung up out of the ground's dark soil. Her flawless, delicate features and slender waistline were not what Sandra expected to see. Jealousy seized her heart. Sadly Sandra thought, she is beautiful, how can Mark say that she is nothing to him?

After spying on Mira for a short while, Sandra made her way back to her car and sat there for hours crying in confusion. She thought, dear God how can Mark not want her when she is so beautiful? Please don't let him be lying to me.

After seeing Mira, Sandra was more dissatisfied than ever. Every time Mark left her she imagined him being with Mira and her heart ached. Who is this woman, Mira? What is she really like? Sandra needs answers but she had promised to believe Mark and she didn't want to pester him with her insecurities or reveal her smoldering jealousy.

While Sandra had so few Trinidadian friends and none of them knew Mark, she had a larger number of Haitian friends and maybe some of them know Mira. The problem is getting them to part with any information. Islanders do not talk to outsiders freely. Nevertheless, since Mark had not satisfied her curiosity about Mira, she felt that she had to get some answers for herself.

In the course of her immigration paperwork, Sandra had met a high priestess that conducted church services in the apartment building next to hers. They had spoken on several occasions and Sandra had been invited to attend their services, but, upon learning that the service consisted of séances, voodoo and fortune telling, she gracefully declined the invitation. Since learning that Mira was Haitian she hoped that this woman could have some information about her and Mark.

Early that Friday evening, Sandra sat by her

window and watched for Madam Marie to walk through the apartment's complex courtyard. Upon seeing her, Sandra raced down the stairway and caught her before she entered her apartment building. When Sandra reached her, Madam Marie was standing before her open doorway attempting to gather the packages that rested on the floor while she unlocked the door. Sandra's sudden appearance startled her and she turned quickly to face her. She relaxed when she recognized Sandra.

Sandra said, "Hi! I didn't mean to startle you. If you will please give me one minute, I need to talk to you."

"What have I to say that you would want to hear?" asked Madam Marie.

"Maybe much, if you wish too." said Sandra.

"Come then," said Madam Marie.

Inside her apartment she instructed Sandra, saying, "Take off your shoes."

Madam Marie points to a white porcelain washbasin filled with water that sat on a stand near the doorway and said, "Wash your hands there."

Sandra did as she was instructed, then Madam Marie led her to the dining room with walls covered with draperies and multi-colored curtains that hung heavily at each window. There were incenses burning amidst many-lit candle and crosses hung everywhere. Clear glass urns filled with roots, herbs and leaves lined a long shelf in the wall. A very strange, sweet, spicy, potent and peculiar aroma filled the room, an eerie feeling swept over Sandra. Once inside of the dining room, Sandra was asked to sit down at a round tapestry covered table. Madam Marie came in and sat across from her. She lit a white candle and started burning more incense. Reaching out to Sandra, Madam Marie said, "Let me see your hands!"

This was not what Sandra had in mind. She merely wanted to ask about Mira and Mark and find out if Madam Marie knew them. Yet, she stretched out her hands.

Sandra looked at the woman's dark, ivory smooth face, whose large brown eyes peered down onto the backs of her open hands. She began to massage and rub Sandra's downturned palms. After performing a short ritual resembling a prayer, she turned Sandra hands over with her palms upward and began starring into them, saying, "This is your lifeline."

Then there was an eerie silence in the room, as within minutes Madam Marie seemed to go into some kind of trance. The deep long, drawn in breaths she took shattered silence that once filled the room. She began caressing Sandra's hands. Then she slowly blew her hot breath onto on Sandra's palms. Fear began to possess Sandra. She had heard of this sort of thing, but had never seen it. Suddenly Madam Marie spoke in a forlorn voice saying, "There is much fog surrounding your life that holds many secrets. There is a wall between you and a loved one that must be shattered, for many hands with binding threads have done much in the dark, but the light will come soon. Love, patience and understanding are your only weapons. Much strength, belief and patience will be required of you if you are to prevail. Often true love comes with a very high price. Beware... Beware!"

Then Madam Marie went someplace beyond the realm of reality her body gave a sudden, violent jerk as a look of horror covered her face. Shaking uncontrollably, she seemed to be struggling to break free of the place that she was in. Her eyes suddenly flew open and she leaped up and looked at Sandra in the most frightening way, saying in a loud demanding Haitian voice, "Go now. Go! There is nothing more for you here. There is nothing for me to tell you. Go right now I say."

Shocked by Madam Marie's unexpected change of attitude, Sandra quickly got up and rushed towards the door.

Breathing hard with trembling hands Madam Marie was almost running ahead of Sandra to the door and she hastily opened it for her, saying, "Go now! Go right now and may God protect you."

Completely puzzled by the woman's rudeness, Sandra watched as Madam Marie tossed hands full of table salt behind her all of the way off of the steps.

Sandra left Madam Marie's apartment more confused than ever. She wished that she had never gone there, as she wondered what had she really seen?

One week later, on a Friday, it was a local government holiday, which meant that Sandra had the day off. She took the opportunity to prepare an early dinner for herself and Mark. She went all out because it had been such a long time they had a long free weekend. There were no weekend band engagements for Mark and there was no unexpected overtime for her to pull at Robbins and Robbins. It was a perfect time for them to be together. Sandra really thought that the shadow of Mira, as well as Diana, had faded and no longer effected her emotions.

Sandra broiled lobsters, grilled large steaks, tossed a green salad, made potato salad and chilled a bottle of wine.

By the time Mark arrived, the table was set with a white linen tablecloth and colorful dishes. It was times like these that enriched her hours with Mark. Sandra always viewed these moments as a preview of the life that she would eventually share with him.

Sandra knew that pretending did not make her dreams a reality, nevertheless she did. Realizing this made tears well up in her eyes. She sat misty-eyed, gazing at Mark across the properly set table separating them.

When he saw that a forlorn look had replaced the smile that he had basked in just moments before, Mark said, "Let me inside of your thoughts baby."

"Just thinking about us, that's all," she answered softly.

"That's no reason to be sad," said Mark, slightly smiling. "Don't you know by now that I love you? Knowing that should make you happy."

"I'm not sad. I was just wishing, a little," she admitted.

"Wishing what?" he asked.

"Wishing this day and time would last forever. I was pretending that it would."

"Pretending will soon come to an end. I promise you that sweetheart, it will soon come to an end, Sandra."

She smiled. He reached across the table and gave a hard squeeze to her hand to confirm his promise. Smiling, they gazed at each other for a moment then proceeded to finish their dinner.

After dinner, they sat on the sofa, watching the blazing sun take its daily late evening dive into the blue Caribbean Sea as the rolling waves and the frolicking breeze among the palm leaves preformed its exit song. Sandra lay in Mark's arms where any other time she would have been perfectly content, but today she had no peace.

Sandra tried to push Mira into the land of the forgotten, but she would not remain there. Again, as many times before, her shadow slowly emerged. How did she sound when she spoke to Mark? How did she interact with Mark? How did they spend their time together? The bubbling slush pools of unanswered questions in her mind were refusing to let it rest.

She heard herself saying to Mark, "Tell me about Mira. I need to know all about her, Mark. I'll not let it make a difference between us, but I need to know all about her."

Mark said, "Where is this coming from Sandra? I thought we had agreed..."

"We did agree," she interrupted. "But, Mira won't agree. She creeps into my thoughts when I least expect her to. She'll not leave me alone. Tell me about her, Mark. Maybe that will help me to eradicate her."

"There is not really anything to tell. She doesn't matter to me. Don't let her matter to you," pleaded Mark.

"That will not make her go away. I've tried,"

insisted Sandra.

"If you must talk about her I'll tell you this much," said Mark. "I'd seen Mira around mostly during my youth, but I had never known her. One day I turned around and she was in my life. She is secretive, silent and imperceptible. She and I share a house in the rain forest on the west end of the island. She hates the city and I'm glad. I can enjoy total freedom when I'm away from her. Not that she bothers me or questions my comings and goings. I'm just the happiest when I'm not around her. When I do get home she is usually sleeping, so I don't have to deal with her."

Sandra sat eyeing Mark and detecting the uneasiness in his voice as he spoke of Mira. In her mind her thoughts kept crying out, why is this even happening? She has no right in our life.

"Even before you came into my life I stayed away from Mira. When I wasn't working at Robbins and Robbins, in the store, or in the shop I was playing at clubs or hotels. Before I met you almost two years ago, I was quite content to live and work as I had. Sex, love, and passion weren't a part of my lifestyle with Mira, but every since the first time I laid eyes on you a lightening bolt of life suddenly energized my world. At that moment I knew, no matter what, you were the one. I knew with everything in me that I had to have you. I believed that you knew and felt the same way too.

"For a long time I fought my feelings for you until I faced the fact that running from you was useless. I loved you and I began tapering my life toward that end.

"It took me a long time to gain your trust. But when the possibility of a life with you became a reality I took fewer hotel engagements and stopped putting in overtime at Robbins and Robbins and took fewer orders for furniture. I needed time just for you, Sandra. I needed time for being in love, for being loved by you and making love to you; that was all I really cared about."

Sandra sadly moaned, "Mark, for almost two years of knowing you in which for over a year you've let me live like we were the only two people in the world. Now I find that I am sharing you with Mira."

"No! No! No, Sandra," protested Mark. "What can I say or do to convince you that you don't share me with anyone? If we were the only people in the world before why aren't we now? You never have and never will share me. I am all yours. I live, sleep, eat and breathe you. You are in my heartbeat. You are my life. No one has any part of me except you. Don't you ever doubt that fact, Sandra! You are my heart's regulator. There is no one else."

"Make me understand all of this, Mark," she pleaded. " Better still make me believe it. I want that more than anything in life."

"You must believe it, Sandra. You must. Mira and I is a very long and complicated story. Right now is not the time for it. Just say that you will always trust and love me no matter what. Promise me that. I have only been in love twice before you and Mira was never, ever one of those times. Please believe me, she was never one of those times. I swear. So will you promise to believe and trust in me?" begged Mark. "Just let me love you."

Sandra laid her head on his chest and said, "I promise. I love you too much to do anything else."

Even though Sandra gave Mark her promise, questions still lashed her mind like rolling tides lashed the reefs rising out of the sea just beyond her windows. She knew no peace.

Mark and Sandra spoke very little of Mira for a little while, but the lack of knowledge concerning Mark's marriage and his relationship with Mira still emerged at the most unexpected times to cast a shadow over Sandra's emotions. At times it overpowered the effect of their love life, as insatiable and utterly consuming as it had become.

Less than several weeks after Mark had told Sandra that he was married, exhausted from swimming, hiking, and playing in the sand, they laid side by side in the sand at Creamer's Park, a large beach area on the east end of the Island,

They had plans for spending the entire day at the beach, therefore they traveled with a well packed picnic basket, containing drinks, food, battery powered radio, towels, blankets and all of the necessities for comfort.

Sandra laid tanning on a blanket beside Mark with her eyes closed against the bright sunlight without sunglasses. She didn't want her sunglasses to make an outline around her eyes. Her breathing is low and her thoughts are happy. The weather is beautiful. Everything is in place to make their day perfect.

From time to time Mark rubbed splashes of suntan lotion on all of Sandra's skin that her bikini didn't cover. Sandra moans as the touch of Mark's hands inflames her and the cool lotion renders a soothing, refreshing and pleasing feeling.

Mark's voice was low and solemn when he said, "Sandra, I have given this much thought-- I have asked Mira for a divorce.

Sandra was completely unprepared for his words. She didn't expect him to even have this conversation, especially when Mira was supposedly the last thing on their minds. Sandra was speechless.

Mark explained, "I can't go on like this any longer. Since we have been together you have given my life fullness and meaning. It's not as if Mira doesn't know about us. She has a way of knowing everything, but she hasn't really been hassling me, because you are a stateside woman. She thought that you were a sex toy that I became overly preoccupied with for the moment. She has said as much. She said that she didn't think that I was serious about you until now. But now she knows that I don't intend to ever give you up."

In order to enjoy their lives for sometimes Sandra had dismissed Mira from her mind, especially today. It was easier just to forget that she ever existed so she seldom spoke of her anymore, neither did Mark. As much as she wanted him, she would have never asked him to divorce Mira, it had to be his decision.

As Mark's words sunk in Sandra's eyes sparkled with delight. She could barely control her excitement as Mark went on talking.

"I asked her yesterday," he said.

Sandra looked at Mark with wide, happy eyes.

Now he was saying words that she wanted to hear and they were sounding unreal. She heard herself asking, "Are you sure this is what you want?"

Mark answered, "I'm very sure. I've thought about it for a long time. I should've done this a long time ago before we ever met. Now, since I've met you there's no way I'll stay in a useless, dead end marriage."

"You say you should've divorced her a long time ago."

"Yes, I should've," he replied.

Looking at him she asked, "What stopped you?"

"Things!"

"What things?"

Heaving a restless sigh, Mark repeated, "Just things."

Looking intently at him, Sandra said, "We've never really talked about Mira. I had to know what she looked like so I made it my business to see her.

Surprised, he asked, "When did you do that? When did you see her?"

"A few weeks or so after you told me about her," said Sandra while thoughtfully scooping up a handful of sand and letting it slither down through her long, slender fingers, back onto the beach.

Looking over at him she said, "But I still don't know anything about her, except that she is beautiful. Whenever we do talk about her, you never really say anything except you don't love her. Why did you marry her anyway if you don't love her? Was it because of her looks?"

He answered saying, "I've often asked myself

that same damn question. To be honest, that's something that I've never really understood myself so how can I make you understand? But I will do all I can to make you understand to the best of my ability."

Curiosity etched it way into Sandra's voice, "You married her, so there had to be something. Does these things that you speak of hinge on Mira?"

Still playing the sand, Sandra whispered. "Do you think that at one time it was love?"

Mark quickly shouted, "Hell no! Hell no! It was anything but love. As I've already told you, I've been in love twice in my life and Mira was never either of those times."

Looking very puzzled as she lay on her side in the sand, Sandra said, "Now that is what I really don't understand!"

Mark timidly replied, "That makes us even unless I believe in destiny or something else."

"Something else like what? Tell me what!" Sandra insisted, "Tell me about you and your wife. Tell me everything about it."

"All of it sounds stupid. So just forget it," muttered Mark.

"No, tell me about Mira anyway. Tell me all about her" pleaded Sandra. "There is still much that I need to know if I am to go on."

In a low voice Mark said, "It's like I told you before, it's a long story and not a nice one. I hadn't planned on spending today talking about Mira and the past. I just wanted to make you happy by telling you about the divorce. Let's just forget about Mira. Pretend I never mentioned her name," he said.

"No I can't, because you did mention her name.

So tell me about her. We've got all day," Sandra insisted.

Mark had set his mind against recalling the dreadful facts of all he knew now Sandra was asking that he open up and share his memories with her.

Sandra braced herself for whatever it was that she must hear. Together, beneath an innocent clear blue sky that was to blanket their romantic outing on a marvelous sun drenched day upon a picture perfect beach. However Mark's mind bolted back to the darkness of his past, and he mentally quaked as emotionally he was forced to step backward into an episode of the most painful days of his life.

As Mark began to speak sadness overshadowed his face. His journey backward had begun and there was no turning back until Mark had told Sandra about Mira and Mira only. His love for Twila was something he didn't care to relive or share at the moment. Even now thoughts of her were too unbearable.

He thought Twila, like Diana, was a precious part of his past that was forever lost so why do we need to talk about them?

Sadness veiled his eyes as he remembered and his thoughts caused long dark shadow of pain to sprout within and cast their reflections over his face like dark clouds rising at high noon covering the sun's bright face. Sandra watched as distress etched lines on his brow and turned the corners of his tightened lips downward. She saw Mark's body when it suddenly gave a tremendous jerk. She was unaware that he had slammed shut the door of his mind trying to flee what he deemed a living hell. Mark's body jerked again so violently that Sandra asked, "What in the world is happening to you? Tell me what went on with you just then?"

The look on his face immediately caused her to withdraw her question. She saw a mask of agony sweep over his face and she decided that it was better just to allow him to simmer in his caldron of smoldering memories of whatever he found too horrible to share with her. Sandra was fully aware of how Mark was bleeding from probing so deeply into his obscure wounds of his past. She had no desire to invoke any more misery or to keep his gaping wounds reeking with pain. She knew that the very best remedy was diversion

Attempting to put a lighter spin on their conversation, Sandra laughingly said, "Try as I will, I damn well just don't understand why you married her, or better still, why did she marry you? Now...if you had ever laid that man root thing on her like you did me, I would understand the entire whole saturation. If you had dipped her just once she would had the 'can't help its.' But since you say that never happened, I just don't understand a damn thing."

Mark looked at Sandra for a moment. He saw the impish smile dancing around her lips. He gave Sandra a long, hard kiss and said, "Well then I guess you will never understand, cause she never got one damn little bit."

Kissing her again he said, "Now see if you understand that and guess why I am divorcing her, you inquisitive little nymph."

Instantly she seized the brief hint that his attitude indicated playfulness and she immediately retaliated for his teasing remark by pelting him with a handful of sand.

Then she leaped up and raced off as fast as she could toward the sea. In fast pursuit Mark took off after her. Sandra couldn't escape Mark's reprisal. Catching her at the water's edge, he grabbed her and they plunged into the water. There he vigorously dunked her several times for her bad behavior.

Sandra wrestled with Mark until she managed to fling one arm around his neck. Facing him, laughing hysterically, she swung up onto him and wrapped her legs around his waist with her hips straddling his. She crushed her lips to his. He tightly embraced her.

With one arm securely locked around Mark's neck Sandra slipped her free hand beneath the seat of his swim trunks and clutched his hardness partially encircling it. While clinging to his firmness she opened her thighs as she pulled the solid muscle free of his tight fitting swim pants and used it to shove aside the narrow seat of her swimsuit and she began to stuff herself with it.

Grasping Sandra's hips and with a forceful upward thrust, Mark completed the entry and filled her with the swiftness that she desired.

The breast high waves swirling around them added to the momentum of their performance further churning the fervor of their enthusiastic sensual rhythm. Their entwined bodies lurched and rolled with the swelling tides as they administered to each other the required healing for their raw emotions.

Embracing they rose and fell as they swirled

and lurched about. Sandra soon cried out with explicit joy and Mark uttered a deep satisfying groan, each knowing that this was all the solace their souls required.

CHAPTER TWENTY-THREE

The Past and the Stranger

A few weeks later Sandra went into her office at Robbins and Robbins to learn that she had to launch a drive for hiring additional manpower. There was an unscheduled 'turnaround' coming up in the Hess Oil plant in several days and she needed to get prepared.

The morning surge of new employment seekers had passed and the afternoon applicants were few. Sandra was reviewing the new applications when a man about thirty-seven came in to apply for a job as a pipe fitter.

Sandra gave him an application and went on reviewing the earlier applications that she was piled up on her desk.

When the man finished the application he handed it to Sandra and returned to his seat. As she went over it she noticed that the man named Delroy Clemmons had listed his place of birth as Port-au-Prince, Trinidad, which was also Mark's hometown.

This immediately grabs her attention and she begins a conversation with Delroy Clemmons by saying, "A countryman of yours from Port-au-Prince is employed here as pipe fitter and carpenter."

"Oh really?"

"Yes! Maybe you two know each other."

"It's quite possible," said Mr. Clemmons. "What might his name be?"

"Mark Landers," she said. "He is one of our best employees."

"You are kidding me aren't you, Mrs. Dubois? Mark Landers doesn't really work here does he?"

"I assure you that I have no reason to kid you, Mr. Clemmons. I don't even know you. But it is apparent that you know Mark Landers."

"You are darn right I do. I haven't seen or heard from Mark in years. We were once very close friends."

"Really!" Then she asked, "How close?"

"He replied, "Very close. We shared a lot of our younger years. Our families lived in the same area. We slept over each other's house from time to time. We told each other just about everything."

Fingering his application Sandra looked curiously at him and asked, "What happened to change that?"

Mr. Clemmons change of voice denoted a sorrowful tone, as he said, "Well, after the horrible automobile accident that killed Twila, everything about Mark's life changed especially after he married that strange Haitian woman. That was something that I've never understood. It was as if I didn't know Mark anymore. He was there walking, breathing and sometimes talking. Had it not been for those facts I would have sworn that the man was dead.

"Soon after his marriage to that woman he seemed to have dropped from the face of the earth. I've wondered so many days where he was and what happened to him, but his family was closed mouthed about everything. Twila's death practically destroyed that family, especially Mark.

"I can't believe that Mark is really here. I often wondered where he went. I must look him up as soon as possible. I hope that he will want to see me. He is one hell of a nice person. I've missed him so much. He certainly was the best friend I ever had. I hope that he's found himself by now."

At the risk of appearing too interested in Mark's past, Sandra asked, "Who was Twila? Was she one of his family members?"

"Oh no! Of course not, to my knowledge she certainly was the only woman that Mark Landers had ever loved.

"From childhood they were inseparable. It was like they were joined at the hip. I guess you could say that all of their lives they were in love. They were to be married but she was killed in a freak car accident a short while before their wedding date. After that Mark just seemed to dry up and turned into a walking shadow. He was more like the walking dead, if you ask me.

"Everyone feared for his well being physically and mentally. That's why it was so unbelievable when he just up and married that Haitian woman that popped up from out of nowhere. Then they just disappeared from Trinidad without a trace. It was the strangest thing I've ever seen."

"You mean that there was no courtship or anything between Mark and this woman?" asked Sandra.

"None that anybody ever knew of, not anything. Suddenly she was there and then they were married. At least I was told that they were married. There was no ceremony that anyone knew of. I heard that the marriage took place before a Justice of the Peace.

"That certainly wasn't Mark's family's style. They are a proud and proper people. It seemed like they had no part in it. Like I said, it was all so damn strange," Delroy Clemmons said, as he sat shaking his head still in disbelief.

Any other time Sandra would have completed her work in record time. Now hours later Sandra sat dwelling on what Delroy Clemmons had told her concerning Mark. She wondered, "How much more is there about this man that I don't know?"

She also thought of Delroy Clemmons, the quiet, dark eyed man that wore his life upon his face, etched upon sun dried skin that was worn deep with furrows of worry and squinting lines around his eyes. He may have been Mark's youthful friend but life had taken its toll on him. His weary, narrow eyes spoke of the long hours that he gazed into the bright sunlight and the calluses on his thick hands told of many years of hard work. His natural warmth indicated that a friend was always a valued commodity to him. All of these things made her believe the seriousness of his words concerning Mark.

She felt Delroy's pain when he spoke of Twila's death and how it changed Mark into someone that he didn't know. She saw the grief in his eyes as he spoke of losing Mark to a woman and a world that he neither knew nor understood. His words took up residence in her mind. That very day Sandra determined she could no longer ignore any part of Mark's life that she felt compelled to understand and share.

It was almost five thirty when Mark arrived at Sandra's apartment. After dinner Sandra insisted that they sit in the living room. She had determined that Mark would not put her questions off by using any of his masterful and sensuous distractions.

She prepared him a gin and tonic on ice and took one for herself. Handing him his drink as he sat on the sofa she then sat on a chair across from him. As she fingered her drink she looked at him and said, "I had a very interesting thing happen at work today."

"How interesting?" he remarked as he took a sip of his icy drink glancing at her over the rim of his water beaded glass.

"Extremely interesting," she said in a calm voice. "Especially since it was about something concerning you."

"Concerning me?" Surprised by her answer he leaned back against his seat and asked, "Me? What about me? What?"

She calmly asked, "Do you know a man named Delroy Clemmons?"

"Damn right I do. He was my best friend. We went to school together. Delroy was a grade or so ahead of me but he was my best friend. We sort of lost touch over the years, why are you asking me about him?"

"He came into the office today and applied for a job,"

"Delroy is here? He is here in St. Croix? Delroy is really here?"

"Yes he is, and he was excited about learning that you are here too. He was so happy that it was difficult to restrain himself."

"How did he learn that I was here?"

"I told him. When I learned from his application that he was from Port-au-Prince, Trinidad, I simply asked him if he knew you and you can figure out the rest."

"Well I'll be damned! Who would've guessed the chances of that happening? Old Delroy turning up here in St. Croix after all of these years."

"That's not all, he told me about Twila, the accident and how it effected you after it happened."

Mark's entire countenance changed. His face became drawn, his eyes lost their light and his shoulders slumped. The glass of gin that he was holding leaned towards the floor, spilling its contents. It was like a vacuum suddenly sucked the life out of him. He made no reply.

Sandra caringly asked, "Mark, why didn't you tell me? Why did I have to hear it from a complete stranger?"

Mark sat there. His mouth developed a dry feeling. His body felt numb. An emptiness that he had almost forgotten instantly consumed his insides. Mark

felt like a man dangling between two worlds completely
undecided which he preferred, heaven or hell.

Anxiously Sandra asked, "Mark, are you going
to answer me? You said that you love me but today I
was told about Twila the only woman that you were
known to ever love. Try to imagine how I feel. I am
still reeling from learning about Mira, the wife that you
finally got around to telling me about, and learning
about Diana. Now just like Jack in a surprise box, up
pops Twila. Isn't it time that you told me everything? I
do mean every damn thing. Frankly, Mark, I don't
know how much more of this I can take of having you
piece meal your life out to me. How do you expect us to
have a future together when you constantly refuse to
share your life with me. Time after time you snatch the
intimacy out of our relationship by its roots when you
only tell half-truths or say nothing at all. Tell me
everything right now Mark or get the hell out of my life.
I can't keep going on like this."

Mark managed to say, "Sandra don't you think
that I have tried to tell you? Don't you think that I
would have if I had thought there was any chance in
hell that you could understand or even believe me?"

"Mark, you never gave me that chance. You are
always second-guessing me. Tell me! Let me decide.
You've just handed me bits and pieces of your life, or
nothing at all including a wife. Then you said, 'Just
forget about her. Forget about them, forget about it.'
I've dealt with Diana, now I've got Twila to deal with,
and like Diana she too is gone. But Mira is still here
what am I suppose to do forget about her too? How

much am I expected to forget? I can only endure so much Mark. If you love me like you say you do please tell me everything else there is to know. Do it right now if you really care about me and value our life together."

"Sandra, this night I promise that I will do the best that I can to tell you everything concerning Twila, Diana, Mira and me," mournfully, he solemnly said.

"Mira is a part of my past just like Twila and Diana. You are the only future that I hope to have. Just give me a chance to explain and please accept things as they are told."

Sandra placed her hands under her chin and with quizzical eyes and open ears she waited.

Mark began his story by saying "Having to tell you is as bad as if it was happening right now. This is hard for me Sandra. Now if at anytime this is too much for you I'll stop. But after today don't ever ask me about it again. This is something that I really want to forget."

Then reluctantly he began to speak in a low and drawn out voice. Painstakingly Mark vividly revealed his past with such details that it mesmerized Sandra. When he told her of his trip to Haiti, she said, "That must have been beyond awful."

As Mark explained his past to Sandra she dug the fingers of one hand into the arm of the plush chair and in the other hand clutched the empty glass that she had drained during Mark's painful revelation.

At one point Mark paused. Realizing that she really needed another drink, with her drained glass in hand, Sandra slowly stood up, went over and refilled her glass. Then she went over to the sofa and sat down beside Mark and began stroking his forearm with the palm of her empty hand, saying, "Go on Mark please. I really need to hear every word of this story. You have really captivated me with this almost unbelievable tale. It certainly sounds like a tangled web that originated in some sort of bizarre mystery novel. Now after hearing about Twila I can't figure out why you married the likes of Mira unless you were deaf, blind, and crazy. But you weren't so go on and tell me everything. Make me understand."

After several deep breaths Mark went back to telling her everything about his past.

Sandra sat up straight, barely breathing, hanging on Mark's every word. After Mark's long revelation, shocked and bewildered at hearing about the Doctor Fish and Twila's death and his marriage to Mira, Sandra cried "My Lord! What a story! Mark, this is far too much for me. You are right it is completely unbelievable. Oh my God! Wow!"

Completely amazed, Sandra asked, "If Mira was pregnant whatever happened to the baby?

Mark angrily shouted, "There was no baby. It was all a lie,"

"Why would she say she was pregnant if she wasn't?"

"Who in the hell knows why except to force my family into seeing that I married her without their interference or questions. I certainly couldn't help myself at that time. Who knows what really goes on in the mind of that damned woman? All I know is that she wasn't pregnant and I made damn sure that she never would be by me. I had enough will power to refuse to sleep with her. If she was a virgin when she married me and if there wasn't anybody else, as far as I know, she is still a virgin."

Blinking her eyes in astonishment several times at Mark's statement with a voice of disbelief she said, "Mark forgive me but I still find it hard to believe that you haven't ever touched her. Not even one tiny little bit?"

Skepticism reeked throughout Sandra's voice as she said, "Remember I have seen Mira. She may be sort of weird but she is a very good-looking woman. She could turn any man's head."

Mark snapped. "Look Sandra don't make a joke out of this thing having it happen was bad enough."

She snapped back, "I wasn't joking. I was just surprised. In view of all you have said so far tonight I guess nothing should really surprise me so just calm down. I guess I find it hard to believe that you passed her up as much as you enjoy getting it on."

"Well, you are not the only one that thinks that way. Nobody believes me. Not even the people that I trust the most," he moaned.

"Sandra you are forgetting that for a long time Twila was with me. Remember how I told you that she never left me alone not even in death? Twila came to me every night as real as you are now. Although I was dazed and half out of my mind I lived for those times; she was more to me than any woman could ever be. I realize now that I must have been dreaming but for me then it was real then. My dreams became my life. This went off and on for years then one day she was completely gone."

"Loving you as I do I can relate to that. I only pray that I will never lose you. Did anything else ever turn up about the accident to explain what may have caused it?"

"No, not really. However I did learn later that on the day after the accident an investigator went back to the place where it happened and took pictures of the surrounding area. Like everyone else he found nothing to support my story."

"Your story certainly is stranger than strange but what is stranger is why you continued to stay with Mira, especially with everything being as it was."

Mark simply replied, "Things."

"What do you mean things? You are always saying 'things'. Explain these things to me Mark."

Mark said, "Sandra, you must learn to keep an open mind. This is a strange world with strange things that are hard to explain. There are things that even defy all natural and scientific explanations even in these days and times."

Becoming a little irritated, Sandra demanded, "Please try to explain these so called things to me. I have a right to know what these things are because whatever they are, if they are a part of you and now you are all mixed up in my life, they are a part of me too. So take all the time you need.

Mark asked, "Sandra can I explain the wind to you? No! I can't. I can't see, touch or taste it. But still I know that it is there because I can feel it, stronger at some times than at others. That is the same way other things are. Sandra you must accept the fact that there are many things in this life that defy all explanation, you can feel them, but you can't touch, see or taste them, sometimes you can't even name them, yet you know they are there.

"Three years into my marriage with Mira, I happened go to a party and a seer was there. She was a Haitian and she was reading people. When she got to me she became reluctant to deal with me and began to seal up her wares.

"I looked at her questioningly but she cast a cold look at me and continued to pack up and refused to read me. She paused long enough between putting away her paraphernalia to say, 'Man yu got plenty trouble. Me can't tell yu nothin'. So don't yu stand der givin' me dat what fo' look but dis I kin tell yu', yu done eat de Doctor Fish and now de Doctor Fish don' eat yu. Yu need somebody better dan me to help yu now. God have mercy on yu.'"

Bewildered Sandra asked, "What is a seer? What is this about her reading people and you? What in the hell is all this Doctor Fish business?"

"I believe in that stateside you call these seers, 'readers or fortune tellers'," said Mark.

"You mean in this day and time you believe in those phony people?"

"Maybe I do and maybe I don't."

"Now tell me what in the hell is it with this so-called Doctor Fish?" asked Sandra. "You keep talking about it. What in the hell is it?"

Mark explains, "It is just a fish except when it's fixed. In the states you all say root it. When it's fixed it takes your will. After you are rooted you will marry the woman or be her man slave and you can't help yourself.

"When a woman conjures up that fish and cooks it up a certain way and you eat it then she got you messed up real good."

Flippantly, Sandra remarked, "I really don't know what you mean when you say fixed? There are only so many ways to fix a fish, you fry it, bake it, broil it or stew it. What in the hell else can you do to a damn fish? So, what in the devil are you talking about?"

Mark reply angrily, "That is all you know but there is plenty more that you don't know Sandra!"

"What else is there to know?" Sandra heatedly inquires, "Black Hand?"

Mark made no reply. He just looked away.

Sandra burst out laughing, saying, "You mean in this day of so much enlightenment and education you are telling me you married up with a woman because she fed you some damned fish that she had fixed? Don't be so damn naïve, Mark, or play me for a fool."

Mark voice seethed as he sternly cautioned her saying, "Sandra, if you don't know what you are talking about don't talk."

"Well I may not know much but I don't believe no fish can make you marry someone that you don't want to, or love, no matter how much you conjure it up. That is simply stretching it far too much. I asked you for the reason that you married Mira and you are blaming it on a damn fish. Get real Mark. Confess and say you got carried away or something, anything!"

Submissively Mark said, "If those are your thoughts I won't try to change them as long as you know that I never loved Mira and never had any intention of marrying her."

Then he added, "Sandra there is enough that you don't know to make a new world. Every since the day that Christ ordered the fish caught and that gold piece was taken out of its mouth fish have been a powerful religious symbol. Like all symbols even money can represent good or evil depending upon who is using it. The fish is no different. If it is used for evil then evil will be. 'Become a fishers of men' has been taken literally by some women and they will use all manner of evil to do it.

"Believe me, Sandra, I know what evil is. From the day I set foot in Haiti to deliver that furniture I have been the victim of evil and my life has been a living hell. I spent years standing on the sidelines of my life watching it go on without being capable of having any control over it. Like a sleepwalker unable to awake I became a part of events that were repulsive and humiliating like my marriage to Mira. I've had a desire to do one thing only to find myself doing another. I lived like a puppet with someone else pulling the strings. If you haven't been hypnotized or been a sleepwalker, lived with your hands and feet in bondage or lived through an out of body experience where you observed what was taking place and were helpless to change it, if you have never known or experienced any of these then you will never know what I am talking about, no matter what I say. Until you have been there don't you ever try to tell me what can't happen ever again, just remember that."

As Mark spoke, his pain became almost tangible and he trembled at remembering his past.

Sandra regretted the attitude that she had taken

and she felt humbled. She recalled even when he delayed sharing with her the fact that he was married he still told her. He showed his love for her every day in so many ways. Mark had never given her any reason to really doubt his truthfulness.

Looking directly into his eyes Sandra said, "Mark, I am truly sorry. I had no right to speak to you as I did. I guess there's much in this world that is beyond my comprehension but I do know you do love me. Forgive me!"

Speaking softly Mark said, "There is nothing to forgive. If I were in your place I might have said the same thing. I couldn't believe it myself until my father told me about what happened to a man he knew."

Sandra sat very still, not being nearly as arrogant as before, absorbing Mark's every word.

"As I told you Mira and I had been married for three years before I came across that seer. When the old woman told me about being fixed I never believed her because I didn't believe in the Doctor Fish tales that I had heard from others. I just went about what I thought was my business."

Mark went on saying, "Sometime later I told my father about meeting the seer. When my father heard what she said about the Doctor Fish he became very upset and began yelling at me asking why hadn't I told him sooner. For the first time my father began to understand some of my strange behavior. My father told me there is truth rooted in the use of the Doctor Fish. He told me of a woman who tried to do the same thing to a friend of his with the Doctor Fish. But he was too smart for her because as a young boy his grandfather had severely warned him of the wickedness of some women. His friend realized what she was up to and when she wasn't looking he fed the Doctor Fish to the dog that was under the table."

Sniggering softly, Sandra said, "Then I suppose the dog married her."

"No!" Mark sharply answered her. "The dog didn't marry her instead the dog ran down to the church and sat on the church steps howling day and night. Nobody could make him go away. The dog was roped and carried away. He broke loose and returned to the church with pieces of the rope tied to him.

Once again he went and sat the on the steps of the church and howled. This went on and on for weeks. Finally someone had to take that dog off and shoot him.

"My father was not lying. He would never make up a story like that. Furthermore, despite what you may or may not believe, I know what has happened to me."

Sandra proposed to Mark, "Let's assume that this Doctor Fish business is true. Why didn't someone see it before? What took so long?"

"When Twila got killed my life went to hell. Sandra I was so grief-stricken over Twila that everyone accredited my strange behavior to my grief. Some people even assumed that I might have turned to Mira out of my grief, because she resembled Twila so much, they were cousins you know. There was just far too much emotion raging during that time for anyone to even consider Black Hand."

"All right let me assume that it was because of Black Hand and that Doctor Fish stuff that made you marry Mira, now what? Are you free of all that fish stuff now?"

Mark declared, "Yes I am. I took care of that some time ago. After confiding in my father we found a high priest with the power that knew what to do. It wasn't easy, but it got done. For over a week I had to consume a strong, bitter, potion to cleanse my body. Then the priest told me to search my house and look for a glass jar with strange contents in it. When I find it he said to open it, stir it vigorously, and immediately burn whatever I found inside of it along with the jar, and wash my body and my house down in sea water."

"What?" Seawater? Why seawater? Asked Sandra, more surprised than curious.

Mark said " Maybe it was the salt or maybe it's Biblical, I suppose. Anyway that's what he said to do. I don't really know why. I just did as I was told.

"I had to pick my time when Mira was in the garden or the woods. It took me more than a couple of weeks but I found a glass jar behind the steps near the front door. It was well hidden in a small space. I noticed a loose board on the outside wall in back of the steps with fresh as well as old scratches on its ends. I pried the planks off. There was a clear glass pint jar, wrapped in some of my old clothes and filled with a lot of stuff. Inside was some transparent glue-like substance with a coloring that looked like an iridescent blue Jell-O-like mess that as you turned the jar it seemed to crawl and move like some incredible living thing. It emitted tiny sparks of light like little lighting bugs were trapped inside. I replaced the plank and took the jar into the woods.

"When I opened that jar it smelled like old rotten earth, fish, foul smelling sea water and when I opened the jar a long, hissing, whirling sound rose up into the air. Suddenly I felt just like I had stepped out of a dense fog or awakened from some long endless nightmarish sleep. My flesh felt clammy and the back of my neck began to smart as did my eyes and nose. But beneath it all I felt brand new. I took a stick and stirred into the jar's contents. Inside that jar were clumps of my hair, my high school picture, pennies, strips of my clothing, finger or toenail clippings, split sticks, roots, wood shavings, herbs and that blue Jell-O-like stuff that I had yet to identify.

"The more I stirred that stuff the more I felt alive. I built one blasted, roaring fire in the yard and I burned everything including the jar.

"I went back and told the priest about it. He warned me not to eat or drink from Mira and to lock my door when I slept and keep my door locked when I was away from the house because she would try it again."

Puzzled and frowning thoughtfully, Sandra said, "Now I'm more bewildered than ever. You say that you are free and you have known all of what Mira did to you yet you are still with Mira, why? I just can't understand any of this."

Mark said, "I guess I just didn't care about life anymore. After I broke the spell that Mira had on me my life changed for the worst. When I gained my freedom from Mira I lost Twila all over again. After that day Twila even stopped coming, even my longest sleep was without dreams of Twila. Life without Twila even in a dream was meaningless. My feeling remained dull. My life became even emptier than ever because now I fully knew there was nothing left for me.

"About six months before I met you, every now and then, Twila began to come to me. But, it was not the same. It was no longer fulfilling. I can't explain it. Maybe it was because of the relationship that I had with Diana. But even so, whatever it was, it was still better than nothing. My dreams of Twila had been all that I had to keep me going after she died.

"Mira was just there like furniture or something taking up space and just watching never really interfering or anything, saying nothing just watching.

"Whenever I went out she knew better than to come any place I was or to complain about anything I did. She watched me like she had some secret that gave her great pleasure, but she never mentioned the jar, nor did I, but I know that she knew.

"She made no sense to me like I probably don't make any to you, but I didn't give a damn about her or life anymore anyway. I'd go my way. I'd lost myself in my work and my music. Mira and I were like as it says in the Bible about the 'dead burying the dead' both of us were emotionally dead just not buried in the ground. Daily we share the same sarcophagus, called a house."

Sandra blinked her eyes trying to process all that Mark had told her. A thick quiet fell between them like a thick blanket covering the room. The sun had set and night had slipped in unnoticed and marched silently towards dawn. Bewildered, drained and exhausted Sandra slowly arose and went into the bedroom without putting on the light. Fully clothed she fell into bed leaving Mark sitting drained and motionless on the sofa buried deep in painful thoughts.

CHAPTER TWENTY-FOUR

Mira's Motions

After Twila's funeral Mark lay crying as his heart busted with unbearable pain. He gazed at the ceiling; his flowing tears saturated his pillow. Twila was gone and he couldn't understand why. All of the kind words, flowers and cards that he received held no meaning for him. He cried out to a God that didn't seem to hear him. All he wanted was Twila.

After long hours of crying, moaning and praying through pale, narrow beams of moonlight that sliced through the darkness flooding his lonely room, Mark saw a slight movement near the doorway. Then the shadow seemed to come alive. Raising his head and blinking his eyes several times Mark attempted to deal with his imagination. But the slow moving shadow slinked out of the darkness diced by moonlight and was coming toward him. As it gradually approached him, brightness emerged from the shadow became dense and took on form.

Mark sat up on the side of his bed and tried to focus his eye on the apparition that he was certain his mind had conjured up. When the figment of his imagination was within hands reach, Mark saw that it was his Twila, his beautiful Twila. He heard her breathing and smelled the scent of her sweet perfume that he knew so well.

Not yet trusting his disbelief, Mark closed his eyes and held his breath as he longed to reach out and touch her face but she appeared so fragile and unreal.

In the dimly moonlight lit room Mark sat gazing at her face not daring to breath too hard for fear that the vision before him would disappear. Then, he slowly arose and stood before her. His heart quickened while with trembling hands he reached out and gently touched her. To Mark's surprise his hands slid smoothly over Twila's tender flesh and he felt her warm softness. After having touched his Twila, he wept at her reality.

Sheltered in the midst of night, viewing Twila through misty eyes and feeling her flesh beneath his trembling fingers his woeful world changed to sheer ecstasy. Her soft face and lovely smile appeared more beautiful than ever. The comfort of her sweet aroma and wonderful presence filled his room. Mark vibrated with excitement as uncontrollably tears of happiness flowed from his eyes.

When Mark reached out his arms to her, Twila quickly went into them filling them with her loveliness. Her eager compassion instantly consoled him. Twila melted beneath each stroke of his hands. As Mark's held Twila his passion intensified and his needs increased.

His heart raced as Twila slipped out of the gown that was meant to be a part of her trousseaus, in doing so she removed every barrier of life and death that stood between them. Even though still doubting the reality of Twila's actuality there was no waiting in Mark.

His pounding heart exploded with happiness and caused Mark to break into hysterical tears followed by short spurts of uncontrollable laughter.

Lost in the night, blinded by grief, vibrating with longing, with groping hands and unrequited desires almost in a fit of madness Mark greedily possessed his lovely Twila.

At all times Twila had remained silent, but when Mark rapidly entered her, she reared up in pain and gave in to intense low sobs with cries of, "Ooh. Ooh ah!"

Mark kissed her and whispered, "Please forgive me, darling. I should have been more gentler."

Then tenderly he proceeded to savor the sweet innocence of his long await love. With gentler strokes he caressed her within until she became attuned to his lovemaking. Afterward her only responses came in short gasps and moans of satisfaction as he entertained her every fantasy and fulfilled his every dream.

Mark relished the joy of her return. He whispered, "Twila, my darling thank God you came back. You really came back to me. Don't ever leave me again my darling. Please don't ever leave me again. Never again my darling!"

Securely lodged inside of her throughout the

night Mark made love to Twila until they bordered on the verge of insanity. To Mark's reality he had his Twila. He had prayed and begged God to return to him the warmth that stroked his very soul. Once again his life became significant.

When at long last Mark completely surrendered to unbelievable satisfaction and slipped off into a world of deep sleep an elated Twila left as softly as she came.

Morning found Mark drained and bewildered. Once awakened he tearfully he sought Twila all day but she was nowhere to be found. Those who he told about Twila's return and of his experience saw it as a very vivid realistic dream and considered his conversation as wild babbling. They believed his hallucinations had been brought on by his grief.

Yet the tenderness of her flesh and lingering vibration of her kisses were testimonies to the realism of her presence. Overwhelmed by their disbelief, Mark spent the day wallowing in despair and grief born out of losing Twila again.

However, through it all, Mark continually insisted that his parents believe his encounter with Twila. He told how her perfume had filled the room and how warm and real she was when they made love.

His father said, "Mark, your grief has become too much for you. Maybe you need to go away for a while. How about London? A change of scenery will help you get through this."

"No, father I can't go away," he said. "When Twila comes back how will she find me if I'm not here waiting?"

"Twila is not coming back Mark. Twila is dead," his father said. "As hard as it may be, son, you must accept that. It's true Mark. It's true. Twila is dead."

"You are wrong. You are wrong. You must believe me," shouted Mark. "I know what I know. Twila isn't dead. You'll see."

"Come Mark. Come with me my son."

Together they went to the cemetery. Standing beside Twila's grave Mark's father placed his hand on Mark's shoulder and said, "Your beloved Twila lies sleeping beneath those flowers that have yet to wilt. She's gone Mark. She's gone."

Unable to accept what his father was saying Mark lost all desire to live. He fell to his knees and wept and prayed for death.

Night fell and Mark lay in his bed still praying for death refusing to accept the reality of the grave that he had seen with his own eyes. He tried to recapture the miracle of the previous night when he held Twila so tightly in his arms and her moist, hot body had totally sheathed his.

Mark pulled the sheet over his head and wept into it. After hours of weeping, engaged by pain and despair, Mark felt a tugging at the sheet that covered his face. He slowly lowered the sheet to peep over it and he saw his Twila standing nude before him, smiling.

He opened his mouth to speak her name but she sealed his lips with her soft, warm finger as she slid into bed beside him. Mark took her in his arms and immediately swallowed her up in the potency of his acute longing.

Their dance of love went on until the hours peeled away the shades of night and slew him with exhaustion just before dawn. Twila seized the opportune moment to slip away in silence.

Night after night Twila returned to Mark and every night Mark accepted her into his yearning arms, with death and darkness no longer obstacles or enemies, because they had delivered to him all that life had not.

Again and again, Mark anxiously awaited the miracle of the night knowing that at dawn Twila would float away leaving him to pray for night's quick return.

Mark had no one to share his happiness with so he kept the bliss of his miracle to himself. Everyone continued to see him as being grief-stricken and filled with delusional dreams. Still he lived for the end of each day waiting for night's arrival to bring with it his loving Twila. Nightly, with each manifestation of their love, the innocent manhood of his youth slipped away as he blossomed into fullness.

After Twila death Mira made sure that Mark was perfectly prepared to succumb to her will. The Doctor Fish that her grandmother helped her to dressed and cooked and she fed him was the first step that she had taken in preparation for his possession. The rooted fish penetrated his mind and began to eradicate his free will.

Mira and Mrs. Arrington had returned to Trinidad knowing that feeding Mark the Doctor Fish alone wasn't enough. The love between Mark and Twila was so strong it proved to be a hindrance, but not a deterrence to the women's plans. So Mira and Mrs. Arrington shadowed Mark and Twila everywhere they went determined that Twila would not stand in the way.

The night that they went to the Flamingo Club provided the old woman the prefect opportunity to complete their plan. It was the first time that she could reach Twila unnoticed.

At the club while Mark and Twila danced Mira's grandmother succeeded in slipping a lethal dose of Ciguatera, a fish induced poison, into Twila's drink. Ciguatera have characteristics that could induce undetectable coronary arrest within the hour of consumption. She also slipped a hallucinating drug into Mark's drink.

Later that night the drug that was given to Mark in combination with the sudden appearance of Mira's grandmother sitting on the top of the car, wearing a hideous voodoo mask with the snake like entity wrapped around her shoulders, and seeing the car in the middle of the dark, curvy road was enough to cause Mark to wreck the car just about the time that Twila would pass out and die leaving Mark to believe that he was responsible for Twila's death.

It was over an hour before the police actually arrived but in Mark's sick mind he believed it was within minutes. It was a telephone call from Mrs. Arrington that bought them to the scene of her handy work. The sense of guilt and the pain of loss left Mark in the right state of mind for Mira, with her Grandmother's assistance, to completely seduce his mind.

After Twila's death her grandmother intensified her plan to complete the spell over Mark. He quickly became lost in his lamenting environment. The Doctor Fish, the hallucinate drugs, the special jar of roots in addition to his grief epitomized him for re-creation. He became the perfect submissive creature for total possession born out of Mira and her Grandmother's dire plan.

Amidst the turmoil that existed in Mark's home, during the wake for Twila, Mira's grandmother stole one of Twila's sheer white nightgowns and a bottle of her favorite perfume. That night after the funeral when the house was still and everyone had surrendered to their grief and physical exhaustion, Mrs. Arrington and Mira immediately put their plan into motion. With her grandmothers help Mira was transformed into the spitting image of her cousin Twila. This was easy because of their physical likeness, Mark's state of mind and Mira, Twila and Mark's virginity.

The moon drifting high in the sky caused the thick shrubbery surrounding Mark's family's house to cast a long wall of dark shadows over it. The shadows provided Mira with an excellent cover as she stealthily moved toward the house where doors were never locked.

Upon entering the house Mira looked up and down the deserted, silent hallway. The still house reeked with the lingering aroma of the evening dinner. The silent, dimly lit hallway made it easy for Mira to move about. She went directly to Mark's bedroom located on the first floor toward the back of the house. It was a place that she knew very well because after the accident she went to the house daily as part of the family under the pretense of grief and sympathy.

Mira paused for a moment beside Mark's door

in an effort to calm down her racing heart. She took a deep breath and let it out slowly before she entered Mark's room. In the silence of the night, moving like a white shadow, she approached the bed where Mark lay with his eyes tearful open staring into a dismal night of nothingness. At first sight of Mira he fought to focus his unbelieving eyes on her. After staring in disbelief, he whispered in a wavering voice, "Twila. My beautiful Twila, is that you? You came back to me. I thought you were gone forever."

Mira never spoke a word as she smiled and moved closer to his bed. Saturated in Twila's perfume that she had absconded along with the gown for a touch of reality. She allows Mark to tenderly caress her face as she touched him with her scented hands.

By the end of a month Mira had become so obsessed with Mark's lovemaking that her grandmother, who was always standing by coordinating Mira's every move, had to keep reminding her that she was lingering by his side to close to dawn. She insisted that Mira depart from Mark's room long before dawn approached.

Each night after Mira slept with Mark, Mrs. Arrington's eyes beamed beholding the glow of happiness radiating from her little girl's face. Not only was Mira a wonderful granddaughter but she was also an excellent student. She willingly learned every aspect of her grandmother's craft and had no boundaries when it came to using it to get what she wanted. She was becoming almost as good as her grandmother. Not like Twila who she saw as a spineless, weak and poor excuse for a granddaughter that frowned on everything that her grandmother did while Mira always gladly walked in her grandmother's footsteps.

By the end of six weeks Mrs. Arrington said to Mira, " See, I told yu that yu had nothing to worry about. There'd be no weddin' except yuz."

"I'm sorry, Grandmother. I should never have doubted you," said Mira. "I just wanted him so badly."

"Well,' said her grandmother. "He's all yuz now. Are yu happy?"

"I'm so happy grandma," said Mira. "I am so very, very happy."

"Well it's time to make sur' that you stay dat way," her grandmother said. Pulling a small vial from her pocket handing it to Mira, she said, "When yu' go to Mark tonight, just 'fore partin', make sur' dat his lips are saturate' wid dis potion. I'll do the rest."

Knowing that Mira had administered the potion in the vial to Mark just before daybreak the next morning Mira's grandmother called to her saying, "Tis' time. We must now call on his lovely family. Tis's time dey know what dey precious son done been doin' wid my beautiful granddaughter and step 'side and not git in our way."

"I am ready grandmother. I did everything just as you told me to do. Here are the sheets from his bed of our first night together. I went back while he and his father were at the cemetery and got them as you told me to do," Mira said.

"Lemme look at dat sheet 'gain," said her grandmother.

She unfolded the sheets and held the bottom one up to the morning light declaring, "Good! Good! De proof of yur virgin blood tis in de center of his momma's sheets. When dey sees dis dey will know dat we done speaks de truth and not stand in our way. He'll be yur husband fore sun down dis day, my darlin'."

"Under the drug that Mira had given him, Mark entered a death like sleep that lasted until late into the day. Upon rising his mind was in a foggy condition. When Mira and her grandmother went to claim him from his household, he remained in a dream like state even though he walked and talked. Although he was the center of attention he was totally unaware of the events taking place between Mira, her grandmother and his family except what he was later told.

In view of Mira's proclaimed pregnancy and the proof of the bloodstained sheet to avoid a scandal his family was forced to agree not to interfere with the marriage.

Later that evening through a nightmarish wall of helplessness, led like a sheep to slaughter, before a Justice of Peace, Mark saw himself in the middle of the marriage that he had no control over.

Almost immediately after the wedding Mark and his family agreed that Trinidad was not the place for him to be. Still unable to control his life Mira and Mark moved to St. Croix.

With her ill deeds accomplished Mrs. Arrington, Mira's grandmother, went back to Haiti.

Despite the drug that made him willingly go into

Mira and her grandmother's plan and remain trapped there he was aware of his unwillingness to marry Mira and denied the pending motherhood.

Mark was unaware of the truth concerning the entire relationship between him and Mira. However, he clearly remembered his lovely nights filled with lovemaking to Twila.

In St. Croix each preferred living in the rain forest. The seclusion reminded Mira of Haiti and she conducted her life accordingly, secretly practicing her voodoo and cultivating her roots.

Mark agreed with living in the rain forest, because it afforded him the solitude that he still desired and allowed him to conceal Mira.

He lived lonely days and waited for Twila at night. His dreams of Twila were always very vivid. Their lovemaking was intense and undeniable. As long as he had that nothing else in the world really mattered.

Mira happiness with Mark was found in the darkness. From dusk to dawn they lived in their fantasies, her love life with Mark, and Mark's with Twila. Each night she became his Twila and Mark became everything she dreamt he would be. She exploited every emotion that he had. She manipulated his body, controlled his mind and feasted upon his longing. Like a love-starved vampire she sucked dry his every desire.

During broad daylight despite the mind controlling roots Mark recalled his nights with Twila, and shied away from Mira. But just having him in her sight daily knowing he could never leave her allowing her nightly to neurotically feasted upon the stamina of his manhood was the root of Mira's pleasure and her furthermost compulsive passion in the world of her creations.

While worshipping him, Mira cooked, washed, ironed, cleaned their house and the shop without gratitude from Mark, becoming satisfied in knowing that each night her rooted potion carried its own reward. For over three years these were their worlds until Mark's father helped him to obtain a portion of freedom.

Mira knew Mark had broken a portion of her spells but not the one that kept him tied to her side and that was where she intended to keep him for life. After Mark's attempt to break free of her Mira still maintained her own agenda. She realized that it would not be easy to regain complete control over Mark again. But as long as Mark remained in a mournful state he was easier to handle and she had no problem.

After Mark broke her primary spell she could no longer gain entrance to his bedroom as Twila, so Twila had to go away leaving Mark extremely sad and depressed and Mira burned within. Each day her demanding ravenous nature caused her to become more beastly, and Mark's increasing despondence presented her the perfect opportunity to rework her depraved strategy.

Mira had just begun a new plan to get Mark completely back under her spell. It was not going to be as easy as the first time because she knew that he was aware of what she had done and now took precautions against her. He refused to eat or drink anything that she prepared or had access to. Whenever he was at home he kept his door locked, burned his old clothes, fallen hair, and finger and toenails. Yet she had a plan in progress when Diana entered the picture because she knew, just as she did with Twila, that Mark was deeply in love again and that he was moving beyond her reach. True love always presented a problem but not impossibility for her grandmother's witchcraft.

When Mark asked her for a divorce so he could marry Diana, realizing that she couldn't handle his freewill alone, Mira went to Haiti to her grandmothers. She gave Mira the help she needed. Upon returning to St. Croix using the key that she had stolen from Mark's key ring at the shop and copied, she planted her instrument of destruction in Diana's house among her gardening tools. Two days later Diana was gone and Mark was rueful and depressed. Once again he was at the mercy of Mira to again become her prey.

For Mira it had been a slow process, but Mark had begun to respond to her portions. All was going well for a year or more. Twila was able to gain entrance to his bedroom. These unexpected intense visits from Twila exciting Mark and cause him to overlook small precautions allowing Mira to gain much needed ground.

Just when Mira's was on the brink of reaping the full benefits of her efforts along came Sandra stirring deep emotions in Mark that he once only had for Twila. The soft, hot flesh and blood of Sandra caused him to resist Mira's handiwork.

At first Mira saw Sandra as a temporary hindrance especially since she knew that sex seemed to be impossibility between Sandra and Mark. But now that Mark had explored every facet of Sandra's emotions everything had changed. He was more fulfilled than ever. For him making love with Twila was only consummated in his realistic fantasies. With Diana lovemaking was preformed under a shadow of guilt because of his nightly encounters with Twila. By the time Sandra appeared on the scene Twila had been forced to practically desert Mark often leaving a long, tremendous void in his world.

At first Mira only considered Sandra as temporary interference, she never really viewed Sandra as a threat to her. But she did have a plan for Sandra if she really became too much of a problem. Mira believed it was just a matter of time before her insecurities would make her go away leaving Mark abandoned giving her the perfect opportunity to regain complete control over Mark again.

But when Sandra surrendered her all to Mark and their lovemaking became unlimited, uninhibited and extraordinary. Mark's passion soared out of control and his blood sizzled. Now that he was demanding a divorce, she knew there was no stopping him with words alone.

Mira knew that without love she alone and his fantasies were destined to rule Mark for the rest of his life. But now his unbridled love for Sandra had gotten in the way. Once again Mira immediately knew what she had to do.

CHAPTER TWENTY-FIVE

Second Chance

The next morning found Sandra and Mark worn out spiritually, emotionally and physically. Mark had spent the night on the sofa trying to vanquish the past while Sandra tossed and turned the night away in bed alone. She awoke to find Mark lying on his back with his arms folded beneath his head staring at the ceiling. His eyes were dull and his face void of expression.

Uncertain of how to approach Mark, Sandra went into the kitchen and began to prepare breakfast. Twenty minutes of clanging pots and pans produced the smell of sizzling bacon, medium brown toast, scrambled eggs and a glass of orange juice mixed with the aroma of fresh perking coffee. However, none of this did anything to motivate Mark into stirring from the couch.

Sandra went into the living room and knelt down beside the sofa where Mark laid, she said, "Look I know last night was far from what we planned but it's over. It's past. Lying here like this will not change anything."

Mark sighed and replied, "I didn't expect it to.

Nothing can undo what has been done. All we can do now is move ahead. I just feel that maybe somehow I could have or should have stopped it all from happening."

"How could you when you said that you couldn't even help yourself? Mark you were hounded by the evil that surrounded you."

Mark didn't say anything.

After a moment, Sandra said, "Look. Get up, shower, have some food, and you'll feel better."

Mark said, "Okay, I'll shower, but I can't eat."

"You must eat. You'll be sick if you don't."

"Sandra please try to understand, every pain-filled thing in my life that I've tried to shield you from has surfaced and rushed in on us. I can't do anything except pray that this won't change our relationship, except for the better. All I can do is pray for that. My life has been so damned ugly. Now it's rising up threatening to take away the most beautiful moments that I've had in over three years. Since Twila's death happiness wasn't ever on my agenda but once."

Remembering back to Diana and all Lola had said to her, Sandra said, "I know Mark. Lola told me. Your happiness was called Diana. You really loved her, didn't you?"

Mark went on trying to explain by saying, "Yes! That was a time when I was really ready to leave Mira."

"Well, why didn't you leave?"

Mark said, "It was what happened to Diana, Diana Taylor. She didn't just die she was murdered."

Mark paused to get control over his emotions.

Sandra patiently waited for him to go on.

Softly Mark said, "As you now know Twila was my first love and would have been my last love had she lived, but she didn't. So Diana became my second love, only I lost her too. Now fate bought me you and you are now my only love. I just can't lose you Sandra no matter what. That is why I revisited hell last night I just wanted to make you understand everything."

Sandra said, "It seems that misfortune is your constant companion, baby. None of your relationships ever seemed to have worked out for you and their ends were so final. Should I worry?"

"No Sandra! No! Ours will work out, I promise you. You have nothing to worry about," said Mark. "I swear to that. You certainly don't have anything to worry about ever."

Mark's voice was solemn and his eyes were earnest as he said, "I love you Sandra, ooh how I do love you."

Sandra asked, "As much as you loved Diana and Twila?"

Mark asked, "How can I compare any one of you to the other? Each of you is so special in your own way. There is nothing you have offered me that I could ever find in anyone else. The uniqueness of you sets you apart from the rest of world and is mine alone. The love I found in you stands in a place all to itself."

Mark doubtlessly said, "If I had to make a choice I would say I love you more because you are a dream that I thought I would ever have again. You are a wish that I thought would never come true in my lifetime. You are a life that I thought I was denied forever. You are my reality, my hope, my love and most of all you are here and all mine."

Tears rose in Sandra's eyes as she moved closer to Mark and lifted her face to receive his kiss. Mark pressed his lips so tightly against her that he hurt her mouth. Realizing what was happening he moved his lips to her neck. He held Sandra in his arms, buried his face in her hair and trembled, saying, "I love you."

Now more than ever, Sandra felt deep compassion for Mark. It was the first time she had seen him so fragile. All she wanted to do was wrap him in her arms so she could love and protect him forever.

Sandra got up from where she knelt and sat down on the sofa beside Mark. He placed his head in her lap and lay there quietly. As he did so, thoughtfully, he pushed his hand beneath Sandra's skirt and begins to very gingerly stroke her bare thighs. She caressed his head and rubbed the back of his neck. With his head resting in Sandra's lap Mark felt free to recall his short-lived happiness with Diana. After a few quiet minutes Sandra felt hot tears running over her legs. He was crying, but she made no mention of it. She just continued to caress him, hoping it eased his pain.

After several minutes of venting his emotions, Mark softly said, "After today we can put all of this behind us and start a new life completely free of the past both yours and mine."

Sandra admitted, "I never thought of it that way."

"Sandra that is why I am so sure about divorcing Mira. It's a must."

Feeling drained and very sad, Sandra said, "It's

strange how you know a person and yet you don't really know anything about them. In the very beginning, when I first met you, I thought so many things about you Mark so many wrong things.

"At one time, until I got to know you, because of your nonchalant attitude I even thought you were a slick New York playboy. Now I find that I still never knew you at all. In my wildest thoughts I would not have ever imagined you as ever having experienced any of those awful things. You act like there have never been any real problems in your life. You smiled, you talked, you played music, but you don't show that huge load of pain that you must be carrying around inside. Why?"

Mark answered, saying, "Maybe it is because I choose not to carry around the pain. I buried it beneath all of the love that once was mine. I treasure that love because in the end that is all I had that really mattered and I found what little happiness the only way I could, never dreaming that I would have another chance at that kind of love again, but I'd never build my life on pain. I just lived through it the best I could. Until I found love again in you my music and my craft was all I really had.

"Now our life together will consist of the purest love. The love that I shared with Twila and Diana gave me strength to go on. They left me their love that is how I survived. I lived in the world they left for me treasuring the beauty and shutting out the emptiness. I learned through their love how to embrace and appreciate the love I'm sharing with you. Love is precious and it has its own strength. Even when we don't seem able to make it love will help us endure.

Sandra said, "Mark, you've walked the embers of hell and can still embrace love and are willing to fight for it. After all of that are you sure that you want to confront Mira? Do you really want to do that? Do you have the strength?"

"I really want to do that. I need to do that," said Mark, as Sandra's bent over and he kissed her lips softly and passionately. Still feeling Sandra's thighs he then rolled over off the sofa onto the floor, lying on his back in the soft carpet looking up at her, saying, " I want to face her and get it over with more than anything else in the world. I've never been more sure of anything."

"Well our breakfast is probably shot to hell by now, but I can't say that you haven't had a very complex and extremely strange life. Somehow I feel that you still haven't told me why you married Mira in the first place other than some damned old Doctor Fish story," she laughed, saying, "Maybe I had better get back into the kitchen and cook you up a fish of my own."

Mark slid his hand further up beneath her skirt caressing her smooth thighs and said, " I prefer that the fish you give me be hot, wet, raw and snapping."

They laughed.

CHAPTER TWENTY-SIX

The Edge of Eden

They were finally able to put their ill fated past behind them after Mark, like Sandra had completely shared his horrible, distressing life with her.

Beginning that day everything in their lives took on even more serious implications but at last they were completely one. The bond between them became almost tangible. Sandra dwelled in a secure place filled with serenity and pleasure. Any thought of Mark's life outside of what they shared was finally understood and without any meaning. It had not bothered her anymore until he had telephoned her at her office that Friday morning. It was nearing mid-morning when he called her at work saying that he had again demanded his divorce from Mira and she had refused him. His voice reflected unusual component anger. Almost shouting he sounded so upset that Sandra said, "Mark I can take off and come home now and you can meet me there if you need me."

Mark instantly refused her offer, saying, "No! No! It isn't anything that I can't handle. Mira is being a genuine ass. She wants to cause complications with the divorce procedure and she can. All that I have to base my reasons for wanting a divorce on is voodoo. Who in hell is going to believe me in this day and time? But I can handle her and I will."

Sandra said, "From the way that you sound, I'm not so sure about that or what you mean."

Mark paused before replying, "Yes I'm very upset but having you to take off wouldn't solve anything. Don't you worry about anything. It will be alright."

Anxiety crept into Sandra's voice as she asked, "Are you sure Mark?"

"I'm sure!" replied Mark, appearing to sound a little more sedate, Mark said, "Just go straight home after work. I'll be there waiting at your apartment. I have my key with me. If I'm not there I'll be there as soon as possible."

Sandra said, "All right then, I won't leave the job but after you close the shop come right on over. I'll be waiting with dinner prepared. Afterward I'll follow up with your special dessert treat."

Mark chuckled as he said, "That sounds just fine to me. You always know what I need. I'll need all of that and then some more after today."

Sandra had been home for over an hour before she heard Mark's key in the door at exactly eight o'clock. As always, she was true to her word; dinner was waiting and so was she. She had become Mark's

Wailing Wall, his tower of strength and the keeper of
his deepest secrets. Mark knew that she was always
there for him as he poured out his heart and reflected
on the torments in his soul. He knew that no matter
what Sandra would always love him.

When Mark entered the apartment his face
appeared strained. His eyes were dull and his features
reflected a great deal of distress.

Taking a signal from Mark's appearance,
Sandra said, "I guess that today has been anything but
easy."

Then she smiled and asked, "Do you want to talk
about it or leave it outside the door?"

In low voice Mark said, "We have to talk!"

She asked, "What in the world happened today
that has you so depressed?"

"All hell broke loose," he said. "Mira never
believed in us, she seriously believed that you would just
go away."

"Whatever made her so stupid? Doesn't she
know you by now?"

"Hell no and she never will. That is why she lost
it when today I made it very clear that I was demanding
that damn divorce. She was totally unprepared. She
never thought it would be you that I divorced her for.
You being a stateside woman threw her off. She acted
like a bush monkey, jumping, screaming and shouting
curses in her native Haitian tongue, she kept saying,
'I'll never let you go,' as if she has any say so about it."

Apparently getting upset, Sandra said, "Doesn't
she know that I already have you? How long did that
scenario go on?"

"All morning-- that is why I didn't come to work

today. I did everything possible to persuade her. I've never seen her go off like that. She has never been so desperate before. All the time she was just standing by never really saying anything.

"I knew that because Twila and Diana were West Indians she always saw them as being more of a threat because you are a stateside woman she saw you differently; not as someone I was serious about. Mira is so piss poor at understanding a damn thing. Love is love no matter who it is with and there are always exceptions to every so-called rule."

"I know that she vowed that she'll never give you a divorce, " said Sandra.

" You are right. She damn sure did."

Mark paced about the living room seeking some physical outlet for his anger as he shouted, "But she has no choice. I told her with or without a damn divorce I am leaving her even if I have to take you and leave this island."

Sandra eagerly asked, "When are you leaving her Mark?"

Banging his fist onto the cement living room wall, he declared loudly, "Now! Right! Right god-damn now,"

"Hallelujah to that," shouted Sandra as she threw her arms around his neck. "This is a surely a day to remember."

Mark responded by giving her a quick kiss on the cheek.

Later, Sandra sat on the sofa and watched Mark as he paced up and down the living room floor

like an enraged caged lion as she waited for his fury to peak and burn out. After a while he walked over and stood before the window looking out over the building's back terrace. He appeared to had calmed down.
Sandra rose up from her seat and went over to him. Standing behind him she slipped her arms around his rigid body and whispered, "Sweetheart, come with me, sit down on the sofa and relax. I will bring your dinner."

"I can't eat. Thinking of that woman's gall took away my appetite. I've never been hers. All she ever gave me is grief and now she wants to deny me what probably is my last chance at happiness. I need you. Without you I don't know what I'd do. You brought sanity into my life. Not even the fire of hell or the fury of a person like Mira will come between us, I promise you that."

With her arms wrapped around Mark, Sandra asked softly, "What now? What now?"

"Whatever it takes," he assured her. "We'll decide tomorrow. I am staying here tonight."

Realizing that the die had been cast Mira took action without wasting anymore time. That same night she grabbed an overnight bag and took off to Haiti. The note that she left behind simply read, "I've gone home."

Her sudden departure provided Mark with the perfect opportunity to peacefully pack his belongings and move out.

CHAPTER TWENTY-SEVEN

The Hose

Mark filed for his divorce while Mira was away and spent every day and night thereafter with Sandra. To her it was almost as good as him being her husband. He was there free to love her morning, noon, night, anytime between and whenever time permitted it.

Now, every morning she left for her office filled with the excitement of knowing when she walked into her apartment she would find Mark waiting to share not just dinner but to lavish her with such extraordinary loving that it made every night a star spangled event and made each morning's sensuous pre-dawn performance worthy of the sun's applause.

Today after her triumphant completion of hiring at Robbins and Robbins, Sandra couldn't get home fast enough because today was so wonderfully different. The mere thought of forever being near him made her as effervescent as a schoolgirl.

Despite their many trials and tribulations time had brought each of them in touch with their fondest dream, total happiness. So often since loving Mark she had longed for this day. Now they would be completely free to share every aspect of their lives. Mark would no longer be required to get up in the middle of the night and go to a place that never was a home nor would they be forced to cut their lovemaking short to keep up public appearances on her behalf. They were going to be married.

Arousing thoughts of Mark caused her head and heart to pound. Sandra was intoxicated with emotion as she rushed home only to have some worthless old hose get her so upset. Additionally, she was disappointed to learn that Mark was not yet there.

She glanced at the hose resting on the floor near the doorway where she placed it. Seeing it caused her temper to soars. Angrily she walked over to the hose and kicked it several times with all of might. Her rising anger became somewhat abated when she loudly shouted, "Shit on you!"

Then she recalled her torrid telephone conversation with Mark only a few minutes ago and calmed down. She said aloud, "He will be arriving anytime now."

Smiling broadly Mark hung up the telephone from talking with Sandra. Looking up he saw Mira standing in the shop's doorway. She had stealthily eased in like a slender shadow and stood silently staring at him. Her dark eyes were hard, smothering and penetrating.

Surprised by her sudden appearance Mark asked, "How long have you been standing there? I thought you were at home."

Without responding to his remark she stolidly asked, "That was your woman wasn't it?"

"Yes! If you must know that was Sandra," answered Mark. "So what?"

In a firm cold voice she said, "You moved in with her while I was gone, yes! When I went home I took a look and I saw all of you things were gone."

Mark sharply replied, "You saw everything clear enough,"

Moving closer to where Mark sat, becoming extremely irritated, Mira eyes narrowed as she asked, "What did she want from you just now?"

Anger exploded in Mark voice as he shouted, "That's none of your damn business. You have no part in me. Besides I know that you must've seen the notice of the divorce proceedings. I left it where I knew you would find it."

"That paper is only a thing. It means nothing to me and you're not going to her tonight or any other night," declared Mira as she stomped around in angry circles flailing the air loosely with her hands. Her voice was determined as she said, "I know she wants you to come but you're not going to her. I won't let you."

Mark leaped up yelling, "Let me! Let me! Like hell you say. You don't tell me what to do especially when it comes to Sandra."

"You'll not see her ever again," Mira forcibly shouted, "I'll not let you! I'll not let you!"

"You will not let me? You will not let me?"
Mark parroted. "What in the hell do you plan to do to
stop me Mira? Kill me and eat me?" He screamed in
her face. "You're too late I was dead already,
remember? I was eaten alive, dead and buried by you.
Everyday of my life that I shared with you was as being
the living dead. Now you can call me Lazarus. Call me
Lazarus! Sandra bought me back to life. Because of
her I'm really alive. Now tell me...how in the hell do
you expect to stop me? Kill me again Mira. Get your
grandma to kill me. You, your grandma, your fish,
your roots and jars will never stop me again. You have
lost your power over me. Love took it away. Love!
Love! Something you don't know a damn thing about.
You'll not stop me."

"You're such a big man Mr. Landers. Such a
big man, yeah," snarled Mira. "Well never you mind I'll
have my way. You will learn to listen to me one way or
another and you will never leave me. Never!"

Utter contempt filled Mark's eyes and contempt
stroked his every word and filled his voice, as he stared
at Mira, with ice coated words he yelled, "You can do
whatever you like, including reading the book of the
dead *Maccabees,* against me, if you think that will help
you but you will not stand in my way anymore."

He spat on the floor before her then ground it
beneath his feet as living proof of his anger and
exhibiting his contempt. Grabbing his keys he headed
for the door. Mira made one huge leap and threw
herself against the shop's door. Her arms were
outstretched forming a barrier attempting to prevent
his departure. Tears streamed down her face and she
frothed at the mouth as she yelled, "You can't go. You

can't leave me my husband."

Mark grabbed her outstretched arm and flung her to the floor.

With the agility of a cat, she leaped up crying profusely as she grabbed his arm. Clinging to it with all of her strength, she pleaded, "You can't go my sweet, loving man. You can't go my darling, please don't go. Don't leave me."

With all of his might Mark gave a hard yank, snatching away from her and bolted for the door.

Seeing that she couldn't stop Mark her cries became like those of a wounded beast almost howling. Louder and louder she cried as bitter tears flowed rampantly over her distraught face and she began slobbering and chanting in some strange dialect. It was like an intense prayer to some unnamed god.

Mira still refused to give up with one last burst of energy she made an energetic leap just as Mark was about to exit the door and seized him by the back of his shirt. Mark grabbed the front of his shirt and in one forceful effort he managed to rip it apart and wrenched himself free of it and her. She fell to the floor while still clinging to his torn shirt Mira reached out and grabbed him about the leg. Mark kicked and stomped until he shook her loose. He ran down the steps and across the yard.

Mira crawled after him calling out to him "Don't go! Don't go my little baby. Please don't go, I beg you my husband. I beg you. I love you. Don't go to that blasted damned stateside woman."

Shirtless, panting and determined Mark cried

out over his shoulder as he fled down the storefront steps and ran across the parking lot toward his parked truck, "I would gladly die right now rather than to remain in this living hell with you another minute."

Inside his delivery truck he slammed the door and locked it. Despite the sizzling heat from the late evening sun he rolled up the windows, turned on the truck's motor and pressed hard on the accelerator revving up the truck's powerful engine several times. The truck reared up in place causing the loud swirling sound of the roaring engine to drown out Mira's horrible cries.

Anger had ravished Mark's body, his physical encounter with Mira absorbed his physical and emotional strength. He required a few minutes before he could calm down enough to release the accelerator, put the truck's gear into drive, and head directly to Sandra's apartment.

Forgetting to use his key to let himself in Mark knocked soundly on Sandra's door.

She called out, asking, "Who is it?"

Mark called back somewhat subdued, "It's me baby."

"I am in the shower; use your key."

Mark fumbled in his pocket a few minutes before finding his key. Upon entering the apartment he tripped over the hose lying in the hallway. Fighting to stay on his feet he loudly shouted, "Shit! So this is it!"

Hearing him stumbling and cursing Sandra guessed what had happened. She said in a disgusted tone, "If you mean that hose, oh yes...that is it all right."

"What are you going to do with it, baby?"

Stepping from behind the drawn shower curtain she popped her head out of the bathroom door saying, "I don't know. I guess just leave it there until tomorrow or the next day. I suppose that Scottie or its owner will turn up to claim it sooner or later. Lord knows I certainly don't need it."

Walking into the living room in a leisurely manner, wrapped snuggly in a large, brightly colored floral bath towel, Sandra was a vision of loveliness to Mark.

He rushed to her and wrapped his arms tightly around her narrow waist and kissed her solidly on the forehead. Embracing her gently, cradling her against his chest, Mark pressed his face into Sandra's damp, soft hair and without any mention of Mira he held her close and cast every memory of those horrible moments with Mira out of his mind. He began rubbing Sandra body slowly with the towel that covered her. After a few minutes of touching her curvaceous body the heat within him made the torrid heat from the Caribbean evening sun seem cool by comparison. He immersed his soul in the flame that was building inside of him.

Mark's tender caresses became brisk, ardent and grew increasingly urgent. He spun Sandra around letting the towel fall from his hand onto the floor, as he pulled her around to face him. Kissing her hard in the lips Mark swept Sandra into his arms carrying her into the bedroom and lowered her into the center of the bed. "I came here with every intention of finishing that shit that you started on the telephone earlier today."

Sandra gave a little sigh and teasingly

murmured, "Well, here I am. Come on. Show me what you got."

Mark's hands reached out and cupped her round, firm breasts, salivating; he caressed them for a moment, before kissing them. Then hastily stripped away his clothing and fell onto the bed beside her.

She eluded him, gently shoving him away, saying, "Silly, go and check the lock on the door. You know that you always forget to lock it. So go and do it now," she jokingly ordered him. "Then if you still have nerve enough you can come back and try to finish whatever it is that you'd think that you can."

Moving quickly Mark rushed to the living room door and called back, "You're right baby, I didn't lock it but I will fix that now."

Sandra heard the lock turn and she also heard the safety lock fall into place. "I'll lock the windows too," Mark said. "No one will rescue you because your mouth made a bill that your behind will pay. You won't escape the hurting I'm about to inflict on you, Miss Fresh Mouth."

As Mark headed back toward the bedroom, Sandra coyly asked, "Whatever gave you the idea that I want to escape? I've been ready for you all day."

Laughing, Mark said, "Tell me anything now that you are at my mercy. But I'm not taking any chances. No telling what you will do when the heat starts to rise. I'm going to make it real hot and heavy for you tonight, I just hope that you can take the pressure."

Mark began walking in a stalking manner towards the bed where Sandra laid laughing hysterically as she anxiously awaited him.

The setting sun's dying rays coming through the bedroom window cast an orange colored glow that flooded the entire room. As he approached her Mark's appearance in the brilliant light surrounding him almost threw Sandra into a hypnotic state. She observed the wondrous sight of his perspiration drenched, nude, brown, muscle lined body sensuously gliding toward her. With half closed eyes Sandra inhaled deeply the strong masculine aroma of sweat and cologne exuding from him. Mark's body never failed to tremendously excite her but tonight even more so. From head to toe Mark's muscles flexed with every move. Her mind was completely wrapped around Mark stroking every inch of him and her body cried out to embrace him. The exciting contrast of his smooth brownness against her almond toned flesh always fascinated her and Sandra never wearied of observing Mark's nakedness or possessing his manhood.

"Mark, you are so damned gorgeous," she whispered, "Your physique is so like that of gods and the wonderful part of all is that you are almost my very own husband."

Despite their many sexual experiences Mark's obsession for Sandra never ceased. Each time he possessed Sandra, her tightness was akin to a virgin. He reveled in her freshness and completely appreciated his rare possession.

Smiling as he came nearer, he leaned over and began lowering his body down onto hers. Sandra raised her arms to receive him. Within seconds they were lost in a world fully ruled by their sensuous adoration of each other.

They were so obsessed with their consuming desires that neither noticed nor cared that the beautiful glow of sinking sun had given way to a sky filled with dark foreboding clouds. Within minutes the shade of night had rode in on the winds of a roaring storm. Nature's sudden upheaval became a syncopation of rumbling jungle rhythms providing a thundering background for their primitive lovemaking. Tightly embraced Mark and Sandra's winding bodies initiated an emotional dance that incorporated natures rumbling sounds, letting them become background to their prelude of a long performance of savage sexual consumption.

Amidst the bright flashes of lighting and loud claps of rolling thunder they began to ride out their own blustering storm of carnal desire that was raging furiously in them. Nature's ferocious outbursts only fueled their ravenous appetites causing their emotions to run rampant and unbridled.

As they thrashed about on the rumpled bed their locked limbs held each other fast while their groping hands explored every crevice of each other's entwined bodies.

With both hands, Mark hoisted Sandra's her hips above the bed and penetrated her with the swiftness of the lightening flash that lit up the room around them. Mark's potent passion and uncontrollable craving for Sandra compelled him to feverishly possess her. Continuously he sent his entire length into her. She eagerly braced herself and fully received him. With each lusty thrust the bed slid.

With the ease of a thistle in the windstorm,

Mark thrashed Sandra about as he verbalized his feeling in the midst of his strives. Sandra's low, throaty sounds of unadulterated pleasure fed the fire inside of him. Her feverish responses gave credence to his phenomenal performance. The pleasure Mark dispensed sent her drifting over the realms of rationality. Her ultimate expression of indescribable gratification came in the form of tears streaming from her eyes.

Perspiration from their gyrating bodies splashed over the crumpled sheets like falling drizzling rain on an arid desert. Their fervent fire recklessly propelled them to the highest peak of absolute gratification. For either of them passing out from sheer exhilaration was not an option.

Experiencing the perfection of total fulfillment as they gave birth to cries that were born in the beginning of time. Sandra's climax abruptly manifested itself with a loud, unearthly, and piercing shrill scream that filled the room.

At that same moment, an extremely long, deep and profound groan flowed from Mark's open mouth announced that he had acquired unconditional ecstasy.

Their simultaneous climax blended their souls together as their exhausted bodies crashed onto the rumpled sheets. Sandra lay prostrate in bed with Mark's drained body spread out on top of hers. Except for heavy breathing and gasping of the exhausted lovers' silence filled the room.

CHAPTER TWENTY-EIGHT

Silent Guest

Amidst the loud sporadic claps of thunder and the intermittent eruptions of flashing lighting came the sudden movement of the hose as it lost its rigidity, shivered and went limp, sliding softly onto the floor. Then very gradually visible raced throughout the hose steadily increasing with vigor until rigorous shudders occupied every section of it. Soon the pulsating movement ran all through its entire length of it. The hose became engorged to an incredible thickness much like an anaconda. It was alive, unwounded and pulsating. The long, large, green serpent like entity slowly stretched outward down the hallway until it completely extended. Then continuously it moved over the floor with the silence of a dropped stitch.

The flashing lightning lashed the darkness as the hose slithered down the hallway crossing the plush white carpeting on the living room floor and moved on to the bedroom. There by design and intention the hose stealthily made its way beneath the bed that nested the exhausted lovers.

The bedroom echoed with the panting, moaning and groaning sounds of their ongoing recovery from their glorious journey to the edge of the world. Meticulously the hose looped over them with such gentleness that each of its feathery brushes was accepted as a touch or a caress from one to the other.

The hose went on rising, falling, looping and crossing them with its methodical maneuvers, completely encircling them several times. Once in place the hose mission began as it tightened around the lovers ever so slowly. It pressure became so uncomfortable that it prompted Sandra to asked Mark, "What are you doing to me baby, trying to squeeze me to death?"

Mark, with his weary eyes still closed, kissed her ear and said, "No! I was just about to ask you the same question. Why are your caresses so tight and why are you so cold?"

Sandra said, "I'm certainly not cold and I haven't any strength. Your loving, like always, has rendered me as helpless as a kitten."

The increasing pressure across Mark's shoulders, waist and buttocks began causing him severe pain. His eyes flew open as he cried out, "What in the hell is going on here? What are you doing baby?"

"I am not doing anything," Sandra cried in agony from the pain that she was experiencing. Just then a burst of lighting lit up the room as bright as daylight revealing the hose with its weaving bright brass nozzle rise high in the air over her head. Sandra's open eyes widened. The hose weaved and quivered above her face like a huge serpent. Knowing what she saw but not believing her eyes, Sandra cried out, "Oh Mark it's the hose. It's alive. It got us. It is trying to kill us."

Sandra's protruding eyes looked over to see Mark's partly severed head entwined in the hose, rolling limply from side to side. She opened her mouth to scream only to have the hose clamp off her voice by looping around her throat. Smidgens of light danced off of the nozzle of the pounding hose as it swung and smashed into Sandra's startled face with such force it sent her teeth crashing against the distant wall. Before Sandra lost consciousness from the tremendous impact to her head she became aware of the brass nozzle sliding between her nearly lifeless legs and up her thighs, then forging its way into her. Then like a blanket being pulled over her face darkness covered her blank staring eyes. The flashing lightning faded just before nothingness swallowed her. Brilliant bolts of flashing lightning had spotlighted the carnage.

There was much concern Monday when neither Sandra nor Mark showed up at Robbins and Robbins. Mark had somewhat mended his record for being absent without proper notice, but Sandra had never missed a day except for illness. No one had seen her since work on Friday. Some of the men from Mark's crew went by his house but the place was locked up appearing deserted. Lola went to Sandra's apartment several times but there was no answer there either.

Some of the workers whose papers she was handling began looking for her. Sandra couldn't be found anywhere.

Finally the police responded to a missing

persons report from Lola, Sandra's employer and concerned friends.

The door to Sandra's apartment had to be forced open because of the security lock inside. There was no access to the windows other than a very long extension ladder. Once inside the apartment the police were horrified by what they found. Behind a securely locked door and windows that showed no evidence of forced entry were the mutilated bodies of Mark and Sandra.

Upon entering the apartment, an officer cried out, "Hold your breath."

The foul smell of death had become the primary resident. The sight horrified all of those most seasoned law enforcement officers. Mark's severed head with its blaring eyes was found a foot away from the bed. Suicide was absolutely impossible.

The chief of police was called to the death scene. After examining the bodies he scratched his head, pondering aloud, "What in the hell did this?"

The question required an answer that no one could give.

After a preliminary examination of the bodies the medical examiner concluded that every bone in their bodies had been crushed and some enormous thing had entered Sandra's private area and exited through her mouth. Marks genitals had been beaten to a pulp.

One officer asked, "Did you see the look in their eyes? It was like they had looked the devil himself in the face before they died."

"Well" said another officer, "There was a

similar case when Diana Taylor was raped and murdered. Do you think that it may have been the same killer?"

"Who in the hell knows?" said another officer. "That sure was one that we have never been able to solve."

The first officer replied, "I hope that we have better luck with this one. Whoever did this must be a damn raving maniac."

"What's stranger still," said the other office, "Diana Taylor was this man, Mark Lander's, woman too. If it weren't for the rape aspect of these damn crimes and the awesome amount of strength required to destroying these bodies I would swear that his wife had something to do with it. She damn sure is a weird one alright with more than plenty of reason."

"Yeah he was doing them both of those women," replied the first officer. "But under the circumstances the rape and all that's just too damned much of a far fetched idea."

"Do you know what else is strange around here?" asked a detective, " Just like that Taylor's case there are no footprints or fingerprints in this place other than those of the victims. There isn't one shred of evidence or any sign of an outside intruder, nothing. All we have here is the fruit of their host, Death."

After a long and fruitless investigation the case of Sandra and Mark was closed and listed as unsolved. The sealed apartment was now open to be cleared out.

All of the remaining debris including the hose that lay coiled up in the living room hallway was deposited into the apartment's trash dumpster just beyond the building.

Very late that afternoon when the cleaning was finished and all of the trash had been put in the dumpster, out of the shadows, an old lady emerged into the uninhabited area and a younger woman followed her pushing a small hand cart. Almost adoringly the old woman plucked the hose out of the trash bin. She wastes no time as ever so gently she placed the hose into the cart.

Upon seeing the hose the young woman trailing behind the old lady began to weep profusely. She repeatedly asked the older woman, "Grandmother, why did Mark have to die too? Why did it kill Mark too, Grandma?"

"Mira," said the old woman, "Yu knowz dat once vengeance done been sought and tis sent forth, its spirit must obey, dat demanded dat it can't return empty handed. We sent it to kill Sandra not knowin' dat Mark and Sandra was completely inseparable. Dey had become one. Mira not even yu could separate dem not even fo' one night. Yu needed to destroy Sandra but she had consumed Mark and he had consumed he', dey lives had become indistinguishable. So as it twas ordered, so twas done. De spirit took all life de life it saw which was one. You shoulda been able to keep Mark 'way from he' lik' yu done wid Diana, but yu couldn't. Dey love was too strong.

"When Twila was killed de hose only spooked Mark. Even through dey wer' together 'cause no death twas ordered dat 'llowed Mark's soul to be spared, wid

Twila, death had already made its visit and de spirit twas gone, de drug killed Twila. Vengeance twas mine and a soul twas received and vengance twas satified, cause, no matter what vengeance always require' a soul."

"Why Mark's this time Grandma? Why Mark's? I tried to keep him away Grandma," moans Mira. "I tried to keep him away. I did everything that I could. I loved him so much. He was all I ever wanted. I loved him, but his love for her was too strong. I couldn't control him anymore. He wouldn't listen to me. There was nothing I could do! There was nothing I could do! Now he is gone what am I going to do?"

"Now at last yu know de answer, my little one. Now yu at last yo' know der twas nothin' yu could do. Dey lov' won out 'gainst everythin' dat we don' don', and now she is don' gone takin' him wid her," the old woman told her. "And der twas nothin' yu or I kin do 'bout dat."

Leaning over the cold, supple, neatly coiled hose the old woman caressed it before she gently finished piling it up neatly in the cart. She whispers to her beloved hose, " Com' and let's go home, lov'. Yor work her' tis finished. Som' yu win, som' yu looses, some yu say yaa-yaa. We hav' a long journey 'head us, all de way back to Haiti. One day yu may hav' a reason to return her' again. Who knowz? It may be sooner dan yu think my pet. Maybe soon, someday, some way, or neve', who really knowz?

The End

Maybe?